Embracing Destiny

To Charlie,
Every day is a new adventure!

12/1/12

To Sweetness and the joy we have shared
and the adventure that awaits

Chapter 1

An automatic meeting reminder popped up in the middle of the computer screen, accompanied by a loud dinging noise. Sara Taylor positioned the mouse over the notice and clicked on it. The thirty-minute countdown started. She stared wistfully at the collection of pictures on her desk. These pictures, as well as a few irreverent, work-related cartoons, livened up the ugly, steel gray cubicle.

A simple gold frame held a high school graduation snapshot of Sara with her best friend, Laura. Most people mistook the tall, thin girls as sisters. It was an easy mistake, considering they both had long brown hair and blue eyes. Sara remembered graduation day well—the excitement, the anticipated freedom, the endless opportunities. Their grand plans had been filled with hope for the future and of making a difference in the world.

Another picture, in a wooden frame with a grizzly bear etched in the lower right-hand corner, contained the happy Taylor family, posed in the foreground of the Grand Canyon at sunset. With her left hand, she picked up the picture. A fellow tourist had snapped the shot. It represented a minor photographic miracle for the Taylors—no bunny ears or weird faces. Sara's two older brothers, Robert and John, prided themselves on screwing up family pictures. Sara treasured this picture, the last one of her entire family before the accident.

Sara wiped the dust off the top of the frame with her fingers. She recalled that the temperature in the canyon that day measured ninety-five degrees Fahrenheit. The humidity had been equally unbearable. Despite the uncomfortable weather, she would rather endure that heat and humidity than be stuck in an air-conditioned cubicle with a view of a plain, drab hallway wall. She situated the picture back on her desk.

Sara wondered how anyone could work for a single company for thirty years. She just couldn't fathom it. The boredom and monotony of DAGS Engineering had overwhelmed her after only a year. There must be a job out there better than this one. She simply needed to find it.

Residing in a four-person cubicle—in the middle of a sea of small, identical, uninspiring cubicles—was not what she envisioned for herself. However, she rationalized it in her mind. After all, she went to college for industrial engineering. It wasn't rocket science or going through medical school with the intention of finding the cure for cancer. On the other hand, she had graduated near the top of her class and had landed a good-paying job. So what if she wasn't challenged and was bored out of her mind?

Sara gathered some papers on her desk, stapled them together, and inserted them into a green hanging folder in her lower left desk drawer. Her attention turned to the clock on the wall, which always read two minutes slow and drove her crazy. She inhaled deeply and let out a long sigh. Multiple phones, with slightly different ringtones, rang throughout the area. She decided to review her presentation materials one last time. The layout proposal to renovate an old office area in the building was due today.

Given free reign, Sara believed she could have designed a really creative and comfortable space. However, the layout group published strict guidelines of the options at her disposal. As a result, Sara's office design only varied slightly from the same conservative office design found elsewhere in the building.

The guidelines for meeting rooms were less stringent. Therefore, she injected some personal flair in the conference rooms. For Conference Room Alpha, she chose seven odd-sized triangular tables. That would thwart any employee's urge to push the tables together to make rectangles out of them. Conference Room Delta possessed the latest in teleconferencing gadgetry—

microphones, speakers, wireless capability for computers, and a large viewing screen for global meetings.

For both conference rooms, Sara had selected interesting geometric pieces of art with bold colors for the walls. When a well-intentioned colleague suggested she should utilize inspirational framed posters, she barely refrained from screaming aloud. She loathed "Aim high!" and "Reach for the Stars!"

Although these posters littered the walls throughout the building, management squelched most questioning views or breakout ideas. Despite being sent to workshops to learn to think outside the box, employees were encouraged to do the opposite upon returning to their desks. Therefore, it remained doubtful whether inspirational posters could truly inspire anyone in this building. Any person desiring an atmosphere where personal creativity was rewarded and true inspiration was appreciated would choose to work elsewhere.

Sara discovered she couldn't concentrate long enough to get through her well-rehearsed spiel. Too many conversations were being conducted around her. Two male colleagues debated how to fund Social Security. A larger group of men outside the copier room rehashed baseball highlights from the last couple of days. In the next cube over, a woman tried to keep her voice down while making a doctor's appointment for one of her kids.

Flipping through the stack of papers in front of her, Sara verified the contents. She had e-mailed her presentation to the secretary already. However, she always carried a backup hardcopy, just in case. The secretary possessed the unenviable task of consolidating all of the presenters' materials into a slide show for the meeting. As Sara placed her backup presentation into a blue file folder, George, the cube-mate on her right, caught her eye.

"Ms. Taylor, how about joining me for a cup of coffee in the break room?" he asked.

"No, thank you, George. I'm rehearsing a presentation I have to give in a few minutes. Thanks anyway."

Sara didn't really like George Russell. Because she shared a cube with him, she made the best of it. She couldn't provide a specific reason why she didn't like him. It was just a weird feeling. Perhaps it was the fact he called her "Ms. Taylor."

At fifty-four years old, George epitomized the company lifer. In the same position for the last eight years, staying under the radar was his specialty. That way he didn't get assigned to special projects that required overtime or travel. It afforded him time to spend with his family. In his mind, he lived the American dream.

"Perhaps another time then?" George replied hopefully.

"Sure. Another time. I'm just really busy right now," she responded, rather dismissively.

George nodded and wished her luck.

Her watch, set five minutes fast, indicated there was plenty of time for a quick trip to the ladies' room prior to the meeting. She walked down the dreary aisle without encountering anyone. As she leaned into the ladies' room door, the usual blast of cold air greeted her. The temperature in the bathroom measured an average of ten degrees colder than the rest of the building. The secretary had mentioned that management believed the cold temperature would discourage loitering in the bathrooms. When Sara heard the explanation, she thought managers should have better things to worry about than monitoring employees' bathroom habits.

As she entered the facilities, she encountered a young woman in the lounge area sitting on the hideous green couch. Sara prepared to engage in friendly conversation until she realized the woman was half-naked and in the process of hooking herself up to a breast pump.

Sara had encountered women breastfeeding on airplanes, in shopping malls, and in other public places. However, walking into this situation at work was unexpected and felt somewhat awkward. So Sara focused her eyes straight-ahead on the full-length mirror against the far wall.

The breast pump was hard at work now. Sara could hear the humming from the pump's motor as it sucked the milk from the woman's breast. She checked her hair and makeup in the mirror, smoothed her charcoal gray suit, and straightened the collar of her plum-colored blouse. Pleased with her appearance, she leaned closer to the mirror and smiled a large, toothy smile to verify no remnants of lunch remained in her teeth.

Sara headed for the door and tried to avoid glancing in the woman's direction, but peripheral vision has a way of thwarting even the best of efforts.

The woman reclined on the couch—one breast connected to the pump; the other peeked out from the unbuttoned blouse, waiting its turn. Sara thought the woman should show some discretion and pull her blouse over herself. Perhaps she even could have used a wad of paper towels as a last resort. After all, this was a public place, and, when the door opened, anyone standing in the hallway by the door would have a full view of the couch. Sara merely desired to escape from the ladies' room. As she passed, the woman spoke.

"Hi, Sara. Beautiful day outside, isn't it?"

Sara recognized the woman now—Tammy What's-Her-Name from accounting.

"Yes, Tammy, it is a lovely day." It took all of Sara's concentration to maintain eye contact.

Tammy smiled. "It's the kind of day that makes you want to play hooky. I used to do that back in school. Those were the good old days. No cares in the world."

"Right. The good old days," Sara agreed, despite the fact she had never skipped school. That was an irresponsible thing to do. Sara had striven to please her parents and teachers and had done what was expected. She hadn't wanted to disappoint them.

"I guess I shouldn't complain. I've been on maternity leave for four months. This is my first week back. This breast pump is a pain in the ass, but my doctor says breast milk is best. So, here I am." Tammy gestured with both arms in a manner that caused Sara to think of a magician finishing a trick with "ta da!"

Tammy continued, "I'm still trying to get used to the pump. It's just weird."

Not knowing what else to say, Sara replied, "I'm sure you'll get used to it."

"Yeah, I know. And I have to bring a cooler to put the milk in. After all of this trouble, I'm not about to let the milk go bad."

Sara shifted her weight uncomfortably from foot to foot and inched closer to the door. Then she caught a break—the bottle was full. Tammy would have to switch sides. It was a perfect opportunity to vacate the ladies' room.

"I wish I could stay and chat," Sara lied. "But I have a presentation to give in a few minutes. Bye." She departed without giving Tammy an opportunity to respond.

The presentation that afternoon flowed well, as Sara had anticipated. There weren't any computer glitches, so her backup material proved unnecessary. In addition, she encountered no difficulties answering the questions posed to her. The overall layout design for the area pleased the staff and remained within budget.

Several high-level managers attended—typical managers of an engineering organization—men in their fifties and early sixties. A few of the older men wore shirts and ties, but most dressed as if waiting to tee off at their favorite golf courses.

"That's a workable design and it fits the budget. I'll approve the work orders as soon as you can get them to me. Good job, Taylor," Ben Roberts said, slapping her on the back.

Ben, Sara's supervisor, a portly man of sixty-one years, insisted on calling her by her last name. She disliked being referred to by her surname, as well as the slap-on-the-back gesture, but she wanted to fit in and be treated like one of the guys. So she endured his routine.

The first time Ben had slapped Sara, she had fallen forward. Fortunately, there had been a table in front of her at the time. Its mere presence had saved her from hitting the floor. After that encounter, she learned to anticipate his movements and steel herself against them.

Ben didn't accomplish much except for attending meetings and consuming large quantities of donuts and coffee. The company calendar on his office wall, with each expired day crossed out in black permanent marker, indicated he looked forward to retirement. That auspicious day was circled and highlighted in yellow.

Sara smiled and excused herself. She returned to her desk and filed the materials in an overhead cabinet. Next she checked her e-mail. There was nothing important that couldn't wait until morning. She logged off and powered down her computer.

She collected her keys from the center compartment of her desk. A picture tucked in the corner of the drawer caught her attention. She gently touched the face of the man in the picture. After a few moments, she shook her head, grabbed her big, black purse, closed the drawer, and locked up for the night.

Making her way to her blue Impala in the company lot, Sara walked around a telephone company service van blocking the main walkway into the lot. As she sidestepped the van, her cell phone rang. Startled, she fumbled to locate the phone. The unzipped purse produced sunglasses, a wallet, and some feminine products before it rendered the phone. The screen displayed the name "Joe Lazaro," the man in the desk drawer picture—the former love of her life.

Joe and Sara had started dating in high school as the result of a bet. During warm-ups one day, a few members of the junior varsity baseball team had noticed Sara and Laura in the bleachers. The two freshman beauties stood out in the crowd. Joe, the team's pitcher, couldn't take his piercing blue eyes off Sara. Her smile was infectious. Joe's best friend, John Lombardi, bet his fellow sophomore he couldn't get a date with Sara. He told Joe that this particular freshman was out of his league.

Joe accepted the bet and deliberately threw a ball past his teammate and offered to retrieve it. The ball landed directly in front of Sara. Before jogging over, the six-foot, two-inch tall pitcher ran his hands through his wavy black hair. After picking up the ball, he leaned on the chain-link fence and smiled, revealing deep dimples. Engaging Sara in a few minutes of flirty conversation, he mustered the courage to ask her out on a date. She accepted.

The first time they had kissed, it literally took Sara's breath away. Silver stars darted in front of her eyes, and her knees buckled. Instinctively, Joe pulled her closer, so she didn't fall. The chemistry between them was pure magic. From that point on, they were inseparable—attending every function, sporting event, and dance together.

During Joe's senior year, he decided to major in foreign languages in college and won a scholarship to study abroad in Italy. The news devastated Sara. They had planned on attending St. Peter's University together in their hometown of Clear Brook, New York. However, the opportunity afforded Joe an experience of a lifetime.

In the beginning of their separation, they wrote long love letters every day. Over time, Joe's letters became less frequent because of his course load. Sara understood and continued to write faithfully. After two years, Joe announced he would remain in Italy after graduation and would not return home. The Italian countryside invigorated him. He proclaimed his love for Italy and everything about it—the sights, the sounds, and the food. Sara didn't want to move to Italy and still had three years of college to finish. Although there were impassioned pleas from both lovers, neither changed his or her mind. Reluctantly, they agreed the only viable option was to move on and remain friends.

Halfway through his senior year of college, Joe had astonished everyone when he returned home to finish up his degree at St. Peter's University. Although enamored with the beauty of Italy and its trappings, the novelty had worn off. It lacked the one thing he truly loved—Sara.

Of course, by that time, Sara was playing the field. With her beauty and personality, there was always someone waiting in line to date her. Even so, Joe assumed they would pick up where they had left off. However, Sara played hard to get. Joe could not understand why Sara wouldn't take him back, and he dated other girls to get his mind off her. Sara misinterpreted Joe's actions and believed he wasn't interested in her any longer. Crushed, she continued to date other boys.

After graduation, Joe accepted a teaching position at St. Peter's

University to stay close to Sara. Since then, their dating lives had never been in sync, until now. For the first time in three years, they were both available.

Sara pressed the green answer button on her phone. "Hi, Joe."
"What are you doing tonight?" Joe asked.
Pressing the unlock button on her key fob, she replied, "Nothing much. I figured I'd stay in and watch a movie with Anna and Laura."

Sara shared her parents' house with her friends, Anna Cristo and Laura Delaney. Sara's parents, Nick and Chris Taylor, had gone down South to help hurricane victims several years ago and had extended their stay indefinitely. Sara felt awkward living in the big house alone. So when Anna, a close friend from college, needed a place to live after graduation, she invited her to move in.
Her other roommate, Laura Delaney, had been Sara's best friend since kindergarten. The girls grew up next door to each other and shared every facet of their lives, behaving more like sisters than friends. Laura's parents had moved from their home in Clear Brook to a condo in Florida a year ago. It had seemed natural for her to move in with Sara as well. The girls had revamped Sara's brothers' rooms, and the living arrangement worked for all of them.

Sara yanked open the car door, tossed her purse on the passenger seat, and settled into the driver's seat.
Joe was not going to give in so easily. "Forget the girly movie. Come to a party with me instead. Tell Anna and Laura that they're invited too. You girls need a more intriguing social life. There will be a lot of interesting people there. Of course, with your gift of gab, you never have a problem fitting in anywhere."
Sara closed the door and started the car. "Thanks a lot! I'll assume that was a compliment. I guess I could go for a couple of hours. I'll ask the girls when I see them at home."

"Great. I'll pick you up at seven o'clock."

"Hold on a second, I need to transfer to speaker phone." Sara switched the phone over to the speaker function and pulled out of the parking space. "Can you hear me?"

Joe pretended he couldn't hear her and mimicked static noise. "What's that?" He simulated more static noise. "You're breaking up. Are you there?" His laughter intermingled with some additional static noise.

Exasperated she said, "Oh, cut it out, Joe. You can hear me fine. What kind of party is this, and what should we wear?"

"You're no fun. It's casual. Wear whatever you want. You look fantastic in anything." He paused. "On second thought, you'll look better wearing nothing at all," he said flirtatiously.

Sara turned on the air conditioning and cracked the sunroof to let the hot air out. "Dream on. I'll see you later."

"Okay. See you then. *Ciao.*"

"*Ciao.*"

Sara was encouraged by Joe's call. She had high hopes that tonight would be the night for their long-awaited reconciliation. *He mentioned wanting to see me naked. But he did invite the girls along. Hmm ... he probably did that to make his motive less obvious.*

Sara was convinced that this was her opportunity for a second chance at true love. She mentally sorted through her closet, immediately deciding on her short, black skirt. She knew she looked hot in it. That was the easy part. After a few minutes, she settled on an electric blue blouse to bring out her eyes.

Joe had called Sara from his new condominium on Maplecrest Court, six blocks from Sara's house. He had dismissed his last class early. In his opinion, a beautiful summer day should not go unappreciated; not to mention that a great deal of unpacking awaited him.

Joe had vacated his parents' house a week prior to move into his own place. The two-bedroom, one-bathroom condo commanded a partial view of Clear Brook Park. He paid extra for an enclosed garage.

The amount of guilt and disappointment he endured from his traditional Italian mother had caused the move to be a less-than-pleasant experience. Moving out of the house before getting married was not viewed favorably, especially since he was staying in town.

When Joe broke the news to his parents, his father, Salvatore, had remained silent and glanced at his wife of thirty-one years.

In typical fashion, Rose Lazaro's body movements had mirrored the words she spoke. "You rip out my heart and throw it on the floor and then you stomp all over it. Joey, you're breaking my heart."

Rose pulled out a tissue from the pocket of her floral apron. She dabbed at her eyes as she sat on a kitchen chair. "I take good care of you. I cook your favorite food—even when you come home late at night. I clean up after you. I do all of your laundry—I've never seen one person generate so much laundry. But I don't complain. I nurse you back to health when you're sick. I welcome your friends ... and feed them too. And *this* ..." she lamented, extending her right arm toward her son and gesturing with her palm facing upward, "*this* is the thanks I get." Rose turned to her husband and asked, "Aren't you going to say something?"

Salvatore knew better than to jump into the conversation at this point. The question was rhetorical. She wasn't done ranting quite yet. Accordingly, Sal shrugged his shoulders and threw up his hands as if to say, "What can you do?"

"What did I do to deserve this? I tried to be the best mother I could. Obviously, it just wasn't enough for you."

"Ma, it's not you, it's me."

"Please. What a bunch of baloney."

"It's the truth, really."

"Truth, huh? I don't think so." She studied her son's face for a moment. "Oh, I get it now. How could I have been so dense?"

"Ma ..."

Rose resumed immediately. "So, who's the girl?"

"What girl?"

"There must be a girl. Why else would you leave all of this?"

She gestured again with open arms. "Your older brother, Anthony, still lives here at home. *He* still loves me."

Joe shook his head and attempted to put his arms around his mother. She refused the overture and pushed her son away.

In an effort to defend his decision, Joe said, "Ma, you know I still love you. And do you really want me to be like Tony? Last time I checked, he still doesn't have a paying job. He's really not the poster boy for role models."

Rose gave her son a disgusted look. Wagging her right index finger at him, she scolded, "You shouldn't talk about your brother like that. He's a good boy."

"Right," Joe said sarcastically, walking away from her. Reaching the refrigerator, he opened the door and peered inside.

Rose stood up. "Don't you walk away from me, young man," she ordered. "Look at me when I'm talking to you."

Joe pulled his head out of the refrigerator and leaned on its door.

"Don't lean on the door, you're going to break it. And you're letting all of the hot air in. Close the door and come over here."

Joe complied with his mother's instructions and stood with his arms crossed in front of his chest.

Rose continued, "Don't change the subject. It's about a girl. I'm sure of it."

Joe argued, "It's not about a girl."

"Uh huh. Sure, there's no girl. You just want some space then? Is that it? We give you space." She turned to her husband. "Sal! Tell him we give him space."

Sal raised the newspaper he was reading slightly higher to block his face from view.

Rose didn't miss a beat. "How much space does one person need? Maybe you should have become an astronaut. Then you'd have all of the space in the world!" She crossed the kitchen, lifted the lid of the pot, and stirred the sauce inside vigorously. She fumed silently.

Joe leaned over and spoke softly to his father. "Dad, a little help here?"

Sal lowered his newspaper and whispered back, "You're on your own with this one, Joe. I still like my meals cooked for me." He noisily turned the page and resumed reading his newspaper.

Joe joined his mother at the aging, harvest gold stove. Standing on her left, he wrapped his arm around her, resting his hand on her right shoulder. "Ma, you know I love you. I just think it's time to be out on my own. I need to take responsibility. You're always telling me I need to accept more responsibility."

Slipping out of her son's embrace, Rose tilted her head sideways. "Huh! Now you're using my own words against me. You're a clever one, aren't you?" Rose rolled her eyes and drew her lips tightly together.

On the losing end of the conversation, Joe replied, "It's not like that. I'll still see you all the time. I promise. I'll even swear on the Bible."

"Sal, did you hear that? He's going to swear on our family Bible now."

Sal said, "Well, if that will help ..."

Rose cut her husband off with a disgusted look. After tasting the sauce, she tapped the spoon against the side of the pot and replaced the lid. Looking from her son to her husband, she shook her head in displeasure. She placed her right hand over her heart and announced, "I need to lie down. I think *I* need some space. There's only so much a mother can take."

The entire week following this exchange, Joe had endured similar moments of his mother's grief and guilt trips, while Sal remained silent. Anthony, on the other hand, basked in his newly crowned "favorite son" status and milked it for all it was worth.

When moving day came, Joe had declined help from his family. A few friends helped him move in exchange for pizza and beer. He told his parents that he would invite them over for a special dinner once the place looked decent. Rose begrudgingly agreed.

Joe's search through the stacked cardboard boxes yielded the box labeled "bathroom stuff." Although he had planned ahead and packed a few necessities in an overnight bag, the reserve was depleted. The time had come to break into the boxes. Using his keys, he punctured the tape securing the box. Pulling the flaps up, he removed a few fluffy blue towels, shaving cream, and a razor. After he showered and shaved, Joe threw the wet towel into an overflowing laundry basket in the laundry room.

Joe entered the common room, stopped, and went back for a pair of shorts. His mother's voice, with her unmistakable rapid-fire delivery, rang clearly in his head.

"Joey, make sure you don't run around that condominium naked. It's a sin, and someone might see you. *God forbid!* It's bad enough you left my house without getting married. How much humiliation must I endure? *Well?* And what would the neighbors think? I could never show my face again in public. What would the church ladies think? That I was a terrible mother. *That's* what they'll think. They'll whisper and gossip behind my back. *They will,* you know. You just mark my words, Joey. You love your mother, don't you? Be a good boy. If you love your mother, don't run around naked!"

He thought of taking a digital picture of himself to send to his mother via e-mail to prove he wasn't turning into a degenerate. After a moment, he decided against it. She didn't check her e-mail account that often anyway. He grabbed the television remote off the coffee table and turned the unit on. It was already tuned to a sports channel. He tossed the remote on the tan leather couch before heading into the kitchen.

The refrigerator contents were sparse. The top shelf held a carton of chocolate milk, two energy drinks, and five bottles of beer. A box of leftover pizza occupied the middle shelf. Exploring the bottom shelf, Joe discovered a moldy sub, which was promptly relegated to the garbage can. Examining the carton of chocolate milk, he learned its contents wouldn't expire for two more days. He set the carton down on the counter. He removed the pizza box from the refrigerator, grabbed the milk off the counter, and headed to the couch.

Joe threw the pizza box on the coffee table. Within minutes, he had wolfed down the remaining four slices of cold pepperoni pizza. Still hungry, he raided the pantry. The pantry contained a few more items than the refrigerator. There were pouches of tuna, some granola bars, three different varieties of potato chips, and a few boxes of cookies. The barbecue potato chips and a box of chocolate chip cookies emerged victorious and were chased down by the remainder of the milk.

"Wow! Look at the time. I have to get dressed." Joe paused and surveyed the boxes stacked chest high—kitchen stuff, sheets, shoes, and, finally, pants. The tape on the pants box was peeling, so he tore it off. Peering inside, he found a blue pair of pants and shook them out before putting them on. "Thank God for wrinkle-free pants. Now, for a shirt."

He scanned the next stack of boxes and located the box with "shirts" written on it. Rummaging through the box, he discovered a beige, wrinkle-free polo shirt to match the blue pants. He put the shirt on and tucked it in as he strutted over to the bathroom mirror to check himself out.

"Damn, I look good."

Sara pulled up to the house she had grown up in on Springhill Drive. The Taylor family's brick ranch, located in a small, quiet neighborhood in Clear Brook, consisted of four bedrooms, two and a half bathrooms, and a two-car garage. It had been a very happy home until her oldest brother, Robert, died on vacation several years prior. The accident had occurred during a two-week winter vacation in the Rocky Mountains in Colorado. Sara and her mother had planned to meet her father and two brothers during the second week. One fateful morning, a group of teenagers disregarded the ski patrol's warnings and triggered an avalanche that set off a chain reaction on several slopes. Robert and two other skiers could not escape the wall of snow that bore down on them. The remaining family members, including Sara, had gone to counseling for several months to help cope with their loss.

Approximately a year after the accident, her parents had embarked on a new passion to help them cope with their grief—volunteer work. They travelled year-round to help hurricane and flood victims and relocated frequently. Sara's older brother, John, had married his high school sweetheart and moved to Albany for a better job.

Sara turned into the driveway and pressed the garage door opener. The door didn't budge. She shook the opener, turned it sideways, and pressed again. The door opened. "I have to remember to get a new battery for this stupid thing," she said.

After parking, she grabbed her purse, exited the car, and closed the car door with a swift hip bump. Sara squeezed past Anna's yellow Volkswagen Beetle, closed the garage door from the wall unit, and unlocked the entry door. In the mudroom, she kicked off her shoes and dropped her purse on the desk in the corner, next to the dryer, and continued into the kitchen.

"Anna, I'm home!" Sara yelled.

Anna emerged from the bathroom looking pale, her blonde hair pulled back in a ponytail, wearing an oversized gray T-shirt and sweatpants. Her green eyes were bloodshot. "Thanks for the announcement. I came home sick from work around lunchtime. I think I caught the flu or something." Anna plopped down on the mauve-colored couch and pulled a blanket over herself.

"Well, I guess you won't be coming to the party with me tonight. Where's Laura?" Sara inquired, flipping through the pile of mail on the counter.

Anna coughed, then answered, "The workaholic is staying late at work for a meeting. She called to say not to wait up for her. Like we would anyway. And what party are you talking about? I thought tonight was movie night." Anna blew her nose.

Peering into the refrigerator, Sara saw various leftovers. After selecting which leftovers to eat, she scooped some meatloaf, potatoes, and peas on a plate. On her way to the microwave, she ripped a sheet of paper toweling off the roll and placed it on top of the food. She opened the microwave, positioned the plate, closed the door, and set the timer for two and a half minutes.

Maintaining her distance, Sara explained, "Joe called and

convinced me to go to a party with him for a couple of hours. And since you're sick, I'd rather be with some noncontagious people, thank you."

"Fine. Be that way. I'll run into your room later and cough up a storm. So there." Anna stuck out her tongue as Sara headed for her bedroom. Sara returned the gesture.

Sara was thrilled—not that one friend was sick or the other was stuck at work—but that their misfortunes ensured that she and Joe would be alone together.

Sara didn't bother closing the door to her room as she removed her work clothes. Anna couldn't see her from the couch. She found the blue blouse and black skirt easily in the closet. Dressing in front of the mirror, she turned from side to side, critiquing herself. She wasn't a hundred and ten pounds anymore—more like a hundred and thirty pounds. That still wasn't bad for a five-foot, seven-inch frame. She comforted herself with the fact that some of it actually went to her boobs. While she was thanking God for small favors, the microwave beeped. She instructed her reflection in the mirror, "Stand up straight, shoulders back, chest out, and suck in that stomach. Now, if I could only hold this pose for the next few hours." She let out the deep breath and laughed.

Sara breezed by Anna on the couch and gingerly removed the plate from the microwave with a red plaid potholder. Then Sara settled in the chair farthest away from Anna, food in hand, and watched the news with her. After she ate, Sara freshened up her hair and makeup. The doorbell rang as she turned off the bathroom light.

"Bye, Anna. I hope you feel better. I'll see you tomorrow."

Anna waved, tissue in hand, as Sara crossed the room. "Thanks. Have fun, and don't do anything I wouldn't do."

"I'll try not to." They both laughed.

Sara opened the front door. "Joe, it looks like you're becoming more responsible in your old age. You're actually on time for once."

"Yeah, yeah. Living alone has had a huge impact on my timeliness. It's next to godliness, isn't it?" Joe responded, beaming.

"No, Joe. It's *cleanliness* that's next to godliness. But leave it to you to try to become more godly. Let's go." She closed and locked the door behind her.

As they made their way down the sidewalk to Joe's red Pontiac Grand Prix, she handed him her driver's license and house key. Accepting them automatically, he deposited them in his wallet. It was a routine they had established years ago. Sara didn't like to carry a purse when they went out to clubs, and her outfits usually didn't have pockets.

As he shoved his wallet into his back pocket, Joe commented, "Apparently, the girls aren't coming."

Sara shook her head. "No. Anna's sick, and Laura's still at work."

"That's too bad. Maybe next time." Joe gave Sara the once over. He admired the way her skirt accentuated one of his favorite distractions and remarked, "You look fabulous, by the way."

Her pulse quickened. Without turning to look at Joe, she said, "Thanks for noticing. And you can quit looking at my ass now."

"Do I have to?" Joe whined.

Sara wanted to respond *no*. However, she replied, "Behave! We have a party to go to. Oh, by the way, you clean up pretty good yourself."

Happy that his ensemble had made a fashion hit, Joe reciprocated the thank-you and held the car door open for her.

"At least chivalry isn't totally dead." Once settled in the seat, she added, "Thank you."

Joe removed his imaginary hat, bent low, and used his best British accent. "'Tis not, my lady. I am your knight in shining armor for the evening. I await your next command."

Not at all surprised, she responded in character. "Thank you, kind sir. I only beg that you engage this chariot quickly so that we may reach our destination posthaste."

"Aye, my lady. Your wish is my command. To Camelot, anon." He closed the door and pretended to ride a horse to his side of the car, dismounted, and entered the vehicle.

Buckling her seat belt, Sara declared, "You are such a dork sometimes."

Joe smiled and winked at her. "Yeah, but you love me anyway." He buckled his seat belt and started the car.

Sara agreed silently. She loved that he always made her laugh. His dreamy blue eyes broke through her defenses every time. "So, what's new, Joe?"

"New York, New Jersey, New Mexico ..." he responded with a twinkle in his eyes.

"Ha, ha, ha. It's *so* funny every time you do that. *Not.* Really, what's new?" she pressed.

Joe talked about his work as a translator for visiting tourists over the past few weeks in addition to teaching summer school. Sara inserted the occasional "uh, huh," "oh really?" and "that's interesting" remarks as appropriate. He loved his work, and it showed. Although happy for him, Sara wondered if she would ever find something equally as exciting—something that would inspire her the way his work inspired him.

Joe took the scenic route to the party on back roads. The roads narrowed, but the breathtaking scenery by the shores of Lake Ontario made the increased danger worth it. She noticed how much darker certain areas became because of the multitude of trees. She could see the expansive lake for the majority of the drive. The water varied in shades of blue, with darker blue hues the farther she looked from shore. Several speedboats zigzagged on the water as their occupants enjoyed the last hours of sunlight. A water skier tumbled into the water. Eventually, the boat's driver swung around to retrieve him. In what seemed a matter of minutes, Sara and Joe arrived at their destination—26 Azalea Drive.

As they debated the best place to park, a valet attendant appeared. The valet opened the door for Sara. After the valet helped Sara out of the vehicle, Joe tossed his keys to him and joined Sara.

On the walkway, Sara stopped. She clenched her teeth in a fake smile. "Joe, you said this was a *casual* event."

Joe took her hand in his. "Sara, you look beautiful, and Frederick told us that this was casual. Just relax and enjoy yourself."

Frederick Devonshire, the dean of St. Peter's University, and his wife, Margaret, both in their early sixties, hosted the party at their summer home. Frederick, a dashing older man, sported a goatee and a full head of silver hair. Wearing a green St. Peter's University polo shirt and khaki pants, he met them on the sidewalk almost immediately.

Frederick waved his hand in a dismissing way, "Oh, don't be fooled by the valet. We worried that parking would become a problem and didn't want to violate any codes or upset the neighbors. Welcome and make yourselves at home. Joe, great to see you." The men shook hands. "Glad you could make it. And who is your lovely companion?"

"This is Sara Taylor."

"Oh, yes! How daft of me. I remember you from some of my lectures. My eyes aren't what they used to be. Maybe I should have Margaret light some more of those tiki torches. Please, go in and make yourselves at home." Frederick turned and greeted additional guests who had arrived behind the couple.

Something about the quaint white cottage appealed to Sara. The idea of owning a simple beachfront home intrigued her. Well-landscaped flower beds bordered the walkway and appeared to extend around the sides of the house. Daisies, black-eyed Susans, forget-me-nots, snapdragons, hostas, and many different types of roses grew in the healthy, colorful beds. To her surprise, she didn't see any azaleas. Sara thought it odd to live on Azalea Drive and not have any azaleas. The indirect lighting in the gardens provided a wonderful, romantic feel to the place. The wraparound porch possessed ample rocking chairs and side tables for glasses of iced tea.

Margaret Devonshire was a tall, thin woman. She carried herself primly and with refinement. Sara envisioned the woman practicing for hours with a book balanced upon her head. Margaret's beautifully coifed short blonde hair bounced very little as she moved. The gracious hostess appeared in a crisp, blue and white linen dress. She welcomed them dutifully. The friendly greeting was followed by a grand tour of the house and grounds. The interior, simply decorated, consisted of a large kitchen, great room, three small bedrooms, two baths, and a library. It was nothing to write home about. But the back porch and outdoor sitting areas were lovely. It appeared as if the motto for outside decorating had been "spare no expense."

Sara surmised the Devonshires spent most of their time enjoying the great outdoors rather than sitting inside. Two gazebos, one significantly larger than the other, contained an assortment of chairs and couches. Benches, some made of wood, others wrought iron, were strategically placed under the larger trees. Several white Adirondack chairs sat in the sand facing the water. Sara imagined the peaceful and relaxing view of the sun setting on Lake Ontario—quite an experience from any of these venues.

The party, well under way, hosted small cliques of people scattered over the property. Joe introduced Sara to professors she hadn't met previously. All seemed nice, but none dazzled or impressed. She did her best to make polite conversation.

One group of professors discussed the odd departure of Dan Whitman, a chemistry professor, two weeks before the end of the spring semester. Apparently, he had requested an extended leave of absence for personal reasons. No one had seen nor heard from him since. Another peculiar incident concerned one of his lab assistants, Marah Clemmons, who had withdrawn from all of her classes a week earlier. The note her roommate discovered stated she was going home to Oklahoma for a family emergency. It seemed more than coincidental that both left around the same time. Rumors circulated about an affair and a pregnancy that may have resulted.

Then the conversation turned to Fran Feinstein, the librarian, who had gained sixty pounds after her divorce. Her husband left her for some well-endowed waitress after twenty-three years of marriage.

Sara had heard enough gossip for one evening. She excused herself and poured a tall glass of iced tea.

Joe watched Sara's every move. He had tuned out the conversation around him. Instead, he studied the way Sara's skirt clung to her curves. He imagined what type of lingerie she wore underneath it and calculated how quickly he could remove it.

Sipping her tea, Sara scanned the room and spotted Jessica Davis. The bubbly blonde wore a pale yellow sundress adorned with little white flowers. She cornered Joe and began to fawn over him. Sara felt a sharp pang of jealousy.

Jessica's appearance caught Joe entirely by surprise. Deep in thought over Sara's undergarments, he didn't even hear Jessica greet him. It wasn't until Jessica touched his arm that he registered her presence.

Jessica taught art at the university. Last week, Joe casually mentioned to Sara that he was thinking about asking Jessica out on a date, anticipating that Sara would object. Instead, it took Sara by surprise. Dismayed, she half-heartedly encouraged him. This confused Joe, who determined that he had read her incorrectly—again.

After depositing her empty glass on the nearest table, Sara stared at them for what seemed an eternity. She chastised herself for being so strongly attracted to Joe. They fit together so well; they knew each other's likes and dislikes. When there was news to tell—good or bad—he was always the first to come to her mind. She told herself repeatedly to stop thinking about him so much—so far, to no avail.

Sara wanted nothing more than to march over to Jessica Davis and knock her on her perky little ass. However, this wasn't the type of party at which to make a public spectacle. There was also the pesky fact that she and Joe weren't technically a couple. So, her hopes of a romantic reunion dwindled by the minute. Sara couldn't bear the sight of them any longer. She exited the house and wandered toward the beach. *Time to get some air and find a place to sit alone.*

Although mildly distracted by Jessica's attempt at conversation,

Joe focused on Sara. He was concerned when Sara left the cottage. He wanted to follow her. However, Jessica countered each of his moves with one of her own, effectively preventing his timely departure. Preoccupied with thoughts of Sara, Joe wasn't fully engaged in the conversation with Jessica. Therefore, he answered "uh huh" at the wrong moment and inadvertently accepted a lunch invitation for the following day.

Reaching the sand, Sara removed her shoes. The sand felt warm and gritty between her toes. She strolled near the shore, stopping where the water met the sand. The cool water wrapped around her ankles and receded. She closed her eyes and inhaled as the breeze blew in off the lake. The warm wind whipped her hair around, causing her to appear disheveled. She didn't mind. She stood there a few minutes before continuing the search for a quiet place to sit. A wicker loveseat with bright floral-patterned cushions in the small gazebo, away from the main party action, beckoned. The sound of the water lapping on the beach soothed her. The water rushed up and wiped her footprints from the sand. All traces of intrusion were erased.

CHAPTER 2

As hard as Mark Collins tried to block out the nightmare that had become his life during the day, there was no escaping it at night. He had run into trouble with the law several months earlier. His actions had landed him at the Stonewood Correction Facility, the area's state prison. Since his placement there, a series of unfortunate events had led Mark down a dark and lonely path and had brought him to his current residence at the Misty Pines Institute, a mental health care facility.

As he examined his pale reflection in the shatterproof mirror, he didn't recognize the man looking back. The light blue, institute-issued clothing hung loosely on his thin, five-foot, ten-inch frame. His shoulder-length light brown hair had been reduced to a buzz cut. His dark brown eyes were bloodshot and emphasized by dark circles. He looked much older than his twenty-four years.

Mark dreaded bedtime. As soon as he fell asleep, the recurring sequence of nightmares replayed. It disturbed him how his mind would vividly replay select events of the last several months, night after night. It had begun in identical fashion, on the first day of his incarceration.

The metallic sound of prison doors closing echoed in his dream. To Mark's dismay, a large, heavily tattooed inmate in his cellblock had taken a liking to him. By Mark's estimate, this man stood at six feet, four inches and weighed close to three hundred pounds. His head was shaved bald, and muscles rippled from under his prison-issue shirt. The menacing hulk sat next to Mark in the cafeteria and held his right arm tightly. "Welcome to Hell, *friend.* Everybody calls me Butch. I'm Stonewood's perversion of a Welcome Wagon."

Surprised and stunned, Mark barely managed to swallow the food in his mouth without choking. The man's deep-set eyes were dark, almost black.

Butch continued, "After lunch you're going to give me some dessert, pretty boy. What do you think of that?" A devilish smile spread over the man's face.

Mark fought the urge to scream—which was exactly what he wanted to do when faced with the idea of being this monster's dessert. Running wasn't a viable alternative, because the man had a vice-grip on his arm. Throwing up or faking a seizure seemed like good options. Unfortunately, his throat only yielded a muffled whimper.

The pitiful sound satisfied Butch. He released Mark's arm. Before leaving, he flexed his muscles and growled at Mark and the other inmates at the table. They all kept their heads lowered. Laughing aloud, Butch returned to his table of jeering inmates. For the remainder of mealtime, the prisoners at Mark's table focused solely on their food and didn't make eye contact.

Mark felt nauseated. He'd seen this sort of thing in movies. It couldn't be happening to him. It must be a joke. He tried to calm down; it was probably just a scare tactic used on the new inmates.

To Mark's chagrin, he soon discovered Butch was not bluffing. After lunch, Butch waited for him, cornered him in a hallway, and dragged him into a barely lit food pantry. He shoved Mark against the far wall. A musty, dank smell permeated the pantry. Large, commercial-size cans littered the old wooden shelves. Sacks of potatoes and onions leaned against one wall, sacks of flour against another.

After checking the hallway, Butch shut and locked the door. Positioned in front of a stack of flour sacks, Butch sat. "It's time, pretty boy. Let's see what kind of skills you've got."

Petrified, Mark remained pressed against the far wall. He didn't know what skills he was supposed to have but knew he'd find out shortly.

Butch pulled down his pants and revealed an already erect penis that Mark swore was at least eight inches long. "Get started."

Mark stammered, "I don't understand."

Impatient, Butch growled, "Don't play stupid with me, or you'll piss me off. You *don't* want to piss me off."

Mark crawled forward, within a foot of Butch's position, facing him.

"Good choice." Butch reclined comfortably on his throne of flour sacks. He warned, "The penalty for biting is worse than death."

Mark nodded, indicating he understood. Struggling with his conscience, he resigned himself to the fact that compliance remained his only option. He inhaled deeply in front of the sweating, eager inmate. Then he rubbed his hands nervously on his thighs.

Butch barked, "Well, get on with it already!"

Mark prepared mentally and closed his eyes. He could not bear to watch what he was about to do, let alone see Butch's expression. But just when the act was about to begin, Mark heard footsteps.

"Son of a bitch." Butch jerked Mark to his feet with one hand and pulled his own pants up with the other. Mark's eyes flew open. Butch spoke in a low and forceful tone. "We're not done here. *Understand?* I'll find you tonight." He roughly released Mark from his grasp. Mark lost his balance and fell. He scrambled backward, trying to distance himself from this beast.

Butch listened at the door. Mark remained on the floor, not moving a muscle. A voice inside him wanted to yell out to the mystery person. But he knew he would be pummeled for his efforts.

The faceless man stopped at the door and tried the handle. "Who the hell locked this door? Now I gotta find a fucking guard with a key." The inmate kicked the door for good measure as he departed.

Butch grabbed Mark by the shirt and lifted him off the floor. Opening the door, he pushed Mark through. As he closed the door behind them, he promised, "Later, Collins."

Mark's mind shifted into overdrive, trying to devise a plan to avoid another horrifying encounter. That evening, Mark lifted a spork from the mess hall. After breaking it to create a sharp edge, he used it to slice his arms in a fake suicide attempt in his cell. A guard found him and escorted him to the infirmary. Although he spent the night there for observation, they released him the next morning in time for breakfast.

Butch sought out Mark. Bending over Mark, he rested his hands on Mark's shoulders. Exerting pressure, he leaned over. Mark didn't need to see the face associated with the hands that touched him. He cringed, and his stomach soured.

Mark could feel Butch's breath on his neck, his lips almost touching Mark's ear. In a low voice, he said, "Missed you last night. Heard you had an accident."

"Yeah. Something like that," Mark replied weakly, picking at the bandage on his left wrist.

"See to it that you don't have any more accidents." Butch rose and left the mess hall.

Mark's appetite vanished. He did not finish his breakfast.

Desperate to avoid any encounters with Butch, Mark resorted to self-detrimental behavior. Instead of going outside to the yard, he went directly to his cell. He pretended to hang himself with his bed sheets. A guard notified the warden and prison doctor, who placed Mark on suicide watch.

Although Butch couldn't get Mark alone, he made his presence known. He would sneer at Mark when the guards looked away, unnerving him.

Despite the prison's precautions, when the guard fell asleep, Mark orchestrated another fake suicide attempt using his prison-issue pants to almost strangle himself. After that episode, he was transferred to Misty Pines Institute for evaluation and treatment. It was determined that he would serve the remaining five months of his prison sentence at the institute.

Misty Pines Institute, the only mental health care facility in the area, was located twenty-five miles from the prison—exactly where Mark wanted to end up—far away from Butch. The institute housed a variety of patients who covered the spectrum of mental health issues. The prison transported Mark to the facility via ambulance—handcuffed and strapped to a gurney.

Mark rolled over in his sleep as his dream transitioned.

After the transfer took place, two orderlies wheeled Mark into his new room. They didn't release him from the gurney, but they removed the handcuffs. A female in a white lab coat entered the room. She introduced herself as Dr. Wendell and reassured Mark that everything would be fine. Mark remained silent and nodded.

Dr. Wendell continued. "We, at Misty Pines, want to help you. So we are going to get to know you and develop a plan for your recovery. But don't think about that right now. First, you need some rest. I am going to give you something to relax you. It will help you sleep." After she removed the cap and verified the lack of air bubbles, she injected the contents of a syringe into his arm.

"There. You should feel calm and peaceful very soon, Mark." Turning to the orderlies, she said, "He'll be sedated in a few minutes. You can remove the restraints."

Those were the last words Mark heard before drifting into a drug-induced sleep.

Mark awoke the next morning groggy and slightly dizzy. After the room stopped spinning, he sat up to examine his new surroundings—sparse and white, alone and safe. His plan had worked perfectly.

On a table, in the corner, rested a tray of food. He examined his breakfast selection. It consisted of a banana, two blueberry muffins, four slices of buttered toast, two strips of bacon, a carton of two-percent milk, and a carton of apple juice. Nothing that required utensils, Mark mentally noted, peeling the banana.

After Mark finished eating, an orderly unlocked the door and entered the room. He announced, "Time for your therapy session with Dr. Wendell. Come with me."

Mark followed the orderly to the doctor's office. The door was ajar. They entered the room. The first thing Mark noticed was the doctor's desk—an imposing, old mahogany desk. It overpowered the woman sitting in the high-back, dark brown leather chair behind it. A few bottles of water occupied the corner of the desk nearest to the patient's chair, which was crafted from the same leather as the doctor's chair. Tall, steel filing cabinets lined both sides of the room. Pictures of flower gardens and walkways hung on the off-white walls. The barred window beyond the doctor provided a view of a grassy area.

The doctor dismissed the orderly and offered Mark a chair. He sat and assessed the doctor. She was attractive enough, slightly overweight. Her not-so-natural blonde hair was pulled back in a French braid. She wore rectangular, black-rimmed glasses, which she removed after reading the file in front of her. A white coat covered her street clothes. He guessed her age to be around forty-five.

Dr. Wendell folded her hands and rested them on her desk blotter. "Mark, I'm going to start you on some medication that I think will make you feel better. The medicine will need to build up in your system and often takes a few weeks to fully take effect."

Mark sat up straight in his chair. Defiantly, he replied, "I don't need any drugs."

"I disagree. You have a list of suicide attempts in your file. I believe that we should try medication in conjunction with traditional therapy."

Mark moved his head back and forth, indicating he still disagreed. "No, really. I think regular therapy will work just fine."

"I understand your apprehension, but, as a licensed professional, I must insist on this combined approach to begin with. I can alter the dosage as I see how things progress. My decision is final."

Every morning, a nurse conducted rounds, giving all of the patients their medication. Mark's little white cup contained only one pill. Some patients received an entire cup full of multicolored pills. In that respect, he considered himself lucky. The nurse dashed his hopes of hiding the medication. She insisted on watching him swallow the pill. Then she checked his mouth to verify he had indeed swallowed it. It was a small pill, so Mark didn't think it would make that much of a difference.

Mark and Dr. Wendell conducted daily appointments to discuss his outstanding issues. He spoke about his deceased parents. He missed them greatly. The doctor observed how he lit up when he talked about his sweetheart, only to see him deflate as he related how things went terribly awry. He emphasized his ongoing feelings of loss and abandonment. Dr. Wendell wrote copious notes and said little. After a few days, she inquired as to how Mark thought the medication was working. He told her he didn't notice much of a difference, which was accurate at the time.

For the next week, Mark felt odd, almost detached, floating. Shortly thereafter, those feelings changed to a mixture of sadness and depression. The antidepressants opened a disturbing world—a world filled with deeper depression, abandonment, and death. The sadness he experienced now surpassed the profound sense of loss he had felt when his parents died. This altered state of mind brought real thoughts of suicide. He was losing control.

Mark planned to relay this development to Dr. Wendell during that day's session. Instead, the orderly informed him the doctor had been called away for a family emergency and would return in a few days.

The impact of this news hit Mark as betrayal and abandonment. Walking with his head down, he returned to the common room. "The one person I'm supposed to count on in here abandoned me. I guess I shouldn't be surprised. Everyone leaves me. No one cares about me. No one loves me. I am all alone. All alone."

"You are not alone," said a voice, emanating from the opposite side of the room.

Mark raised his head to identify the speaker.

A small, frail older man sat by a window, playing solitaire on a small wooden table bolted to the floor.

"Are you talking to me?" Mark asked the man.

"Not as good as De Niro, but you'll do," the man responded.

"Huh?" Mark asked, approaching the man.

"Robert De Niro, the actor."

"What about him?"

"That line was from one of his movies. I'm guessing you're too young to remember. Oh well. Why don't you sit and join me?" The man extended his hand, gesturing toward the empty chair across from him.

Mark accepted the invitation and gazed out the window.

The man put his cards down. "What's your name, kid?"

"Mark. What's yours?"

"Brandon Wellington. Nice to meet you, Mark, with no last name."

"What does it matter in this hellhole?" Mark felt his temper building.

"I guess it doesn't. You can treat it like an AA meeting if you want. It's your choice." Brandon pushed back from the table and folded his hands in his lap.

Agitated, Mark answered, "*My* choice? If I could choose anything, do you think I'd be stuck in a godforsaken place like *this*?" He gestured outward. "*My choice? My choice? Nothing* has ever been *my* choice." Mark slid back into the chair and balanced on the back two legs.

Calmly, Brandon said, "If you keep making a commotion, the nurses at the desk are going to pin you down and drug you up. So I suggest you calm yourself down."

Frustrated, Mark dropped down so the front two legs of the chair were touching the floor, reached across the table, and grabbed Brandon's cards. Shoving them at the old man, he replied, "Screw you."

"You'll just end up screwing yourself, if you don't cool off," Brandon responded, without breaking eye contact. "They're staring at you. If you don't believe me, look for yourself." Unfazed, Brandon collected the cards on the table and shuffled them.

Mark tilted his head toward the desk and confirmed the nurses were indeed staring at him. He sat properly in his chair. Lowering his voice, he said, "All I know is that everyone leaves me. I didn't choose for everyone to abandon me."

"I wish I had your problem. I have a whole bunch of characters that are with me. They won't ever leave me alone, no matter what I do."

Mark glanced around and reported, "I don't see anybody near you now. There are a few ladies sitting in wheelchairs watching television over there. There's a kid making circles in the air. And there's a guy roaming around singing to himself in some foreign language. There's no one else close to you except for me."

"No, they're all here, just waiting to make an appearance," Brandon replied nonchalantly as he dealt the cards.

"If you say so."

"I *know* so. You'll meet at least one of them if you sit here long enough. In the meantime, let's play gin rummy. That is, unless you have another pressing engagement."

Resigned to the situation, Mark said, "Just deal the cards."

The two men played cards for about ten minutes before the lunch bell sounded. At that moment, the cards dropped out of Brandon's hands. His eyes rolled up into his head, and he started convulsing.

Pushing back his chair, Mark yelled, "Help! He's having a seizure."

A nurse nearby assured him. "Don't worry. He'll be fine. It happens all of the time, especially when he hears bells or alarms."

Brandon stopped shaking. His eyes regained focus. Relieved, Mark sat back down.

"Brandon, you gave me quite a scare there," Mark declared.

In a high-pitched voice, the man responded, "Brandon's gone. I'm Celeste."

"What?"

The old man stood and sashayed to Mark's side of the table. Before Mark registered what was happening, the old man was sitting on his lap. Running his fingers over the top of Mark's head, he bragged, "I can do all sorts of things to make you happy, if you'll let me."

Mark pushed the man off him and stood up. "What the hell? What's wrong with you?"

The old man leaned into Mark, trying to get him back into

the chair. Mark quickly grasped the top of the wooden chair and swung it around, positioning the chair between them.

"Brandon got tired. He's resting. I wanted to come out and play." Celeste licked her lips. "But you're no fun."

Now Mark realized what Brandon meant about the bunch of characters. He wondered how many more characters there were inside the old man's body.

In the meantime, Celeste began strutting around the room in search of fun and stopped in front of the singing man.

Off the hook for the moment, Mark turned the chair back around, sat, and glanced out the window at some birds. A few moments later, a redheaded young man sat down across from him.

Mark acknowledged him with a nod and wondered what he was in for now.

This patient was tall, skinny, and jaundiced, and his green eyes kept darting around, watching everyone and everything. His untamed red mane stuck out in every direction.

The young man leaned forward and whispered, "Be very quiet. We don't want them to hear us."

"All right," Mark whispered back to the disheveled patient.

The skinny man continued, "They're all conspiring against us. They want to keep us locked up in here forever. They want us to be alone, away from anybody or anything that means anything to us."

"You're right about that," Mark replied in a normal voice.

"Shh!" The young man fidgeted as he scolded. "You know that's how it starts. They separate us from everyone we love, so we'll be loyal to *them* instead."

Mark saw truth in that statement.

"It's a conspiracy against us. *They're everywhere.* They get to your parents, then the rest of your family and friends. They weasel their way into every facet of your life, until you have nothing left. You have nothing left, don't you?"

Dejected, Mark agreed. "I don't have anybody left. My parents are dead, my girlfriend is gone, and everyone else has abandoned me. Even the doctor left me."

The redheaded patient bounced up and down on the seat of the chair in excitement. "*See? See?* I'm right. I *knew* I was right. We need to band together to fight them. We need to have a plan of attack. I've been working on a plan for quite some time now," he confided, scanning his surroundings. "We can't use our real names. We have to use secret code names. My code name is Mercury."

"Uh huh. That sounds like a good code name for a guy with red hair."

Mercury corrected him. "No, after Mercury, the clever messenger of the gods. You know, Roman mythology."

"Oh, sorry."

"Do you have a code name?"

"No. I've never needed one," Mark replied.

"You do now."

Despite Mercury's explanation of the connection with mythology, Mark was thinking about planets. He suggested, "How about Mars?"

"Mars—god of war. I like it," Mercury replied enthusiastically. "We will meet under the shroud of darkness, when it is safe. I will contact you when the time is right. Do you know Morse code?"

"Sorry. Can't say that I do."

"Don't worry. I'll devise another communication method," he replied, rechecking their surroundings. "I must go before we are discovered."

In the blink of an eye, the young man slid out of the chair. Mark watched Mercury crouch down and slink behind the furniture to cross the common room. He peered around the far corner before standing erect and walking down the hallway.

As Mark's dream progressed, he unknowingly curled up into a fetal position.

The night before Dr. Wendell's return, Mark bolted upright in his bed, dripping with sweat and screaming. Confused and shaken, he regained his bearings and realized he was in his room at Misty Pines. The sheet and blanket lay twisted in a heap on the floor. He wiped the sweat from his forehead with his sleeve. One glance into the shatterproof mirror on the opposite wall revealed that the dark circles under his eyes were more pronounced. He knew he needed sleep, but sleep subjected him to the never-ending nightmares. He sat on his bed, back toward the wall, knees pulled up to his chest. He rocked back and forth, plummeting further into the depths of despair.

He recounted the nightmare from which he had just awakened. It had felt so real. In the darkness, thick fog surrounded him. Ethereal sounds came from all directions. A cold breeze blew on his face and neck, producing goose bumps. A dog howled from parts unknown. Frightened, Mark ran down a trampled gravel path until he came to an old, ornate wrought iron fence. Mark turned. The fog dissipated slightly. He could see a few feet to his left side. The sight of an angel perched on the small stone structure allowed him to identify his location—an old cemetery. Footsteps approached—slowly, heavily. There was nowhere to run. As the figure emerged from the fog, Mark closed his eyes. The face of his pursuer remained a mystery, for at that moment he had awakened, terrified.

As the dream continued, Mark pulled into a tighter ball as his subconscious anticipated the next series of events.

Mark's inner voice rambled as he rocked. *I hate my life. No one cares if I live or die. I don't care if I live or die. If I killed myself, who'd miss me? Really, who'd miss me? Right now, the only person who might miss me is that crazy kid, Mercury.*

The voice reconsidered. *And maybe Brandon. Aside from them, there's no one. Absolutely no one. How sad is that? Pretty sad. My only two friends in the world are crazy people.*

He lowered his head until it rested on his knees. *I should just* kill myself. I've faked it so many times. It's not like it's not expected. But if I do that, they win. Mercury's right, they'll all win. I lose again.*

Raising his head, he yelled, "Why can't I win? For once in my life, why can't I win?"

Mark stopped rocking and fought back tears. He crawled off the bed, knelt beside it, and clasped his hands together in prayer. "God? Are you listening? I really need you to be listening. I hope you're listening. If I could just get some rest, maybe I'd feel a little better. But every time I close my eyes, I have another nightmare. The next is worse than the last. God, can you *please* stop the nightmares? I promise I'll be good. *Please?* I know this is punishment for trying to avoid prison. But I can't go back there. I just *can't*. Please God? There has to be another way. Please show me the way. I don't want to feel like this anymore. Please God? *Please?*" He continued pleading with God, and some time later he cried himself to sleep.

The next day, the orderly called for Mark for his visit with Dr. Wendell. As they marched down the hall, Mark held his right hand above his eyes.

The orderly asked, "What are you doing?"

Mark blinked. "The light is too bright. It hurts my eyes."

"Whatever. They're the same lights as always." The orderly stopped in front of the doctor's door.

When Mark entered the office, the doctor sat facing the window. Without looking up, she told Mark she'd be with him in a minute and motioned for him to take a seat.

After a few moments, the doctor turned and started to ask, "So, Mark, how are ..."

Then she saw the condition of her patient. Her mouth hung slightly agape. Realizing that her reaction was inappropriate, she closed her mouth. The Mark Collins in front of her looked like death warmed over. The dark circles, the glazed-over look in his eyes, and his overall haggard appearance startled her.

Mark mustered the strength to respond to the question she hadn't finished asking. "I'm not doing well at all. The light hurts.

I'm tired but don't want to sleep. When I sleep it's all nightmares. I feel like hell. I want to die."

Regaining her composure, she asked, "How long have you felt like this?"

Squinting, he answered, "Since the day you left me."

The doctor frowned. "Mark, I am going to take you off the medication. However, due to the nature of it, I have to decrease the dose gradually. Do you understand?"

Mark lowered his head, covered his eyes with both hands, and pleaded, "Just make the nightmares stop."

As promised, Mark was fully off the medication in two weeks. Unexpectedly, his original five-month stay was extended for an indefinite period of time. It took another week for the nightmares to dwindle down. However, they did not disappear completely.

During their sessions, the doctor agreed to try therapy without medication. She gave Mark a journal and instructed him to write down his thoughts and ideas. She promised not to read it, unless he gave it to her to read. Dr. Wendell also encouraged him to set goals for the future—goals for his life outside the walls of Misty Pines.

Mark returned to his room and sat cross-legged on his bed. He flipped through the blank pages of the journal, forward and back. As he searched for inspiration, he chewed on the cap of the pen. Determined to write something, he opened the book to the first page. For his first diary entry, he wrote:

Dear Diary,

This is stupid. I'm supposed to write about my feelings. That's what girls do.

Then he tossed the book to the other end of the bed. He stared at it for a long time before picking it back up. Hesitatingly, he wrote:

Dear Diary,

I can't believe I'm here. But where else could I be? I can't go back to jail. I'll die if I have to go back there. I think I'll actually kill myself if I ever have to go back. The thought of having any kind of contact with that monster, Butch, makes me want to die. I can't go back. I just can't. I'll be safe here. His eyes—they were evil.

Pure Evil!!!

He slammed the diary shut and hid it under his mattress before leaving his room.

Mark became more melancholy as the night wore on. Before getting into bed that evening, he removed the diary from its hiding place and opened it to a clean page.

Dear Diary,

All I want to know is why people keep leaving me. One by one, anyone who has ever meant anything to me has left. Why does God let this happen? Why can't I be happy for once? What's wrong with me? I wish somebody would stay. I don't want to be alone. I miss the way things used to be.

After he reviewed his entry, he closed the book and tucked it into its hiding place. The next day, he logged two short entries. His ever-growing loneliness and despair were evident.

Dear Diary,

My heart is beating in my chest, but I don't feel it. There is an emptiness. A hole. A huge void of nothingness. I sometimes pray for death to come and free me from this pain.

Dear Diary,

Death. That's all I can think about. Death and dying. Then my suffering would finally end. I could be at peace. No more loneliness. No more sorrow. No more anything.

The following day, the only words he penned were:

Dear Diary,

I'm scared.

Gradually, Mark accepted the diary as a trusted confidant. He learned to explore the depth of his feelings and pour them into its pages.

Dear Diary,

I wish those people who killed my parents had lived. I would have loved to see the man pay for the crime that he committed by smashing his car into their car. And his wife should have had to visit him in that wretched jail.

That drunken son of a bitch killed them in cold blood. The papers called it a tragic accident. It was no accident. It was murder. He should be in jail, paying for his crime. With any luck, Butch would have terrorized him the way he terrorized me. Then he would have had to confess to his wife the sexual acts he was forced to commit to survive. That would have been just punishment. Yes, they should have lived to suffer—like I've suffered.

Writing down his feelings proved quite cathartic. It worked better than he had anticipated—better than confessing his sins to a priest. The ugliness and anger were neatly trapped between the covers of the journal. At the end of each writing session, he felt relieved and refreshed, as if he had been given a new, clean slate. Best of all, it enabled him to maintain a normal demeanor, which he knew would be crucial for his release.

After a particularly positive session with Dr. Wendell, Mark felt that happiness was possible again. She asked him to read a passage from a book. Its message was that hope springs eternal. That compelled him to create an uplifting journal entry. It was his first optimistic view of the future.

Dear Diary,

I can make things right again. I won't have to be alone. I'll have a perfect life with my sweetheart. If only I could see her. I could talk to her and remind her of our love for each other. What I wouldn't do to touch her.

I'm determined to set things right. I'm going to convince her that I love her. I'll do anything for her. We'll be together forever. I can picture our wedding day. She'll look so beautiful. I'm going to give her my mother's ring. It's going to be wonderful!

Mark tossed and turned in his sleep as the dream continued.

Mark Collins resided at Misty Pines Institute for another month before Dr. Wendell proposed outpatient therapy. One condition of this type of therapy was that he could not live alone. Dr. Wendell contacted Mark's brother, Matt. Matt declined, stating he did not want the responsibility thrust upon him. She invited Matt to visit the facility to witness Mark's progress. That overture was refused as well.

Matt's unwillingness to help only served to fuel Mark's depression and anger with his situation. The doctor attempted to console Mark, unsuccessfully. Retreating to his room, he released his emotions into the journal. Mark yearned to be set free, to reclaim his life and move on. Matt was preventing this from becoming reality.

Dear Diary,

Matt is going to regret this. I hate him with everything I have in me. He is going to have to pay for this someday. I don't know how or when, but it's going to happen. He needs to make up for every terrible thing he's done to me ...

Writing for a half an hour, Mark inked his feelings on the pages of the journal and returned to the common room, pretending to have no cares in the world. The nurses and orderlies watched. Mark was well aware that maintaining the facade of normalcy was imperative.

He sat down calmly in a chair at a wooden table in front of the window. Brandon wasn't there. Mark was glad. He didn't want to talk to anyone. After a few minutes, Mercury appeared across from him.

"You look like you're trying not to be pissed off," Mercury observed.

"So?" Mark snapped.

"They've done it again, haven't they?" Mercury asked, resting both of his arms on the table, leaning closer to Mark.

Mark didn't reply. Instead, he kept looking out the window.

Mercury insisted. "They did. I can tell. They got your hopes up just to kick you back in the gutter. They're conspiring against us. I told you they're trying to destroy us." Mercury tried to follow Mark's gaze, craning his neck. "What are you looking at? Do you see something out there?"

"It was my brother this time," Mark answered, looking directly at the redheaded boy.

"Are you sure? Are you sure it wasn't *them*? *Pretending*?" Mercury imitated a man pulling something toward him with a rope. "Luring you into a trap? They're good, you know."

Mark shrugged. "I guess it's possible. But this time, it was my brother that betrayed me, not them."

"How can you be sure?"

Mark scratched his forehead. "Because it sounded like something Matt would do to me. He'd refuse to help me, especially if there wasn't anything in it for him."

Mercury's eyes opened wide. "You can't trust your brother? I always wanted a brother. An older brother would have been great, but I would have even taken a younger one. Beggars can't be choosers. I thought then I'd have an ally, someone on my side."

Mark crossed his arms. "I hate to disappoint you, but it's nothing like that. I've never been able to count on him at all. He played me from the time we were little. You're lucky you didn't have a brother. He could have turned out like mine."

"But now we have each other, don't we? We're better than brothers. We can protect each other like no one else can." Mercury looked around. "I'd better go before they see us together. I don't want our plan to be ruined."

"You still haven't shared the plan with me. What's it a plan for?" Mark inquired.

"When the time is right, you'll know," Mercury answered.

Mark watched as his friend crouched low and darted out of the room.

The following week, an orderly entered the common room and approached Mark, who was sitting alone at the wooden table, playing solitaire and waiting for Brandon to show up.

"Collins. It's time for your session with Dr. Wendell now."

"Fine." Mark put his cards down on the table and stood up. They strolled to the doctor's office. She motioned for them to enter.

"You are looking well today. How are you feeling?" Dr. Wendell asked.

"I was doing fine until Sasquatch here broke up my card game," he replied, motioning at the orderly.

The orderly muttered something inaudible and closed the door as he departed.

Dr. Wendell reviewed Mark's file and closed it. "You've made tremendous progress lately. I know you were disappointed that the outpatient therapy idea didn't work. I have a new idea I think you'd be interested in. Do you think you're ready for a change of scenery?"

Mark's heart raced. "What do you mean by change of scenery?" He hoped the doctor didn't notice his voice had cracked. He was terrified she might send him back to prison.

"I have recommended you for an in-house work program. I think it will be beneficial to you."

A wave of relief overcame him. "What kind of work program?" Mark asked.

"You will be working laundry detail. You'll pick up dirty laundry, towels, and linens, and deliver clean items to the residents. You'll have contact with the laundry service personnel as well as the institute's housekeeping staff." Dr. Wendell paused for a moment to gauge his initial reaction. "How does that sound?"

Mark perked up. "It sounds great. When do I start?"

"You can start tomorrow. I'm very hopeful this will be a positive experience for you. If all goes well, you should be released back into society very soon."

"How soon?"

"Maybe another month or so."

Another month sounded like an eternity. Nevertheless, Mark smiled. "I'll be counting on that, Dr. Wendell."

Then Mark was abruptly awakened from this recurring sequence of nightmares and dreams by the screams of a distraught patient.

Chapter 3

From the gazebo, Sara glanced toward the house. Faint jazz music played in the background. It seemed the Devonshire party was still going strong. From this vantage point, she observed the activity inside for several minutes before turning her attention back to the water. She preferred to stay outside for now. She stretched out across the loveseat, knees bent, with a multi-striped pillow behind her. In this position, she relaxed and absorbed the peaceful atmosphere and the sound of the waves. She sought to float away her worries and problems under the cloudless sky. Millions of stars joined the moonlight to glisten on the water. The atmosphere made her pensive.

Sara hoped a shooting star would make an appearance, so she could make a wish. As she contemplated what she would wish for, a pleasant-looking woman approached. The woman, with gray waist-length hair, wore a peasant-style blouse, a multicolored skirt, and too many necklaces and bracelets to count.

The woman introduced herself. "Hello. I'm Eva Seville, a creative writing professor at St. Peter's. Have we met somewhere before?" The woman studied Sara with a moderate degree of intensity.

Sara didn't recognize the woman. "No, I don't believe we have. I'm Sara Taylor. I came here with Joe Lazaro, one of the foreign language professors."

The woman nodded and smiled. "Would you mind if I joined you?"

Sara didn't want to appear rude. "No, I don't mind at all."

Eva lowered herself into a wicker chair on Sara's left. "Beautiful evening. Perfect for clearing one's mind and renewing one's spirit."

"Yes, it is a beautiful evening," Sara responded, hoping that would end the conversation.

Eva persisted. "I sense that you are out here to regain your spiritual center."

Sara couldn't believe her luck and wondered why eccentric people tended to gravitate to her. She replied, "No, I just wanted a little fresh air, that's all."

Eva nodded and smiled again. "Well, while you are just getting a little fresh air, would you like to look into your future? I have my tarot cards with me."

If Sara had any doubts before, they were gone. She definitely had a flashing neon sign over her head, directing all weirdoes to her. Sara politely protested. "I wouldn't want to trouble you."

"Oh. It is no trouble at all, I assure you. Quite the contrary, it would be my pleasure."

"Well, if you insist," Sara reluctantly agreed. Her peaceful moment gone, she swung her legs around and sat up properly, hands in her lap. "I'm sure it will be quite enlightening." Sara thought Eva might pick up on the sarcasm and leave her alone. She didn't.

Eva heaved her large bag onto the table. In a matter of seconds, Eva had set a candle in the center of the table. Sara didn't think it was necessary because of the torches surrounding the backyard. It could also be a potential fire hazard—although there was plenty of sand available to put out a fire.

Eva prepared to light some incense.

The incense reminded Sara of church, when the priest would use it on Christmas and Easter. She disliked incense. "Could you please not light the incense? It gives me a headache."

Eva returned the incense to her bag. "Sure, dear. No incense. Is the candle all right?"

"Yes, the candle is fine," Sara replied. She wondered what else was in the seemingly bottomless bag.

"Excellent. Let's get started then." Eva removed a wrapped bundle from her bag and situated it on the table. She grasped a piece of the material at the center, which looked like black velvet, and peeled it back to lay it flat on the table. The movement was repeated three additional times, revealing a deck of cards in the middle of the cloth.

"Do you have a specific question that you would like answered? Or would you like a general reading?" Eva inquired, picking up the cards.

"I guess I'll take the general reading."

"Please clear your mind, and shuffle the cards until you feel comfortable. Then place them into three separate piles on the table," Eva instructed, handing Sara the deck.

Sara shuffled the cards awkwardly. The cards were larger than a regular deck of playing cards and were difficult to handle. After shuffling for a minute or so, she split the cards into three uneven piles. Eva picked up the first pile, then the last pile, then the middle pile. Sara assumed there was a reason for that, but she didn't ask.

Eva dealt the cards into three rows. The first row consisted of three cards. The middle row contained one card, positioned under the second card of the first row. The third row included three cards, mirroring the first row.

Sara eyed the arrangement. It resembled the capital letter I.

Eva studied the cards. She touched the card in the bottom right corner, from Sara's perspective. Eva explained, "The first card of the first row represents your past."

Sara realized her view was upside down. Apparently, the cards were placed so that Eva could read them. Therefore, Eva's top row was her bottom row. The card Eva touched pictured a man in a tunic, holding a cup with a fish coming out of it in front of a body of water.

"This card is the Page of Cups. This could have been a man in your life, a fun-loving person. The astrological signs associated with this card are Cancer, Scorpio, and Pisces."

Sara edged closer to the table. "I'm sure that's Joe. He's a Cancer. He's an old boyfriend of mine."

Eva looked up from the cards. "The same Joe that escorted you to tonight's party?"

"Yes. We're still friends." She wanted to add, "Yeah, yeah. I know. I can't let go of the past. I need to get on with my life. I've heard it all before." But she didn't feel the need to explain herself and wanted this to end quickly.

"Friends? I see."

Sara's blood pressure started to rise. She sat back, crossed her legs, and folded her arms. She wanted to know what gave this woman the right to judge her. She also didn't care for the tone in her voice.

Oblivious of her impact on Sara's mood, Eva continued. "Let's move on. The next card represents how you felt in the past. Your card is the Chariot, and, interestingly enough, it is also connected with Cancer."

Sara thought this card appeared mystical. A man with a scepter in his hand rode on a chariot. There were two sphinx-like creatures in front of it.

"The Chariot represents a journey. You will notice the two sphinxes in front—one is black, the other, white. They represent the good and bad aspects of your quest. The decision you made as a result of your journey helped you move forward."

Intrigued, Sara uncrossed her legs. "I didn't really go on any trips. I went on some family vacations. Do those count?"

"My dear, a journey does not necessarily indicate that you took an actual trip. Rather, think of an emotional event, an exploration of sorts—something that transcended you to a different place in a spiritual sense."

"Oh." Sara started to twirl her hair around her right index finger. After a moment, she realized what she was doing and stopped. She hadn't twirled her hair in years. She used to twirl it while she studied for tests. She shouldn't be nervous now—annoyed maybe, curious maybe, but not nervous.

Eva interrupted Sara's internal dialogue. "Did you have an experience that you feel impacted you profoundly?"

Sara paused before answering. The laughter from the main house had grown louder, which threw off her concentration momentarily. Then she thought about her life. She had had a lot of emotional experiences, especially in high school. Raging hormones, peer pressure, parental pressure—all there for the choosing. However, there was one experience that topped them all. And she knew it.

"The biggest tragedy of my life was when my brother died. That brought on a lot of emotions, probably every emotion I had and then some. I wouldn't wish that on anyone. I learned a lot about myself and other people. I learned who my real friends were. I also learned that I was stronger than I thought I was." Sara glanced at Eva for some confirmation that she had picked the right experience and received none. So she continued. "The only other thing I can think of was when Joe went to college. That was a significant emotional event at the time. Well, then there was this guy I dated in college ..."

Eva interrupted. "It is not for me to say which event is the right event. I just interpret the cards. It is up to you to decide what they relate to."

"But one of those events should be what the card is referring to, right?" Sara searched Eva's face for a clue.

"Perhaps it will become clearer to you as we discuss the remaining cards," Eva replied. "The last card in the row represents what you have learned. It is the Six of Wands. Wands are associated with the fire signs—Aries, Leo, and Sagittarius."

Sara thought the wands looked more like long sticks than wands. In her mind, wands were devices that wizards carried. The man on horseback held a wand. He didn't look like a wizard to her. A wreath crowned his head, and he wore a cape, as did the horse. Other men carried wands, but they could not be seen clearly, as they stood behind the horse.

"This is a good card. It means that things in your life were resolved well. Remember, you need to think about different areas in your life, such as love, school, or a job. There was a time when good things happened after your journey."

"After my brother died, I realized the importance of relationships. A lot of friends and neighbors did what they could to help. I even joined a grief support group for a while. Emotionally, I don't think I could have made it without the support of friends and family. They helped me realize that I had to go on with life. I worked hard and graduated with a good grade point average from college. Some of the courses were really tough. I guess all those hours I spent studying paid off. I landed a really good-paying job."

Sara realized she had been rambling and stopped, looking at Eva for some acknowledgment or reassurance that she was on the right track. Eva offered none. This lack of interaction and the vague answers irritated Sara. In her mind, there should be a right answer and a wrong answer.

Eva tapped her index finger on the lone card in the center row. "I find this card most interesting. This is the Eight of Cups. It represents your present. I am not surprised by it at all. Not all at."

"Why? What does it mean?" Sara unconsciously bent closer to the cards.

There were eight cups stacked in the foreground of the card, nothing too bizarre. It reminded her of a carnival game she played as a child. If you knocked down all of the bottles, you won a prize. She regained her focus and studied the man in the background. He wore a red robe and shoes and clutched a walking stick. He seemed to be wandering into a mountain range with a winding river.

"You appeared to be pondering something when I approached. Apparently, I was correct. This card tells me you are discontent. You are looking for something. Perhaps another journey is on your horizon."

"I have been thinking about changing jobs. I just don't know what I'd rather do. I guess I need to figure it out. But you're right. I'm not that happy with the way my life is at the moment. My job is boring, and I figured I would be married or at least engaged by now."

"You control your destiny. You can change the course of your life, if you choose."

"I just don't know what to choose. *That's* the problem." Sara stiffened and sat upright, crossing her arms in front of her.

Laughter from the main house swelled again. Sara turned her

head to see what had caused the commotion. She saw nothing out of the ordinary.

Eva bowed her head. "Perhaps the cards will help you find a new direction. Let's continue on."

Sara resigned herself to her current situation. "Sure. I've come this far. We might as well."

"The next card represents things that will be entering your life shortly."

This card's appearance concerned Sara. The picture portrayed a man sitting up in bed, his hands covering his face, with nine swords hanging over his head.

Eva continued. "The Nine of Swords is not exactly a welcome card. It signifies suffering brought on by others or an upcoming battle. The signs for this suit are Gemini, Libra, and Aquarius."

"Oh, great! Just what I need—pain *and* suffering," Sara muttered sarcastically.

Eva explained, "This could mean something as simple as catching a cold, or perhaps mental anguish—such as when trying to make a decision—that can cause physical pain, like stomach aches or headaches."

"Great. I can't wait." Sara rolled her eyes.

"Whatever it is, do not sit around and feel sorry for yourself. You must gather your strength and take control of your situation."

"Well, *that's* easier said than done."

"*Everything* is easier said than done. You just need to be mindful when dealing with upcoming events," Eva persisted.

Sara's frustration got the best of her. "I'll try. It's hard when you don't know what to look for. But if I see a bus trying to run me over, I'll know to jump out of the way."

"I sense your frustration. Just be aware of your surroundings, and you will not be caught off guard. We are almost done. The next card indicates how the events will affect you."

Sara raised her eyebrows. "It doesn't look like a friendly card either. A lightning bolt is hitting the tower. Flames are shooting out from the windows, and two people are falling from the burning building. No matter what, it can't be good."

"Your assessment is correct. The Tower symbolizes disaster and destruction."

"So I get to look forward to a disaster, as well as pain and suffering? Oh, this is just getting better and better."

"But you must look deeper. Disaster might not strike every facet of your life. It might simply be in one area."

"Wonderful. So disaster might not strike every part of my life, but could it?"

"Yes. It is possible, depending on the nature of the situation."

Sara laughed uncomfortably. "You've got to be kidding me."

"No. Try not to dwell on the negative. Although the Tower falls, what you gather from the ashes should have a stronger foundation as a result."

"Whatever doesn't kill me will make me stronger? I've heard that one before, more times than I'd like to count."

"Perhaps your negativity will lessen when you hear the meaning of the last card. That card is the outcome of the upcoming events. Are you ready for the last card?"

"Sure. Why not? At least the man on that card doesn't look like he's being tortured." Sara thought the man actually looked happy. He sat with his arms crossed. Nine cups were placed above him.

"Your card is the Nine of Cups. Some people like to call it the wish card."

Sara asked incredulously, "The wish card?"

"Yes, the wish card. What you dream could, in fact, become reality."

"If I dream something tonight, it might happen? I don't always have good dreams. I don't know if that's a good thing."

"Do not take it literally. I am talking about your hopes and dreams for the future, not your nightly dreams. This is a good card. I believe its placement is crucial in this reading."

"Why is that?"

"You have seen that the future holds some unpleasantness. This card provides hope that what you truly desire will be yours."

Sara searched for a straight answer. "So I just have to get past the pain *and* the suffering *and* the big disaster, *then* everything will be fine?"

"I didn't say that. You will get what you wish for—that doesn't necessarily mean everything will be fine. It is important to remember that these cards do not predict the future. You have the power to change the course of your life and your destiny. Do not be discouraged by what you saw today—use it to your advantage instead. Depending on how you handle upcoming events, you can change your future. *You* hold the key. Remember that. *You* control your own destiny, and you should embrace it."

"I'll remember that." Sara glanced at her watch. She couldn't believe how long the tarot reading had taken. It was four minutes before ten o'clock. "Wow! How time flies! I really must be going. Would you like me to help clean up?"

"No. I am going to sit here awhile longer."

"Okay, it was nice meeting you."

"It was my pleasure. Have a lovely evening."

"Thank you, you too," Sara replied, picking up her shoes. She walked toward the main house.

Eva dealt four more cards around the Tower, placing them clockwise, starting above the Tower. She viewed the cards, knitted her brow, and blew out the candle. "Poor dear. She will have a difficult road ahead, no matter what path she chooses." She gathered the cards together and wrapped them in the black velvet cloth before depositing the cards back into her bag.

Sara dwelt on Eva's words as she trudged through the sand. Now the sand felt cold and irritating between her toes. *Disaster, gloom, and doom. Great way to spend an evening, Sara. But hey, I can change my destiny. All I have to do is try. Yeah, but try what? That is the million dollar question, isn't it?*

Sara worked her way through the crowd that had migrated outside and entered the cottage through the kitchen. Brushing the sand from her feet, she slipped her shoes back on.

Across the room, Joe was talking to a man Sara didn't recognize. Jessica Davis was gone. The mystery man with thick, brown, curly hair wore black pants and a blue shirt.

As she crossed the room, Sara subconsciously sucked in her stomach. Reaching the men, she addressed Joe, "Miss me? I've been outside for a while."

He had missed her. Once he had freed himself from Jessica, he had started searching the side yard and immediate grounds. He had been worried that she had called for a cab and gone home without him. He was relieved to see she had stuck around.

"So, Joe, are you going to introduce me to your friend?"

"Oh, yeah. Sara, this is David Turner. He started teaching biology a few semesters ago." Turning to David, Joe introduced Sara. "This is Sara Taylor. She works for DAGS Engineering."

David flashed a brilliant white smile, which extended to his chocolate brown eyes, as he offered his hand to Sara. "Nice to meet you, Sara. We were just talking about the great water view out back."

As his warm hand enveloped hers, Sara admired David's handsome face and muscular frame. She decided he must spend hours lifting weights to maintain that physique.

She agreed, "The view is wonderful. I was just out there enjoying it myself." Then she heard herself ask David, "Would you like to go to dinner sometime?"

Joe looked at her, stunned.

Sara couldn't believe the words were coming out of her mouth, but she kept talking, rapidly. "I really like Italian food. If you like Italian food, I know of a nice restaurant we could go to. That is, if you are interested."

David smiled. "Sure. Why not?"

"How about tomorrow?" she suggested.

Joe had become more confused and jealous as the conversation progressed. He and Sara had agreed to see other people, in theory. So he put up a good front, but he always believed that he and Sara would wind up together in the end. He had hoped that they would rekindle their romance later that night. Now that seemed highly improbable.

David said, "Tomorrow won't work for me. I'm actually booked for most of the week. I'm the volunteer coordinator at St. Peter's Mission. I'm short people this week. I'm pulling double and triple duty. Could I interest you in a Saturday night dinner? Around six-thirty?"

"Sure," she agreed.

"Sounds like a plan. I'll get directions to your place from Joe." Turning to Joe, David confirmed, "Right, Joe?"

Startled, Joe replied, "Huh?"

David clarified, "Directions."

Unenthusiastically, Joe said, "Yeah, sure."

Sara smiled. "Great, it's a date. I'll look forward to it."

David caught the time on the wall clock. "I hate to meet and run, but I have a long day tomorrow. I really have to go. Have a good night. Until Saturday."

Sara's smile widened. "Until Saturday then." Turning to Joe, she said, "It's past my bedtime, I think it's time to go."

Joe gazed at her, perplexed. "What the hell was that?"

"Nothing. Why?"

"Nothing, my ass."

"Whatever," she replied in a dismissive tone. "By the way, where have you been hiding him? He seems a little older. Has he been married before?"

Jealously, Joe replied, "No, he's still single. And wouldn't you like to ask him those questions on your first date? You know, small talk? You wouldn't want to run out of topics and have to start talking marriage and babies and scare the guy off after fifteen minutes."

"Are you kidding me? Give me some credit will you?"

"I don't know if I can after the way you just reacted to meeting him. Geez, Sara, it's like you'd never seen a man before. What the hell is wrong with you?"

"I don't know. I really don't. It must be the combination of my tarot card reading and meeting David right afterward."

"Tarot card reading? What are you talking about? Have you

been drinking? At least *that* would explain your behavior." Joe wiped the sweat off his forehead with the back of his hand.

"I am not drunk, you idiot. The creative writing lady, Eva ... Eva ... what's her last name? It reminded me of a Cadillac."

"Seville?"

"Yeah, that's it. She whipped out her tarot cards and did a reading for me. It was bizarre. She kept telling me I could control my own destiny. Some of the stuff she said got me thinking. I figure if I do crazy things that I don't normally do, I can change my destiny. Hence, the bad things won't happen. Then I met David. It was just timing. That's all."

"Uh huh," Joe grunted. "Let's get you home before you get into any more trouble."

Sara placed her left hand on her hip and poked Joe in the chest with her right index finger. "Wasn't it you who said I needed a more exciting social life? Well, I'm doing just that, thank you very much."

Joe backed up to avoid getting poked repeatedly. "You're right. You're always right. Let's go home."

Sara agreed.

As they walked up to the attendant, Joe produced the valet ticket. The attendant, flashlight in hand, jogged down the sidewalk and out of sight.

"So how did things go with Jessica?" Sara asked antagonistically with a singsongy lilt on Jessica's name.

"We're having lunch together tomorrow," Joe replied reluctantly.

Sara's hands went straight to her hips. "Wait a freaking minute. You give *me* grief because I *tried* to set up a date for tomorrow, and *you* actually *have* a date for tomorrow? Give me a break!" She turned away from him and crossed her arms.

"No. It's totally different." He tried to turn Sara around to face him.

Sara shrugged him off. "Okay, Einstein, explain how it's different."

"If you turn around, I'll tell you."

Defensively, she turned toward him again.

His injured pride prevented him from admitting that he had accepted the date by accident. He began, "For the record, she asked me, I didn't ask her."

Sara rolled her eyes.

He continued. "Anyway, a girl asking a guy out for lunch is totally different from a girl asking a guy out to dinner. Ask anyone."

She tilted her head and responded with her arms still crossed. "Sorry. Not good enough."

"Fine," he said with a sigh. "First of all, I already know Jessica from school. Second, we will be meeting in the school's food court at eleven thirty in the morning. We both have to teach a class at one o'clock." *Third, I don't love her. I love you.* He continued. "So my date will be a light, casual event. There won't be any awkward, 'How do we end this date?' moment. Your situation, on the other hand, involves a guy you *just* met. He'll be picking you up in his car and driving you to a restaurant. After the meal, he'll drive you home. God knows what he'll expect. *See?* Big difference."

"Says you."

"Yeah, says me. You have to admit it was forward of you to ask David to dinner."

"*Forward? Forward?* Why? Are you jealous?"

Joe didn't answer, although every part of his being wanted to scream *yes* at her. Instead, he walked down the sidewalk, away from her, in an attempt to avoid a fight. Sara chased after him. When she caught up to him, she maneuvered in front of him and stopped. He stopped but didn't say a word. He just stared at her.

Uncomfortable with the silence, Sara threw her arms up in the air. "Well, if it will make you happy, I'll admit what a forward girl I am. Why don't you slap a scarlet letter A on my chest while you're at it?" Dramatically, she slapped the imaginary letter on herself.

"Oh, don't get so bent out of shape. You demanded that I explain the difference, so I did." Joe saw the valet pulling up with his car. "Here comes the car." He rolled his eyes heavenward.

Joe tipped the valet after he helped Sara get in. He circled the Pontiac to look for any damage and didn't see any. Then he got in, turned on the radio, and drove to Sara's house. They didn't speak for the duration of the drive.

Minutes from their destination, Joe glanced over at Sara, who was sound asleep. He turned on to Springhill Drive and, subsequently, into her driveway. As he turned off the car, he looked at her and reminisced how they used to talk about spending the rest of their lives together. He still wanted that; he just didn't know if she felt the same way.

Joe regretted the time they spent apart. The blame rested squarely on his shoulders. Other lovers might have been more wild or adventurous, but none truly satisfied him. Something was always missing. His heart just didn't connect with the other women, and it was breaking without Sara. He realized that Sara was the only love for him.

Joe was spellbound with Sara's alluring beauty and her dazzling smile. Her caress energized him in ways he couldn't describe. Her come-hither look was totally disarming. The touch of her lips was pure heaven. Longing to embrace her, he whispered, "You're as beautiful now as you were the first time I saw you. I love you, and I want to be with you. I wish you could see that." He gently kissed Sara's cheek.

Sara opened her eyes and groggily looked at him. "Sorry. I must have dozed off. It was a long day." She yawned.

"Do you want me to walk you to your door?" he offered.

She stretched and yawned again. "Sure, why not? I am a little sleepy. I wouldn't want to trip and fall into the bushes."

"Yeah, we wouldn't want a repeat of the last time you fell off the porch into the bushes. All I could see were your feet sticking up."

"Uh huh. That was a laugh riot."

"Hey, I didn't laugh until I knew you were all right. Then we both laughed as I fished you out."

"I remember."

Joe escorted her to the front door, removed her house key and driver's license from his wallet, and handed them to her.

Sara failed to insert the key into the lock.

"Let me help you." Joe took the key from her. In a flash, he unlocked and opened the door. They entered the house.

Sara closed the door behind them.

They stood facing each other. The hallway was faintly illuminated by the porch lights through the windows on either side of the door.

Sara spoke first. "I had an interesting time tonight. It beat sitting on the couch watching a girly movie. Thanks for convincing me to go. Sorry I snapped at you earlier."

"Don't mention it. I already forgot about it."

"Thanks. Did you want to come in?"

Joe laughed. "Technically, I'm already in. But it's really late, and we both have to go to work in the morning. Can I take a rain check?"

"Sure. One rain check it is." Sara looked up at Joe. His wavy hair was a mess, as usual. She reached up and ran her fingers through it to fix it. "There, perfect." Her hands lingered. She caressed his cheek. Their eyes met.

Impulsively, his arms wrapped around her. He pulled her body closer to him. The pent-up sexual tension screamed to be released. Unable to deny the attraction any longer, they kissed. Although the kiss began sensually and sweet, it quickly became passionate, almost frantic.

Sara pulled Joe's shirt out from the waistband of his pants. She kicked off her shoes. He followed suit. He backed her up against the door. The heat between them was still there, burning as hot as ever. With one hand behind her neck, he kissed her as he slid his other hand up her skirt. Sara inhaled deeply, knowing what would happen next. Joe's fingers found their way to the thong Sara wore. He bypassed it. Slowly, he touched her. Joe's massage technique drove Sara wild with desire. Fighting the feeling of being weak in the knees, Sara started grinding against him. Already rock hard, Joe struggled to maintain control. Sara unbuttoned her blouse to reveal a sexy, lacy bra. That inspired Joe to place kisses from her neck to her breasts. Enjoying every second, Sara gasped and stepped back slightly, teasingly.

Restraining himself, he asked, "Do you want me to stop?"

Brushing her hand across the front of his pants, she bit his earlobe and whispered, "No, I want you. *Now.*"

Searching for the truth in her eyes, he asked, "Is that really what you want?"

"Yes," Sara said with a sigh, trembling in anticipation.

That was all the confirmation Joe needed. Urgently, Sara attempted to unbutton his pants. He stopped her. She looked at him, anxious and confused.

Joe explained, "Not here—in the foyer." He swept her up in his arms and carried her to her bedroom. She pretended to protest the change in locale, but that didn't last long. After carrying Sara across the threshold, Joe gently placed her on the bed.

When he did not join her immediately, Sara asked, "What's wrong?"

"The door's open."

"Well, hurry up and close it."

He followed the command and multitasked by removing his clothes before rejoining her.

"That was quick."

Joe reassured her. "That will be the only thing that will be."

"Really?"

"Count on it."

Joe wanted this moment to be perfect. He had dreamt about their reunion countless times. Taking his time, he slipped Sara's blouse off her shoulders while kissing the swell of her breasts. With one hand, he deftly unclasped her bra. It landed on the floor, on top of the ever-growing pile of unwanted clothing. Caressing her breasts, his touch was slow, tender, and warm.

Although they hadn't been intimate in years, it seemed as if no time had passed. She trusted him and surrendered her body to him. They connected on a level she had never felt with anyone else. Although enjoying the foreplay tremendously, Sara longed to make love to him. Desire rushed through her body in waves, like a fever.

After Joe succeeded in slipping off Sara's skirt and thong, he admired her beautiful, smooth skin before resuming any further physical contact.

Sara worried. "You're not having second thoughts, are you?"

"No."

"Then what are you waiting for?"

Joe answered her question with a tantalizing kiss. He loved the way her skin felt next to his. He took his time exploring, touching every inch of her. Sara didn't complain. She loved the feel of his lips and his hands roaming across her body. She felt alive, and compensated by showering him with affection. Joe savored each sensual touch, kiss, and caress Sara bestowed upon him.

Finally, their bodies were united. Synchronized almost immediately, they moved to their familiar rhythm. Joe concentrated to ensure the experience would last long enough for Sara. He knew he had achieved that goal when Sara's moans grew louder and her nails dug into his back.

Sara succumbed to the emotions she could not adequately describe and begged, *"Don't stop, Joe!"*

Joe would not disappoint her. They made love until they climaxed together.

Out of breath, Joe said, "I'm not done with you yet."

"Really?"

"Really," Joe responded.

Joe cupped one breast, while his tongue and lips teased the other. He knew all of Sara's hot buttons and ensured sufficient attention was paid to each and every one. As a result, Sara experienced the first multiple orgasm she had had since the last time they were together. Joe maintained a deep and steady pace for the duration of her orgasm before allowing himself to give in to his own pleasure. Satisfied and exhausted, they separated.

Joe brushed the hair away from Sara's face. They remained silent, gazing into each other's eyes, fearing the moment would end. Sara nudged closer to him and rested her head on his chest.

Joe wrapped his arms around her. She listened to his rapid heartbeat. When they were younger, they would fall asleep in this position. Tonight, they were both too wired to sleep.

Finally, Sara broke the silence and joked, "Gee, it's too bad you couldn't stay."

Trying to catch his breath, Joe replied, "Yeah. Who knows what could have happened." He ached to apologize for screwing everything up, but he wasn't sure she wanted him back. *She didn't say she loved me while we made love. She always used to. This time she didn't.*

He inhaled deeply and exhaled slowly. *Maybe she doesn't love me anymore. After what I did, I can't blame her. But watching her date other guys is killing me. Why can't she see that?*

Instead he simply said, "I guess I'd better get going." But he didn't move a muscle. He hoped she would ask him to stay and never leave.

Sara longed for Joe to spend the night. Apparently, that wasn't what he wanted. So she said, "I could help you get dressed, if you want me to."

Her mind fought with itself.

- *That's not what I wanted to say. I want to tell him that I love him.*
- *But what if he doesn't love me anymore? He has a date with Jessica.*
- *But we just made love. That has to mean something. I felt the connection. It seemed like he did too.*
- *But he didn't say he loved me, so maybe this was just about sex.*

Disappointed, Joe interrupted her train of thought. "No. I think you've done quite enough. If you help me get dressed, I'll never get out of here. Thanks anyway."

Joe mentally kicked himself. *This isn't a one-night stand. I need to tell her that and apologize for everything. And I need to tell her that I love her.*

Despite the internal bickering, neither Joe nor Sara expressed their true feelings.

"Suit yourself." Sara sat up on the bed and watched Joe get dressed. Then she slipped on a robe and escorted him to the front door. She opened the door. They both said good night at the same time.

Joe walked to his car as Sara waved and closed the door. Her heart and body yearned for him. She convinced herself that this relationship was probably one-sided on her part and that to him, good sex was just that, good sex.

Joe drove home battling the feeling to turn around and confess his love for Sara. He managed to make it home. Entering his condo, he threw his keys on the counter. After removing his clothes, he wadded them up and tossed them into the laundry room. He missed the overflowing basket, not caring. Continuing into the bathroom, he relieved himself, brushed his teeth, and fell into bed. Sleep found him as his head hit the pillow.

Joe dreamt only one dream that night. Beautiful, naked women surrounded him on a private beach as he lounged under a large umbrella. Four women fanned him with large palm fronds. Two other women alternately fed him grapes. A water boy spritzed him occasionally with a water mist. The other men on the beach envied him. Women from all around lined up to catch a glimpse of him. He enjoyed his kingly status until Sara walked by. Her long, brown hair flowed with the breeze. She wore a simple, white, gossamer cover-up. She glanced in his direction for only a moment and kept walking.

Joe struggled out of the lounge chair and pushed the attentive women aside, running clumsily after Sara. He repeatedly stumbled in the sand and called out to her. Her gait never wavered. Regaining his footing, he resumed his chase.

In the distance, a gazebo, decorated with colorful flowers, beckoned. As she approached, the linen panels separated and were drawn up like a stage curtain. She entered and seductively motioned him to follow. After what seemed an eternity, he reached the gazebo. As he entered, the panels, which had been tied back, fell into place and blocked out the rest of the beach.

As Joe approached Sara, she tugged on the string of her cover-up. It fell slowly and gracefully to the sand, revealing her beautifully tanned body. Pressing her naked body against his, she touched her fingers to his lips, not allowing him to speak. Joe was at full attention.

Grasping his hands, she led him to the luxurious blanket laid out on the sand. Warm chocolate and fresh strawberries were on a plate next to the blanket and pillows. She reclined effortlessly on the blanket and adjusted the pillows. He quickly joined her.

Sara instructed him sensually, using only her eyes, her lips, and her tongue. Receiving the message loud and clear, Joe dipped a strawberry in the chocolate and offered it to her. She accepted and slowly sucked the excess chocolate off his fingertips. He attempted to repeat this task, but her interest had shifted. She knocked the strawberry out of his hand and whispered, "Make love to me."

After a short time, he felt the water boy spritz them with water. Joe did not want to spoil the moment, so he ignored it. On the edge of climaxing, he felt a strong, cold, pressurized stream of water on his lower back. Unable to disregard the cold water any longer, he looked up. The water boy had morphed into his mother, Rose.

"Joey, what did I tell you about being naked?" As she reached her arms heavenward and dropped to her knees, Rose Lazaro exclaimed, "Jesus, Mary, and Joseph, give me strength! And to make matters worse, you're having sex so everyone in the neighborhood can see you. *There* you are—in *all* your glory. You've humiliated your mother. Are you happy now? Answer me! Are you happy *now?*"

Joe's alarm clock deprived him of the opportunity to see how his dream ended.

Sara climbed into bed, clutched the pillow Joe had used, and inhaled deeply. His intoxicating scent lingered. After staring at the ceiling for half an hour, she finally fell asleep. Nonetheless, her dream started almost immediately.

It began in front of what appeared to be a castle. A music box played a familiar tune in the background. A fairy flitted along and motioned Sara to follow. As they entered the castle, a pair of glass slippers floated in mid-air, accompanied by a handwritten note that rested on a pink satin pillow. Sara removed her shoes and put the slippers on. They fit perfectly. The note read, "Your prince awaits." She turned to ask the fairy to guide her to the prince, only to discover she was alone.

Wandering down the hallway, she found an ornate side table. On it rested a key. Sara believed the key must fit one of the massive doors in the corridor. She picked it up and methodically tried every door in the hall. It did not fit any of them. Disappointed but undaunted, she returned to the foyer to contemplate her next move.

After some deliberation, she mounted the grand spiral staircase. The marble steps were steep, but the prince waited on the top landing. She waved to him. He returned the gesture. For some reason, she couldn't see his face clearly.

With only three more steps to climb, the steps collapsed under her. The spiral staircase transformed into a slippery slide, sending Sara on a downward journey. She clawed at the railings, to no avail. She attempted to use her feet as brakes. That effort proved unsuccessful as well. Closing her eyes, she braced for impact. Despite her efforts to the contrary, Sara hit the floor hard.

When she opened her eyes, Sara was laying on the floor of her bedroom, tangled in sheets. "Stupid dream." Annoyed, she pulled and kicked the sheets off herself. She stood up and threw them back on the bed. However, before she could rejoin her rumpled sheets, the alarm clock went off. "God, I hate mornings."

Chapter 4

MARK dressed and met Mercury in the common room, where they ate breakfast. Mercury wasn't interested in conversation and didn't eat much. He was too engrossed in developing more secret code for them to use. After staying briefly, he performed his "crouch and slink out of the room" routine.

Prior to reporting to the laundry room for work, Mark played a few hands of gin rummy with Brandon. Working laundry detail every day for two weeks had allowed him to befriend the members of the housekeeping staff and the laundry service drivers. They joked with one another. It felt like a normal job—except for the fact that everyone else came and went, while he remained locked up in Misty Pines.

In the middle of Mark's morning rotation, there was an unusual break in the standard routine. Nurses and orderlies desperately attempted to usher all of the residents back to their rooms. They met with a great deal of resistance. Something was definitely amiss.

Out of nowhere, Mercury appeared. Zipping by Mark, he declared, "Mars, the time has come! Watch for my signal."

Mark still didn't know the signal, the secret codes, or any other details about the plan. To humor the redheaded patient, Mark gave him the thumbs up sign as he disappeared around the corner. Curiosity led Mark down the hall, past frantic nurses and residents, to discover what had caused the commotion.

The head nurse, Helga Braun, finally stopped him. She was a solid woman. Her gray hair was pulled back tightly into a bun. Her demeanor seemed better suited for the military. Helga didn't really talk to people. She barked at them. He surmised she had either grown up in a military family or served in the military herself.

"What are you doing over here, Collins? Get to your room immediately," she ordered.

Leaning on his cart, he countered, "I thought I might be able to help or something."

"How are *you* going to help? A water pipe burst. It's flooding the pharmacy and medical supply area. Unless you can shut off the water main, I don't see how you can help," the impatient nurse replied.

Mark thought quickly. "Well, once they shut off the water, I can help clean up the mess. Mops can only do so much." Motioning to his cart, he said, "And I have clean, dry towels to sop up the water."

"Hmm ... you do have a point. Fine. Just stay out of the way until they shut off the water." Short on time, Helga marched down the hall to round up unruly patients.

"While I'm waiting, I'll go get another cart of dry towels," Mark declared to no one in particular as he strolled to the laundry room. When he reached the room, he found himself alone. Normally, Mark would have enjoyed a moment alone, standing on the loading dock, feeling the fresh air on his face. However, he didn't want to miss any of the action. He grabbed another cart, piled it with towels, and headed back to the waterlogged area.

Apparently, maintenance had gotten a late start placing water hogs on the floor to block the water. Therefore, the water continued to spill out of the room into the hallway and common room.

When Mark returned, he navigated through the flowing water and peeked inside the doorway to survey the medical supply room. High-pressured water sprayed out of the ruptured wall. He exclaimed, "Wow! That hole must be at least a foot across!"

Two young nurses ventured to protect the locked medicine cabinets by holding cafeteria trays in front of them like shields. Their efforts proved minimally effective, and this amused Mark tremendously. The nurses were dripping wet and miserable.

While he was laughing at their misfortune, Helga burst his moment of joy. She grabbed Mark's arm and dragged him into the supply room. Two orderlies waded through the water behind them.

Helga raised her voice to be heard over the sound of the rushing water. "They can't get the main shut off. We have to get the supplies out of this room."

The men watched her unlock the cabinets with her master key. Addressing the nurses, she directed, "You girls stay there, holding those trays, until I tell you to stop."

The two nurses struggled to maintain their footing against the force of the water as it pounded their makeshift shields. One girl lost her grip on her tray. She was blasted in the face with the full force of the water. She pinwheeled backward and fell into the rising sea of water.

Helga yelled, "Get up!"

Soaked and embarrassed, the nurse spat out a mouthful of water, pushed her wet hair behind her ears, and scrambled to her feet. Repositioning the tray, she rejoined the other nurse. "This is bullshit," she proclaimed to her fellow nurse.

"You got that right," the other nurse replied.

"Ready?" Helga bellowed, over the sound of the gushing water.

Mark shouted back, "Sure. Just tell me where you want them."

Pointing, Helga explained, "We've set up carts on the other side of the common room. Put these trays on the carts as quickly as you can. We can't afford to get these supplies and drugs wet."

With no time to waste, Helga relayed trays of bandages and miscellaneous medical supplies to Mark and the narcotics and other controlled substances to the orderlies. They hauled as many items as they could handle at a time, careful not to bump into the nurses holding the cafeteria trays, who fought a senseless, losing battle.

Despite the chaos and commotion, Mark paid close attention to the location of all of the drugs. A plan developed in his mind. And, as luck would have it, an entire pharmacy was at his disposal.

After twenty minutes, the orderlies announced they were taking a break. Needed elsewhere, Helga assisted in subduing a panicked resident. The two drenched nurses finally abandoned their posts in search of a more hospitable environment and dry uniforms. The sloshing sound transformed into squishing noises as they wandered down the hall.

Mark wheeled one of his laundry carts through the water, closer to the drug carts. He targeted the cart with the heavy-duty painkillers. It contained different drugs and dosages. Selecting the drug with the highest dosage, he slipped several bottles into his cart. Then he located an older drug, a tranquilizer his mother took years ago, and added it to his cache of drugs. Under the towels, the contraband couldn't be seen. After procuring some other basic medical supplies, he stashed them as well.

Even if someone moved the cart, they wouldn't notice anything amiss. The wet towels were heavy. The poached goods were light in comparison. As Mark congratulated himself, the orderlies returned. They complained that this type of cleanup duty wasn't in the job description. Maintenance should clean up the water.

Despite their objections, the two men joined Mark and dragged the chairs and tables out of the room until all of the room's contents were removed. The supply room would need extensive repairs before it would be useful again. When the water finally stopped flowing, maintenance pumped the water out through a hose that snaked through several corridors to the nearest exit door.

Mark looked at his watch. The laundry service was due to arrive in two hours. Reaching a drier patch of floor, Mark wrung out his pant legs. He needed to change out of his wet clothes and complete a few more tasks in the next two hours.

When the lunch bell sounded, the orderlies left in search of food. Mark took the initiative and dried the chairs and tables in the hall, as well as the shelving units permanently attached to the walls in the supply room. He managed to use every towel in both carts. Piling the wet, dirty towels on his carts, he tried not to smile. It proved difficult.

In squishing sneakers, Mark wheeled the cart with the drugs and wet towels to the laundry room, thankful for the short walk from the supply room, with no patient rooms in between. The staff was serving lunch to the residents in their rooms, since the common room couldn't be used. Roaming the empty halls was eerie. It also meant no witnesses.

Mark's wristwatch indicated there was still ample time. He returned to the scene of the crime and repeated the process with the other laundry cart. After this second trip, he arranged the carts, so the drug cart would be loaded first. He couldn't risk that cart getting left behind. The other loads of dirty bed linens, clothes, and towels were staged behind it.

Hurrying back to his room, Mark changed out of his wet clothes and sneakers and devoured the lunch that awaited him. Before leaving, he slid his diary out from under his mattress, tucked it into his waistband, and pulled his shirt out to conceal its presence. Then he rushed back to the laundry room.

A short time later, the laundry service's box truck beeped as it backed up to the loading dock into the open bay. The driver climbed out of the cab, engaged the dock lock, and extended the dock plate into the back of the truck.

Mark called out to him, "Hey, Chuck!"

"Hey, Mark! Where is everyone today? It looks like a ghost town down here," Chuck remarked.

"Yeah, a water pipe burst. There's quite a mess. Half of the staff is trying to keep the patients calm. The other half is cleaning up the mess. I got lucky enough to help clean up. We had to use all the spare towels we had to soak up the water. So there's a large load today."

"Big load, small load, it don't matter to me. I get paid the same, either way. Let's get this thing loaded."

Mark and Chuck hauled the carts into the back of the truck until three carts remained.

"Chuck, why don't you get your paperwork started? I'll load the last ones. That way you can finish up and still make it out of here on time," Mark offered.

Wiping the sweat off of his brow, Chuck said, "Well, I'm supposed to watch all the carts get loaded."

"It's only you and me here. As soon as I load the last one, I'll bang on the side of the truck. Then you'll know you're good to go."

"I don't know," Chuck hesitated.

"Come on. Who's going to know? It's not like I'm going to tell."

"I guess it'll be fine, just this once."

"Sure it will. Now get moving on that paperwork, or you're going to be late."

Chuck hopped into the cab of the truck and completed his paperwork as Mark finished loading the truck. Mark took one last look around, disengaged the dock plate and lock, and banged on the side of the truck as promised.

What Chuck didn't realize was that Mark had banged from inside the truck, instead of outside. Mark maneuvered to the nose of the truck. Repositioning some of the carts, he pulled a few towels over the edges of the carts, so he would be hidden from view.

Chuck drove up to the guard gate, stopped for inspection, and handed the guard his truck pass. "Shame that water pipe burst today. I heard there's quite a mess."

The guard replied, "That's what I heard too. I haven't seen anything. I've been stuck at this gate all shift. But that's fine with me. I don't mop floors." The guard inspected the vehicle and looked at the cargo. The truck was packed to capacity.

Mark's heart raced as sweat ran down his forehead and into his eyes. His eyes stung and his heart pounded, but he didn't breathe or move a muscle. Focusing on his objective, he willed the guard to keep moving.

Within a minute, the doors closed and locked. Mark breathed a sigh of relief. The guard signaled the driver to proceed, and the truck was on its way.

Mark contemplated his success in the back of the laundry truck. No matter how repulsive it smelled or hot it became, it was worth it—he had beaten the system. Laughing aloud, he extricated the drugs and medical supplies. He deposited them into a clean pillowcase he had thrown into the truck while loading it. The diary in his waistband found a home in the pillowcase as well.

After twenty minutes, the truck stopped and backed up. The cab door slammed. Mark could hear a man engage Chuck in conversation. Then the cargo door opened; a metal crashing noise followed. Mark stayed hidden. Sunlight peeked through the dangling, dirty laundry. A slight breeze entered the truck.

The unknown person said, "We'll have to unload you after the employee meeting. We gotta watch a safety training video."

"Anybody know how long it is?"

"Nope. No matter how long it is, it'll be too long," the man stated. The voices faded.

Mark waited a few minutes and didn't hear any additional vehicles or people moving around. The meeting must have started. He moved cautiously through the carts. Reaching the edge of the truck, he peered out. The coast was clear. A dock plate connected the truck to the dock, which explained the metal crashing noise. Pillowcase in hand, Mark walked casually off the back of the truck.

The door to the employee entrance stood propped open in front of him. Needing street clothes and a less conspicuous carrying case for his newly acquired supplies, Mark sprinted to the laundry service's back door and disappeared inside.

The faded blue sign in front of him indicated that the locker room was to his left. The office area was to the right. He proceeded toward the locker room. The smell—a combination of equally rancid odors—permeated the hall. The filthy floor and walls were illuminated with florescent lights, hanging from the ceiling. Several tubes were broken, so the room was sporadically lit. He tugged on locker handles until he found one that opened. "Empty. Damn."

Continuing to the next row of lockers, he spotted a black duffel bag on the bench. He unzipped the bag and examined its contents—a gray T-shirt and a pair of blue shorts. Confirming they were approximately the right size, he transferred the contents of the pillowcase into the large front pocket of the duffel bag. He removed his institute-issue shirt and pants, stuffed them into the bag, and put on his new clothes.

Retracing his steps, Mark vacated the building in search of transportation. The truck that delivered him posed too high of a risk. The diner parking lot next door teemed with cars. He could get a ride there.

"Collins!" a voice called.

Mark fought the urge to stop and turn, or worse—to run. Panic started to set in. Ignoring the voice, he kept walking.

"Collins! Matt Collins!" the voice yelled again.

An understandable mistake—Matt was Mark's twin brother. Mark relaxed, turned around, and said, "Yeah?"

"What do you mean *yeah*, you dumb shit? How about, 'Hi, Ray! How the hell are you?' Whoa! What'd you do to your hair? Let me guess. You got in a fight with a lawn mower and it won." Ray laughed heartily.

Mark hadn't seen Ray Peters in quite awhile. He was a few pounds heavier, but he was the same old Ray.

"Yeah, I got carried away with the trimmer. It's the new look for summer." Mark ran his hand over the top of his head. "Sorry, you startled me. I was deep in thought." He extended his hand.

Ray shook it.

"Good to see you, Ray."

"Is your truck still acting up? I don't see it parked in the lot."

"Yeah, it's still acting up," Mark replied, going along with the conversation.

Ray removed his well-worn baseball hat and scratched his head. "Told you that you should've let my brother-in-law take a look at it months ago. But no, you said you'd fix it yourself. We see what that got you."

"You know me. I'm stubborn."

"Ain't that the truth. Well, my offer still stands," Ray replied, repositioning the hat on his head.

"And what offer was that exactly?" Mark asked, fishing for details.

"My offer to let you borrow a vehicle for a week or so until you get that old Ford piece of shit fixed."

Those words were music to Mark's ears. "Ray, I think I'm going to take you up on that offer after all."

"It's about time. She's the white Chevy van there on the end, with the grill protector on it. I haven't had time to put the company logo on her yet."

"Company logo?"

"Well, yeah. I didn't buy it for personal use. I needed a new van for the laundry business that I just bought," he explained, pointing in the direction of the building from which Mark just emerged. "I bought it a week or so after we spoke. It just came out of the blue, with Mr. Chen passing away suddenly and all. But I'm not changing the name. I could've, but I decided against it. Everybody knows Chen's Laundry."

"So what happened to your factory job?"

"I ditched it. My foreman was pissing me off. I was this close to decking him," Ray replied, holding his fingers about an inch apart. "I jumped at the chance to be my own boss."

"How do you like it?"

"I love being the boss. Right now, I've got everybody in there watching a boring safety video. I'll never go back to working for anybody ever again."

"Sounds nice."

"It is. You know, I can always use a part-time driver if you're interested in making some extra money to help get that truck fixed. And because you're a good friend, I won't make you watch the stupid video. Whaddya think?"

"I'll think about it. Well, I'd love to stay and shoot the shit, but I've got somewhere I have to be."

"No problem. We'll catch up another time. The keys are in the ignition. Just make sure she comes back with a full tank of gas."

"Don't worry, I will." Mark extended his hand to Ray. They shook hands again. "Thanks a lot."

"We'll have to go fishing one of these days. We haven't been in ages."

"You're right. We'll have to do that sometime soon."

Mark couldn't believe his luck. He got in the van and dropped the duffel bag on the passenger's seat. After readjusting the seat, he started the engine, threw it in reverse, backed up, and shifted it into drive. He yelled out the window, "Thanks again for the ride. See you around." He pulled out of the parking lot and headed south to his house.

Mark felt giddy. He had slipped out of Misty Pines and obtained a vehicle without anyone being the wiser. The staff shouldn't miss him until dinnertime. A cursory glance at the clock display confirmed that event wouldn't occur for approximately three and a half hours. There was plenty of time. It was only four miles to the house.

Chapter 5

Joe met Jessica for lunch at St. Peter's food court. Several options were available to them, such as pizza, burgers, subs, Chinese food, gyros, and salads. After a short discussion, they decided on gyros. Joe waited in line for their order while Jessica chose a table. She picked a table outside, near the fountain, in the center of the courtyard. Red geraniums and low, dense hedges surrounded the fountain. The administration hoped this border would deter students from jumping in the fountain. It proved ineffective most of the time.

As Jessica waited, she crossed her legs and discretely checked her makeup in her compact mirror. After reapplying her lipstick, she slipped the mirror and lipstick back into her purse. Her blonde hair glistened in the sunlight. Without thinking, she flipped her hair over her shoulder. A cloud overhead intrigued her. Her mind transformed it from a butterfly to a dog with floppy ears within seconds. Tilting her head slightly to the left, it became a giant pair of mittens.

Joe passed the time in line talking to a former student. Minutes later, the server confirmed their order and handed it to Joe. A quick search of the courtyard revealed their table. He startled Jessica when he placed the red plastic food tray down. Her thoughts were still in the clouds. Joe didn't notice. He had spilled some soda on his hand, and it was running down his arm. After shaking his hand to remove the excess liquid, he dried it with a pile of napkins.

Joe chuckled. "I guess I wouldn't make it as a waiter."

"I guess not," she agreed, transferring her gyro and drink from the tray to the table. Jessica gushed, "I'm so glad we were finally able to meet for lunch. This is really nice." The art teacher uncrossed her legs, spread a napkin on her lap, and unwrapped her gyro.

"Yeah. We couldn't have asked for better weather," Joe answered agreeably but unenthusiastically. He unwrapped his lunch and took a large bite from his gyro.

Jessica continued, "And the weather for the party last night was so beautiful too. Although it got cool as the night went on, it was really nice." Daintily, she took another bite of her lunch.

Joe remembered it wasn't cool where he ended up last night. It was hot—*really hot.* He replied, "Yes. It's nice around the lake this time of year."

"One day I hope to have a cottage on the lake. Nothing too big, just a place to go every now and then. You know what I mean?"

If he could, Joe would live on the lake year-round. He loved the water, the sand, and everything it reminded him of—Sara. "Yes. I've always loved the water."

Jessica watched Joe dunk his curly fries in some ketchup. "See? We already have something in common. Isn't that wonderful?" Her smile extended to her eyes as she blushed.

A full mouth prevented him from answering. As time passed, Joe realized Jessica was really interested in him. He felt sorry for her. His thoughts and feelings were elsewhere. Jessica deserved better conversation, something with more substance. His heart just wasn't in it. The awkward silence made it evident that even having a simple conversation with Jessica was more difficult than he had anticipated.

Jessica broke the silence. "By the way, the art festival is coming up at the end of the month. It's very exciting. Some of my students will be displaying their work for the first time. Do you think you'll be able to attend?"

Joe didn't meet her gaze. "I'm not sure what my plans are for that week yet. I might have some translation work to do."

Joe did not have any translation work, nor did he care about the weather, nor the art festival. All he could think about was Sara. As a result, their exchanges didn't improve much. Although she was a nice person, Jessica wasn't the right person for him.

"I enjoyed lunch. Maybe we can do this again some time," Jessica suggested, sounding hopeful.

Relieved the clock read twelve forty-five, Joe said, "Look at the time. We'd better get moving. We shouldn't be late for class. You know how kids are if professors are late."

She crumpled up her wrapper and napkin and stuffed them in her empty drink cup on the tray. "You're right. I had a nice time. Thanks again for lunch. See you soon."

Joe gathered his garbage, finished off his soda, and added his garbage to the tray. "I'm sure we'll run into each other, one way or another. Have a good afternoon." He picked up the tray, deposited the trash in the nearest receptacle, and slid the empty tray on top of the stack of other empty trays.

"I will. You too."

They parted ways to teach their respective classes.

After class, Joe graded homework assignments in his office and returned some calls before going home to his condo. After retrieving the mail, he unlocked the door and threw the mail on the counter; he'd deal with it later. Turning on the television, he plopped down on the tan leather couch and put his feet up on the coffee table. As he was channel surfing, there was a knock at the door.

"Come on in. It's open!" he yelled, lowering the television volume.

The door opened, and his parents appeared, laden with casserole dishes. Rose Lazaro was a formidable woman, despite her diminutive size of five feet, two inches. Much to the disappointment of her children, her piercing, blue-green eyes could spot a lie from across a room. Her black hair was styled to perfection, and her pearl necklace and earrings smartly complemented her red blouse.

Salvatore Lazaro, an agreeable man, worked as a master landscaper. His hairline had receded years ago. The hair that remained was salt and pepper. He thoroughly enjoyed his wife's cooking and baking, and it showed on his stocky frame of five feet, eight inches. Joe had inherited his father's dimples and twinkling blue eyes.

"Is that any way to welcome guests? Yelling at them to let themselves in?" his mother, Rose, scolded.

Getting up from the couch and rushing to the door, Joe replied, "No, Ma, it isn't. It's been a long day. And I wasn't expecting you." He kissed his mother on the cheek and relieved her of the items she carried.

Joe's father, Sal, walked into the kitchen and set his load of containers down on the table.

Rose continued, "That's no excuse. You think *I* never had a long day? Every day while you and your brother were growing up, didn't I manage to cook, clean, take care of all of you, *and* answer the door when someone knocked?"

"Yes, Ma."

"Yes, I did. Because that's the way it's supposed to be done. Isn't that right, Sal?"

"Yes, dear," Sal acknowledged. "Your mother is a saint. Remember that."

"You look thin," Rose commented, as she hugged her son. "Sal, doesn't he look thin?"

Sal shrugged, rearranging the casserole dishes covered in aluminum foil.

"He looks thin," she declared definitively. "Since I'm not here to cook every day, we brought you a little something."

"Ma, I'm fine." Joe pulled out a kitchen chair for his mother to sit.

Refusing the chair, Rose replied, "I don't think so, Mr. 'I Can Live on My Own and Take Care of Myself.' I can tell when things aren't fine. Can't I, Sal?"

"Yes, dear. You always know these things," Sal acquiesced.

Rose continued. "Since you haven't invited us over for that special dinner you promised and to see your new condominium, I figured something was wrong."

"Everything is fine," Joe said reassuringly.

Then Rose Lazaro looked beyond her son and husband into

the living area. She stared in disbelief at the state of disarray in front of her. Boxes everywhere, papers piled haphazardly, clothes strewn randomly—all contributors to an unbelievable and unacceptable mess. "Holy Mary, Mother of God, give me strength!" She smacked her son on the back of his head. "*This* is how you're living? *In a pigsty?* You left home so you could live like an animal? What's the *matter* with you? I raised you better than this. This is disgusting."

Joe moved farther from his mother's reach. "I haven't had time to unpack yet."

With her left hand on her hip and her right hand gesturing, she asked, "*Really?* When do you think you'll get around to it? *Christmas, maybe?* Well, let me tell you something. No son of mine is going to live in a pigsty. I'll see to that. I can't believe I let you convince us not to help you move. This place could have been perfect from day one."

"Ma ..."

Rose approached the living area with a disgusted look on her face. "Don't 'Ma' me. Where are your cleaning supplies? I know you have some. I packed them myself."

From the safety of the kitchen, Joe pointed to the tallest stack of boxes in the living room. "They're still in the box you packed. Somewhere over there."

"Silly me. Ask a stupid question. Well, you'll have to amuse yourselves while I clean up this mess. Do you think the two of you can handle that?"

Both men replied in unison. "Yes."

Rose located the box with the cleaning supplies. She questioned her son as she carried the box to the kitchen. "It's a girl again, isn't it?"

Joe tried to ignore his mother and peeled back the foil on one of the casserole dishes. He inhaled deeply. "Mmmm. This smells great. I guess I'll have some of this ziti. I'm really in the mood for homemade ziti. Dad, do you want some too?"

"Don't mind if I do," Sal replied, sitting down on a kitchen chair.

Rose searched for clean plates and glasses in the cupboards. "No, no, no! You are not going to try to change the subject on me, young man. It's girl problems. I know these things. Mothers know these things."

"Don't worry about it."

"'Don't worry,' he tells me. *Don't worry?* What good is a mother who doesn't worry? *Please.*" Rose opened the last cupboard. "You only have two plates and glasses in all of these beautiful cupboards?" Rose removed the plates and glasses and placed them on the counter. Sliding out the drawers, she found no utensils of any kind. "Where are all of your kitchen things?"

"Still in boxes somewhere."

"I could have served the ziti without a spatula if I had a knife and fork. *Or a spoon. Or anything.* But you don't even have those. How have you been eating without silverware?"

"I've been eating out a lot."

"Obviously." Rose turned to Sal and said, "He's your son."

"Guilty as charged," Sal replied.

Hunting for the kitchen boxes, Rose muttered, "This is ridiculous." Turning her attention back to Joe, she resumed the previous conversation. "Don't insult me by sitting there with a sad, pitiful look on your face and telling me there's nothing to worry about."

Sitting next to his father at the kitchen table, Joe surrendered. "Fine. It's girl trouble." Joe resigned himself to telling the truth. It was less painful that way.

"I knew it. It's mother's intuition. I'm never wrong about these things," Rose confirmed as she perused a pile in front of her. She asked sarcastically, "Oh and will wonders ever cease? I found the box with kitchen utensils."

She lugged the box into the kitchen and extracted a spatula and some silverware. Making quick work of it, she cut and served the ziti. "Eat while it's still hot. I just took it out of the oven before we came over. We'll save the lasagna and shells for another time. I'll put them in the freezer."

"Thanks."

"It's what good mothers do," she reminded her son. "We can talk while you eat. *Mangia.*"

With the men occupied with their food, Rose focused on unpacking and stocking the shelves and drawers.

"Ma, your ziti is the best," Joe proclaimed.

Rose smiled. "Thank you. So are we talking about a new girl or someone we already know?"

"It's Sara."

"Sara? Again? Why don't you just tell her you want to go steady?"

"People don't say that anymore."

"Well, that's the gist of it. So use whatever hip phrase you young people use these days and get the job done."

"Uh huh."

"I could talk to her, if you want," Rose offered, filling the silverware drawer.

Joe protested. "No, I'll take care of this myself."

"If you're sure."

"Yes, I'm totally sure. She's got a date with a new guy she just met, David Turner."

"Why?" With the silverware drawer task complete, Rose moved on to the next box.

"When we broke up, we decided to be just friends. So we've been dating other people."

"That was stupid," she criticized, taking glasses from the box in front of her and arranging them in the cupboard.

"When I came back from Italy, she was involved with some guy. So I started seeing other girls. It's just that neither of us is seeing anybody right now. So I thought maybe ..." Joe trailed off.

"Wait a minute." Rose studied her son for a moment. "Did you leave Italy because you missed her? Is *that* the real reason?"

Joe ignored his mother's questions, digging into his plate of ziti.

"It is. I'm right. *That's* why you came back, so suddenly, out of the blue, after your grand declaration that you were going to stay in Italy. I thought it was odd when you came back home. I knew it. Your excuse for coming back was flimsy, but I didn't question it because I was glad you were back home, safe and sound. The truth is that you missed Sara. I know I'm right. It's the only explanation that makes any sense. And you've waited all of this time? It's been years. What are you waiting for?"

"Please just forget about it."

"How can I forget about it? It's just plain stupid. I can fix this for you. I'll talk to her. Better yet, I'll talk to her mother."

"No! I'll handle it myself," Joe insisted.

"Well, if you change your mind, I'm here to help."

"I know. Did I mention how great this ziti is?"

"Glad you like it." Rose smiled. However, the smile faded as she examined the contents of the remaining boxes and the overall condition of the condominium. "No wonder you're having girl problems. Just *look* at this place." She gestured around the room. "No respectable girl would want to visit a place like this. Sal, talk to your son. I have cleaning to do."

The Lazaro men consumed the rest of their pasta in silence and migrated to the couch to watch sports while Rose attacked the condo.

Rose Lazaro—the one-woman cleaning and organizing crew—was on a mission to make her son's condo livable and spotless. As she scrubbed the bathroom floor, Rose yelled, "I don't hear any talking in there. You're supposed to be talking!"

The men rolled their eyes. Joe grabbed the remote and turned up the volume as he shouted back, "We're watching the game!"

In between emptying boxes and cleaning rooms, she laundered the mountain of clothes. As she carried hand towels to the kitchen, she said, "I've never resorted to some methods used by other mothers. I've never set you up on a date. I could have, you know, plenty of times. You don't know how many mothers with daughters I had to turn down for you."

Joe gave credit where it was due. While his mother's friends had fixed up their kids with dates, Rose had let her sons pick their own girls.

After Rose folded and put the laundry away, she returned to

the kitchen to serve dessert. Uncovering the chocolate cake, she asked, "What does this Turner boy have that you don't?"

"I don't know."

She announced, "I brought chocolate cake." Cutting two large pieces of cake, she plated them. "Is he rich?"

"No."

Rose walked over to the couch and handed her husband his cake, without looking at him. Speaking to Joe, she offered him his dessert. "Have a piece of cake. I didn't raise you to give up so easily. You need to go after this girl if you really love her. Tell me, what does this other boy have that makes him more special than you?"

"I don't know."

"You can have more cake if you want. If you can't think of anything special about this boy, there probably isn't anything. If you'd like, I could have your grandmother put the eye on him," she offered, returning to the kitchen to find some napkins.

Sal sank deeper into the couch, concentrating on the television screen and eating his cake. It was excellent homemade chocolate cake. No one made better cake than his Rose.

"Ma!" Joe balked.

"What?" Providing napkins to both men, she said, "Here, take these. I don't want you two making another mess."

They accepted the napkins.

"Joey, you got a problem—I'm trying to fix it. Sidelining the competition would make it easier for you."

"Please, don't."

"What's wrong with trying to help my son? I just offered one solution. Fine, have it your way. No evil eye." Rose threw her hands into the air. "Apparently, I'm only good for other things, like cleaning and cooking," she complained. In a huff, she relocated to tackle the dirty dishes the men had left soaking in the kitchen sink.

"So what happened to the art teacher?" Sal asked.

Surprised, Joe looked at him incredulously. "How'd you know about her?"

Rose replied, "Cousin Tony heard from his wife, Gina, who heard it at the beauty parlor that you were seen with a blonde art teacher at some beach party."

Joe responded, "We went to lunch. It didn't really pan out."

Satisfied with the short answer, Sal lapsed back into silent mode.

While loading the dishwasher, Rose asked, "Why waste time on other girls if you really want to be with Sara? You're not getting any younger, and neither am I. I'd like some grandchildren soon. So get serious and settle down."

"Why don't you ask Tony? He's older than me."

Securing the dishwasher door, she answered, "He hasn't found the right girl yet."

"Will he ever?"

Rose washed her hands. "God only knows. And we're not talking about your brother. We're talking about you. So what about it?"

"I'll see what I can do for you. But you do want a wedding before the grandchildren, right?"

"Don't be fresh. Of course I want it done the right way. Don't make me the talk of the neighborhood, Joey, or God help you," Rose threatened, drying her hands on a towel.

Joe grinned and elbowed his father. Sal smirked back.

Rose announced, "My work here is done. You've been fed. All of the rooms are clean. That ridiculous pile of laundry is done. The dishes are in the dishwasher. You should run it later. Everything here is perfect. Now keep it this way."

"I'll try. Thanks for all the food and everything."

"If you still lived at home, you could have all the food you wanted. But *no*, you moved out so you could be free and independent. Some great idea that was." Pointing to the refrigerator, she said, "In addition to the chocolate cake, there are some cannolis in the fridge too. I made them this morning."

"Cheese or cream?" Joe asked as he got up from the couch.

"Cream for you, of course." Moving her fingers in a sprinkling fashion, she added, "I even put chocolate sprinkles on the ends."

Joe hugged his mother. "Thanks, Ma. You're the best."

Smiling, Rose replied, "Yes, and don't you forget it." She reached up and held his face in both of her hands. "And if you change your mind about me talking to Sara or her mother ..."

Joe bent down for her kiss. "I won't change my mind. I need to do this on my own. Thanks, anyway."

"I just want you to be happy." Rose hugged and kissed her son. He returned both forms of affection. Satisfied, Rose ordered, "Get up, Sal! We're leaving now. I've got another son at home to feed."

"Yes, dear." Sal joined his son and wife. "Take care, Joe."

"You too, Dad. Thanks again for everything," Joe said, hugging and kissing his father.

"You're welcome," they both replied, leaving Joe alone in his sparkling clean condominium.

Chapter 6

MARK was a bundle of nerves. His stomach discomfort increased the closer he got to the house. Time constraints had prevented him from working out all of the details of his plan. Consequently, some decisions would have to be made on the spot. As he drove, he soaked in the familiar landscape. No additional land development had occurred in the last several months. The trees he had treasured and loved to climb as a boy were still there. He had often hidden in the thicket of woods to escape from his parents, brother, and even his babysitter.

His father had selected the land specifically for the abundance of trees. However, many had been destroyed in order to accommodate the house, the barn, and the large yard. Mark had finally reached the end of the tree line at the edge of the driveway. He stopped.

It soothed him that the white, two-story farmhouse remained isolated, surrounded by his beloved trees. Slowly, he pulled in. Mark hated gravel driveways. The sound of dirt kicking up and the popping noises unnerved him. He stopped the van behind the old red pickup, between the house and the barn. Everything remained exactly as he remembered. The house, the barn, and the yard were well maintained.

Mark didn't see his brother outside. He walked to the front of the house and up the steps to the large front porch. The inside door stood ajar. He peered into the house through the screen door. Despite the lack of movement in the house, he heard voices—either a radio or television. He pulled on the door handle, but the door was locked. He knocked on the screen door. It rattled.

"Just a minute!" Matt called out.

Mark turned around, so he wasn't facing the door when his brother reached it.

"Yes? Can I help you?" Matt asked, wiping his hands on a rag.

Mark slowly turned and replied with a smile. "You sure can."

Matt, visibly shaken, dropped his rag. "Mark? Oh my God! What are you doing here? Did you escape?"

"There you go, always thinking the worst of me. I guess I shouldn't have expected anything less. No, I didn't escape. I was let out early on good behavior. Dr. Wendell changed the conditions for outpatient therapy," Mark lied.

Matt picked up the rag. "That's great, Mark. You should have called. I would have picked you up."

"No need. I wanted to see the look on your face. And it was priceless—definitely a Kodak moment. Are you going to let me in or what?"

Opening the screen door, Matt apologized. "Where are my manners? Come on in."

Mark crossed the threshold and looked around the foyer, the hallway, and the family room. It was the same old hardwood floor, same beige walls.

"I'm in the process of painting the whole house, which explains why I'm covered with paint. I'm working on my room today. I finished the kitchen last week. And I just finished painting your room a couple of days ago. Would you like to see it? It's your favorite color—mint green. I guess I must have known you were going to need it soon. It's weird how that happened."

"Yeah, cosmic even." Mark rolled his eyes. "I'll look at it later. Go get cleaned up, and I'll pour us a couple of drinks."

"Sounds good. I'll be ready in a few minutes. There's some lemonade in the fridge. The liquor is still where Mom kept it."

"Take your time. I'm not going anywhere."

Mark waited for his brother to leave the room. As he walked down the hall, he discarded the duffel bag on the floor. He touched the decorative table with his fingertips and plucked a piece of root beer-favored candy from the bowl. Indelicately, he unwrapped the piece of candy and popped it into his mouth—instant gratification.

It amazed him how much pleasure could be derived from such a small sugar concoction. It tasted better than he remembered.

Catching a glimpse of his reflection in the oval mirror hanging above the table jolted him back to reality. Time for frivolous things would have to wait until later. Shoving the plastic wrapper into his pocket, he collected the duffel bag. As he walked into the family room, he caressed the headrest of his favorite recliner and spun the chair around. He longed to savor that moment, but time was of the essence.

He carried the duffel bag through the family room and into the kitchen. The sight of the unusually bright yellow kitchen walls startled him. It was an unwelcome change. "What the hell? This color is beyond awful." Scanning the rest of the kitchen, he remarked, "Well, at least the cupboards and appliances are still white."

Mark tossed the bag on the kitchen table. Shortly thereafter, Mark heard the shower start. Something in the kitchen wasn't quite right, aside from the obnoxious paint color. A visual inventory of the room solved the mystery. The wall telephone was missing. The wall, where it had previously resided, was patched and repainted. Not even a phone jack remained. He wondered why his brother had removed the phone, but he didn't have time to worry about it. He had to focus on the matter at hand.

Mark extracted a bottle of painkillers and placed it on the counter. The drawer in front of him contained the wax paper. He tore off a sheet, positioned it on the counter, and returned the roll to the drawer.

After defeating the safety seal on the outside of the bottle, he broke through the inner protective foil cover with his thumb. He failed to read the patient information leaflet loosely attached to the bottle. The leaflet fell off onto the counter as he shook out three pills.

The drawer on his right provided a spoon. The drawer on the end yielded a hammer. A glass-faced cupboard rendered two glasses. He obtained three ice cubes out of the freezer and dropped them into one of the glasses. Locating the bottle of whiskey in the pantry, he poured two drinks. Mark liked his drinks neat. Matt preferred ice.

After verifying that the shower was still running, he folded the wax paper over the pills and smashed them with the hammer. Crushed sufficiently, he poured the powder into Matt's drink and stirred until the painkiller dissolved. Finished with the whiskey bottle, he returned it to the pantry.

Mark removed the lemonade pitcher from the refrigerator and placed the half-full glass pitcher on the counter. He shook out six more pills, pulverized them with the hammer, poured them into the lemonade, and stirred. After returning the pitcher to the refrigerator, quick cleanup was required. The wax paper was rinsed in the sink before he discarded it. Then he thrust the hammer back into the tool drawer. Wrapping up, he washed the spoon and the sink to remove any residue.

Mark heard the shower still running. Matt took very long, hot showers. Mark recalled how he used to wake up early to beat Matt into the shower. If he didn't, he had to take a cold shower.

Mark swept the bottle of pills and the leaflet into the duffel bag. If he had read the leaflet, he would have seen the clear warning:

> Do not drive or operate heavy machinery. Do not drink alcohol. Do not crush tablets. When tablets are crushed, the entire dose is absorbed instantly, instead of gradually, over time.

The water stopped. Mark carried the drinks into the family room, sat in his favorite chair, and put his feet up. Comfortable in the light brown recliner, he sipped his drink, relishing the progress he had made toward his final goal.

Matt entered the room, hair still wet from the shower. "I just can't believe you're here." Matt sat on the solid blue couch near Mark. "So what do you want to do? Where do you want to go to eat dinner?"

"Actually, I'd like to spend a quiet evening here, with you. We have some business to attend to," he replied, seriously.

"*Business?* What kind of business can't wait a couple of days? You just got out. You need to let loose a little." Matt lifted his glass. "Dude, a toast to you—to brighter and happier days ahead. Cheers!"

Mark raised his glass and clinked it with Matt's. "Cheers to you, my brother." They drank. Nonchalantly, Mark asked, "By the way, what happened to the kitchen phone?"

"I decided to get rid of it and just have my cell phone. It's charging in my room. Do you need to call somebody?"

"No. I'm good for now."

"Dude, you really want to spend the evening here?"

"Yes, really. I'd like to know what you've been up to since I've been away. We need to have some quality time together. You know, catch up. Any girlfriends?"

"No, not currently. I'm living the bachelor life—taking it easy this summer. I figured I'd fix this place up before I have to start coaching again. Football season starts in a few weeks."

"I saw the old pickup parked out back. Does it still run?" Mark needed verification of the truck's status, due to Ray's earlier comments.

"Yeah. I just overhauled the transmission. It was slipping all the time. It left me stranded a couple of weeks ago. But it's running fine now."

"Good. How about another toast? To my brother, for taking such good care of everything. Bottoms up!"

"Bottoms up!" Matt emptied his glass.

"You want another one?" Mark asked coyly, bringing the recliner to an upright position.

"Sure, but I'll get it. You just sit there and relax," Matt urged as he headed to the kitchen. Pouring another glass of whiskey, he yelled, "So have you thought about working at all?" He reentered the room with the glass and the bottle. "Brought it in, just in case you want some more to drink." Matt positioned the bottle between them and settled in on the couch.

"Yeah. I know I won't be able to go back to my old accounting job, because of my record. So I might get a job at Chen's. Did you know that Ray Peters bought the laundry service?"

"I think I heard something about that."

"It's not like all of the businesses here will want to hire an ex-con and a head case you know."

"I hadn't thought of it that way. I don't think other people will either." Matt paused. "People around here know you."

"It doesn't change the fact that I was in jail or the fact that I spent time at Misty Pines. People will remember that."

"Well, if you feel that way, I could call Ray and put in a good word," Matt offered.

"Not necessary. I ran into him earlier. We talked. He loaned me his van. That's how I got here."

Matt slid his empty glass on the coffee table. "Whoa. I'm beginning to feel weird. I guess that's what I get for drinking on an empty stomach. We should get something to eat."

"You sit right there, douche bag. I saw some chicken in the fridge. I'll make you a sandwich."

"I should be making you a sandwich."

"Don't worry about it."

"Dude."

Mark disappeared into the kitchen. He pulled a chair away from the table. The table protested as he pushed it against the wall. The day's newspaper rested on it. Within a minute, a few sections laid unfolded on the floor around the chair. Mark peeked into the family room.

Matt was shaking his head back and forth and slapping his face.

Mark smiled and proceeded to the bathroom to retrieve Matt's hair trimmer and razor. He easily located the items, carried them into the kitchen, and arranged them on the table. Mark waited a few minutes for Matt's grogginess to increase before returning to the family room. "Matt, come on. You need to get into the kitchen."

Matt slurred his words. "Why are we going to the kitchen?"

"To make everything better, of course. You want everything to be better, don't you?"

"Well, yeah. I can't believe how quickly that drink hit me. Remind me, what needs to be better?"

Mark helped Matt to his feet. "My life. *My* life is about to be perfect—like yours. So let's give you a haircut. You let it grow too long. You need to look presentable."

"Right. Mom always taught us to look presentable." Matt swung his left arm over Mark's shoulder and blubbered, "I love you, man."

Mark shook his head in disgust, grabbed his brother by the waist, and half-carried him to the kitchen. "Matt, take your shirt off. That way it won't be covered with hair."

"Good idea." Matt struggled to remove the shirt.

As Matt fought with his shirt, Mark pulled Matt's shorts down and pushed him into the kitchen chair. Matt wasn't wearing any underwear and laughed. Before Mark could make a snide comment, Matt's wallet fell out of the back pocket of his shorts. Mark picked up the wallet and slapped it on the table. After wadding Matt's clothes into a ball, Mark threw them at another chair. Then he draped an old red-and-white-checkered tablecloth around his brother and tied it behind his neck.

Matt said, "Thanks, dude."

"Don't mention it."

"Mention what?"

"Forget it. It doesn't matter."

"If you say so."

Mark spent the next half-hour cutting Matt's hair to match his own. A crew cut is simple under normal circumstances, but Matt's head rolled from side to side. When Mark finished, Matt was singing to himself. Mark slapped Matt's face to get his attention. Matt made an effort to focus.

Mark held his brother's head with both hands to keep it steady. Mark stated, "Matt, you are about to make up for every lousy thing you ever did to me. Refusing to participate in my outpatient therapy program was a big mistake. You should have accepted the challenge, embraced it even. Things could have been so different. None of this would be happening now if you had only said yes. Why didn't you say yes?"

Matt stared blankly. He did not respond.

"You were always Mom and Dad's favorite, their firstborn son. You were born five lousy minutes before me. And since then, you've always been first." Mark imitated his mother's voice, "Matt is on the all-star team. Matt is on the honor roll. Matt won homecoming king. Isn't that wonderful?"

As he released Matt from his grasp, Mark pushed him hard against the back of the chair. Matt's head snapped back from the force of the shove. Not possessing the strength to support his head any longer, it lolled.

Mark reverted back to his own voice. "It didn't matter what I did or how I did it. I was invisible most of the time. I did good in school, but your GPA was a fraction better. I wasn't a superjock like you, but I held my own. I was shy with the girls in high school. So you offered me your rejects—under the condition I didn't tell them I wasn't you. *That* was just messed up. Now it's *my* turn to be the favorite son, the honored one. And *you'll* be locked up, finishing out my time." Mark finished the speech by kicking Matt's chair.

Matt couldn't comprehend Mark's soliloquy through the haze. As Mark untied the tablecloth from his neck, Matt's eyes closed.

Mark demanded, "You have to stay awake a little longer. Come on. Stay with me. You need to get dressed." Mark shook him until he opened his eyes. But when Mark reached to the other side of the table to get the duffel bag, Matt lost muscle control and urinated on the newspaper in front of him.

Furious, Mark screamed, "You think that's really funny, don't you? Well, laugh it up now, ass wipe! Laugh it up because *I'll* have the last laugh—you'll be serving out the rest of my time at Misty Pines."

Mark gathered up the soaking wet newspaper and threw it in the trash. He threw a wad of paper towels on the floor. Using his right foot to spread the towels, he sopped up the urine. He disposed of the mess, then he scrubbed his hands for several minutes. A thorough cleaning of the kitchen would have to wait for later.

From the lemonade pitcher in the refrigerator, he poured Matt another drink. Holding the glass to Matt's lips, Mark said, "Drink this."

Matt swallowed a few mouthfuls and closed his eyes.

Mark removed his institute clothes from the duffel bag. "Time to get dressed for your big debut."

Forcing the shirt over Matt's head, Mark pulled his arms through the sleeves. Missing underwear would look suspicious. So Mark removed his own shorts and underwear and put the underwear on his brother. Mark quickly slipped his shorts back on. Then he struggled to put the institute pants on Matt.

Sweaty and tired, Mark's stomach growled in protest. Frustrated, he yelled at his stomach, "Stop it! There's no time to stop and eat. I have to finish this, or everything will be ruined!"

Mark slid the table back to its rightful place. He rinsed both glasses and deposited them in the sink with the intention of washing them later. "Good enough for now," he said, slipping Matt's wallet into the back pocket of his shorts.

Matt was now unconscious, so Mark heaved him over his shoulder. He carried his brother outside and loaded him into the back of the van. Running back into the house, he grabbed the bottle of pills out of the duffel bag. He closed the kitchen door on his way out and shoved the bottle into his pocket before securing the van's doors. Driving north toward Misty Pines, he glanced at his watch. Dinner would be served in less than an hour. There was no time to waste.

Mark drove to the edge of the property line and located the access road easily. The lock on the security gate in this corner of Misty Pine Institute's yard needed repair. Mark had discovered this on a nature hike with some of the other residents. The trees and bushes in this area provided good cover from a distance. Mark stopped the van in front of the gate. No one was in sight. They weren't searching for him yet.

The gate opened with a swift kick, but the van's back doors stuck. Mark pulled hard on the handle. Matt lay motionless. Mark slid Matt to the edge of the van and cradled him like a child. Carrying him to the Misty Pines side of the fence, he propped his brother against a tree.

Satisfied with the positioning, Mark retrieved the painkillers from his pocket. "They'll see it as another failed suicide attempt," he said, scattering a few pills on the ground for effect. Strategically, he positioned the cap and the tipped-over bottle next to his brother. "I wish I could witness the scene when you try to convince them you're not me. That should be one hell of a show. Hopefully, they won't add too much more time to your stay because of it. In the meantime, I'll temporarily assume your identity. Too bad for you. I guess we'll work things out when they finally release you."

Mark took one last look at his brother and closed the gate. As he shut the van's doors, his wristwatch alerted him there were only minutes to spare. As he drove away, he smiled, careful not to spin the tires. "One down, one to go."

Chapter 7

Sara couldn't help feeling that this day qualified as one of the longest days of her life. The combination of her exhaustion from lack of sleep, her anxiety about her upcoming date with David—topped off with wrestling with her feelings for Joe—overwhelmed her. As the afternoon dragged on, she couldn't concentrate on anything at work. So she left an hour early.

Sara arrived home, pleasantly surprised to find Laura's silver Toyota Camry in the driveway. Sara entered the house and greeted her, "Hey, look what the cat dragged in. I was beginning to think you might have moved out but didn't tell us."

Sarcastically, Laura replied, "You couldn't be that lucky."

"Seriously, Laura, what have you been up to? I can't remember the last day we saw each other, let alone spent any time together."

"I've been working on a project that involved our subsidiary in China. I had daily conference calls with them. The time difference had me working crazy hours. We finished up last night. So I have a bank of comp days to use up. I'm taking one of them today."

"I wish I'd known. I could have taken today off too."

"You're home early, aren't you?"

Sara sighed. "Work sucks. I need to start looking for a new job. Is there anything open at your company?"

"You hate marketing more than you hate engineering. So I'll say *no*."

"Oh well. I didn't see Anna's car. Did she go to work today?" Sara sat down next to Laura on the couch.

"No. She's still not feeling well. She went to see the doctor. She should be back anytime now. Before she left, Anna told me you went to a party last night. How was it?"

"Unexpected, to say the least." Sara relayed the evening's events—going to the party with Joe, getting a tarot card reading, meeting David and asking him out on a date. Then she abruptly stopped.

"And?" Laura pushed.

"And what?"

Laura sensed Sara was holding something back, something important. "What aren't you telling me?"

Sara avoided Laura's eyes. "Joe and I kissed each other. Satisfied?"

Laura tilted her head. "No. What *kind* of kiss? A friendly 'see you later' kiss? Or a 'I really want to jump your bones' kind of kiss?"

Sara looked at her nails. They needed a new coat of polish. "Definitely more of the latter than the former."

"You're kidding. And was there anything else *besides* the kiss?"

Sara fidgeted with her watch.

Laura pressed. "Sara?"

Sara stood up, walked into the kitchen, and reluctantly replied, "Yes."

Laura followed her. "How *much* more, Sara?"

Sara imagined Joe's hands caressing her and the warmth of his breath on her skin. "What you're thinking happened, happened," she confessed.

"No!" Laura exclaimed.

"Yes. And it was as good, if not better, than it used to be. I haven't been able to stop thinking about it all day. That's why I came home early." Sara filled a glass of water from the refrigerator door.

Laura's eyes opened wide. "Whoa. Wait a minute. Let me get this straight. You ask a total stranger out to dinner after a weird tarot card reading at a party. And then you come home with Joe and have awesome sex with him about an hour later. Did I get that right?" Laura questioned, unbelievingly.

"Yes," Sara confessed, staring into her glass of water. Not

really thirsty, she moved the glass, causing the water to swirl in a counterclockwise direction.

"So you guys are back together again. That's great! It's about time. The two of you belong together. So why don't you look happy?"

"We're not back together."

"Huh? Why not? What did I miss here? I'm confused."

"That makes two of us."

"I don't get it." After observing her friend for a moment, Laura asked, "Sara, what's going on?"

Sara rested her water glass on the counter. "I really don't know. I admit I still have strong feelings for Joe."

"Duh. You think? And obviously he still has feelings for you. Otherwise, last night wouldn't have happened."

"Maybe. Maybe not."

"Oh, come on. You love him. He loves you. End of story."

Sara picked up the pile of mail and sorted through it, ignoring Laura's comments. Laura snatched the mail out of Sara's hands.

Sara yelled, "Hey! I was looking at those." Sara lunged for the mail in Laura's hand. Laura jerked her hand back, over her head. Sara couldn't reach the envelopes.

"Give me my mail," Sara demanded.

Laura shook her head. "No. You weren't looking at any of it anyway."

Sara leaned sideways against the counter with her arms crossed in front of her.

Laura persisted, "Hello? I'm not going away."

"Whatever. I don't want to talk about it."

"Too bad. You need to talk about it. Look at yourself. You're a mess."

Sara stomped into the family room and sat on the couch. "I've never denied that I have feelings for him, but we decided to be friends and see other people. That's what we've been doing."

Laura threw the pile of mail back on the counter. "That might have been what you agreed to at the time, but I know *you* didn't mean it. I'm guessing he didn't either. He came back from Italy after he said he wouldn't. Maybe you're the reason."

"That was years ago. Why hasn't he said anything? He's had plenty of time."

"Because he's a stupid guy."

"Maybe I'm the stupid one. This is the first time we've both been available at the same time since he got back from Italy. I was hoping that we would finally get back together. But the way he left last night made me think it was just a 'friends with benefits' hook up."

"Did he say that?"

"No."

"Did you mention it?"

"No."

"What *did* you say to him last night after you had sex?"

"Nothing, really."

"You said nothing? *That's* hard to believe. Anyway, how about him? Did he say anything that would give you an idea of where this might be headed?"

"No. Not really," she answered, clutching a throw pillow to her chest.

Laura sat next to her. "Well, I'll bet you that he still loves you the same way you love him, but you're both too stupid to admit it to each other."

"I don't know."

"What are you afraid of? Are you afraid of being hurt? Is that it?"

"I don't know."

Laura gently pulled the pillow away. "Enough of the 'I don't knows' already. I think it's worth asking him about it. Don't you?"

Finally making eye contact, Sara replied, "I guess so."

Laura placed the pillow behind her back and leaned against it. "Give me a break. You know I'm right. You need to resolve your issues with Joe. I don't think we can handle another meltdown with this new guy, whatever his name is …"

"David."

"Okay, David ... like we did with psycho boy."

"It isn't going to be like that."

"How do you know?"

"He seems normal."

"So was psycho boy at first. We all liked him. It wasn't until after you slept with him that things went to hell."

Sara propped her left arm on the couch's armrest and rested her head in her hand. "Don't remind me. I'm trying to forget about that."

Laura nudged Sara's leg with her foot. Sara wrinkled her nose and squirmed to maintain her claim to her one and a half couch cushions. "Hey, stay on your own side."

Laura gave her a stern look. "Maybe you shouldn't forget about psycho boy. Maybe you should think a lot about him and this new guy and how you're still obsessing about Joe—the way You-Know-Who obsessed about you."

"You can't be serious. I am not stalking Joe. Apparently, I'm just having sex with him."

"Not exactly my point, but close enough. You have this attraction to Joe that you can't let go of entirely. You use him as your yardstick. You measure every guy in your life against him. So far, no one has measured up."

"That's not entirely true," she replied, shifting on the cushion.

Laura asked, "Oh really? What was wrong with psycho boy before he became psycho?" She paused for an answer.

None came.

"Well? I don't hear you saying anything. I'll tell you what—nothing. Nothing was wrong with him. He was a great guy when you met him. He was funny and smart. And then he did the unthinkable—he put you on a pedestal. He treated you like a queen."

"Maybe I didn't want to be a queen," Sara protested, crossing her arms.

"Yeah, right. Every woman wants to be treated like a queen. You said 'Jump!' and he always asked 'How high?' Are you going to deny that?"

"No. He was wonderful. Are you happy now? I didn't mean to screw the guy up. I didn't realize that breaking up with him would send him into a nervous breakdown. How was I supposed to know?"

"You didn't know he'd actually go nuts. But you should have been more understanding. You should have at least given him a reason for why you were breaking up with him. Maybe then he wouldn't have gone nuts and stalked you."

"How could I when I didn't know myself?"

"You knew. You just couldn't admit it to yourself. And you're still denying it now. He wasn't Joe—plain and simple."

Standing up, Sara said, "You always think everything is simple. Don't you know how bad I feel about that? I ruined that guy's life. He thought that I loved him as much as he loved me. He told me that he was saving himself for the woman he was going to marry. A few months later, when he said he was ready to have sex with me, I didn't put two and two together." She took a few steps away from the couch. "I figured he had fed me a line of bull before, and he was just as horny as all the other guys out there."

"Where are you going?"

Reaching for the watering can in the corner, Sara answered, "The plants need to be watered. I forgot to do it earlier."

"Forget about the plants," Laura said, throwing a pillow at Sara.

Sara jumped out of the way, picked up the pillow, and threw it back. Laura caught it. Sara plopped back down on the couch.

Scooting closer, Laura preached, "What's done is done, but you have to learn from that fiasco. If you don't, you're going to keep repeating the same mistakes over and over again."

"You sound like my mother," Sara complained.

Laura grabbed Sara by the shoulders and made her look at her. "Well, right now you need a mother. And since yours is gallivanting around the country helping other people, I'm trying to be the voice of reason. You shouldn't go out with any guy until you're open to having a real relationship with him. You're lucky that you didn't get hurt or killed last time. Who says you'll continue to be lucky? If you're only interested in Joe, then tell him. See where it goes from there."

Laura released her friend.

"What if Joe doesn't feel the same? Then I'll just look desperate."

"Sara. Face it. You *are* desperate. One way or the other, you need to know where you stand. Call him and talk to him." Laura leaned over and picked up the black portable phone on the coffee table. "I'm pressing the speed dial number now." Laura pressed the number one and handed Sara the phone.

Joe answered on the second ring. "Hello?"

"Hey. It's me."

"Hey. What's going on?"

"Not much. I just wanted to call to see how you're doing."

"You mean you want to know how my date with Jessica went," he replied, before taking a swig of beer.

"I forgot about that. How did it go?"

Joe swung the bottle, back and forth, like a pendulum. "It was fine. The weather was nice, and we had gyros. They were good. It's that cucumber sauce they use."

Disappointed, Sara responded, "Yeah, it's really good."

"So Saturday is your big date with David. I hope that goes well for you. I hate to cut this short, but I need to run. Mom and Dad are here," he lied. "I'll talk to you in a couple of days."

"Okay. I didn't mean to keep you. I'll talk to you later. Bye."

"Bye." Joe hung up the phone. Reclining on his leather couch, he emptied the bottle of beer and stared at the television screen in front of him.

Sara hung up the phone.

"What happened?" Laura asked. "You hardly said a thing."

"He had a nice date with Jessica. He wished me luck on my date with David. Then he said he was busy and had to go." Tears welled up in her eyes. "I need to be alone for a while. I'm going to jog around the block a few times."

Sara hurried to the garage door.

Laura chased after her. "I can come with you," Laura offered.

Sara declined. "No. I want to be alone."

"Fine. Be safe."

"I won't stay out too long." Sara laced up her sneakers and left the house.

Laura shook her head as the door closed. "Idiots! Why can't they see what's right in front of their faces? I would love to have a relationship half as good as the one they can't admit they have with each other."

Joe's phone rang again. This time it was his older brother, Tony. At twenty-nine, Tony was a slightly shorter and heavier version of his younger brother. Notorious for his storytelling abilities, Tony loved to brag about his latest get-rich-quick scheme. He was always looking for investors and never at a loss for an idea. His problem was in the execution. This month, he had spun a tale about opening a pizza parlor near their neighborhood. Supposedly, the city only needed to approve the financing and paperwork. In the meantime, he still lived at home with his parents—rent-free.

Joe answered, "Yo."

"Hey, numb nuts! What're you doing?" Tony asked.

Joe was still channel surfing. "Nothing."

"Well, come on over to the house. The guys and I are going to play some basketball, and we need a fourth."

"I'm not really in the mood."

"From what Mom tells me, you're definitely in a mood," Tony teased. "If you don't come over, I'm going to send her back over to your place."

"Fine. I'll be there in a few," Joe said, turning off the television and grabbing his car keys. He drove over to his parents' house—a two-story, yellow and white Victorian-style house in need of a new coat of paint, at least according to his mother. The other guys were already warming up in the driveway. He parked in the street.

Joe ambled up the driveway. "Hey, guys," he said in greeting.

"Hey," they all responded.

Tony asked, "You want shirts or skins?"

"I'll take skins since you're out of shape, doughboy. We wouldn't want to scare the neighborhood kids," Joe teased.

"Okay, tough guy. We'll see who's talking smack after the game. So, it's John and you against Steve and me."

"Wouldn't have it any other way," John replied, removing his shirt to reveal a nicely defined six-pack. John Lombardi, Joe's best friend, still lived in the old neighborhood. He had become a fireman right after high school graduation. He hoped to become battalion chief someday.

"All right, girls, let's get this game started," challenged Steve Gambino, Tony's friend and a licensed plumber. Steve, slightly overweight, proudly displayed his plethora of chest hair by ignoring the top three buttons of his shirt.

Joe and John threw their shirts in the grass. The game commenced.

"So, Joe, I hear you're having girl problems," Steve stated as he dribbled the ball.

"No, I'm fine," Joe replied, trying to steal the ball.

Steve raised an eyebrow. "That's not what I heard." He shot the ball toward the hoop and missed. "Anyway, I've got some great lines for the ladies. I could give you some tips."

As John fielded the rebound, he asked, "What happened with Sara? I thought you were going to finally get back with her."

"Didn't work out." Joe caught a pass from John.

"What'd you screw up this time?" John inquired.

"Long story," Joe replied.

"You're freaking hopeless," John commented.

Steve interrupted their banter. "You should try to catch a new girl. You can borrow one of my lines. I've got a bunch of great plumber-related pickup lines. I'll even let you use my personal favorite."

Joe said, "But I'm not a plumber."

Tony chimed in. "I still want to hear your best line anyway."

Steve replied, "Hey, baby, I'm the best in my business. I can work my snake in ways you can't imagine. So how about we go back to your place, and I'll show you exactly how my anaconda moves."

As he tried to block Joe, Tony snickered and asked Steve, "You actually use that? You're kidding me."

"No. I've used it," Steve declared.

John remarked, "That's got to be one of the worst lines I've ever heard. So how many have you bagged with that one?"

"Enough," Steve replied.

Joe laughed. "I'm betting you haven't gotten any sober chicks with it. They'd have to be pretty hammered to fall for that load of shit." Joe shot for two points and connected.

Tony picked up the ball and threw it to Steve. Steve dribbled and faked to his left. Joe blocked. To Joe's relief, they stopped talking about girls for a few minutes. Their concentration stayed on the game until John spotted two girls about five houses down, walking their way.

John held the ball under his arm, made a T with his hands, and announced, "Time out."

"Time out? We just got going," Steve argued.

"Yeah, I know, but we've got some girls on the sidewalk coming our way," John informed them.

"How many and what do they look like?" Tony asked without turning around, trying not to be obvious.

"Two, but the closer they get, the younger they look," John replied.

"Jail bait?" Steve asked eagerly.

"Possibly," John responded. "They look kind of familiar."

All four men straightened up as the girls approached. They tried to look cool, pretending not to notice the girls until they were almost at the driveway.

"Hi, ladies," Steve said.

"Hi, guys." The girls giggled.

Tony recognized them and immediately intervened. "Hi, Tina. Hi, Sharon. How's your mom?"

Tina replied, "Good, thanks for asking. Tell your mom we said *hi*. See ya around." Both Tina and Sharon waved and continued walking.

Steve asked, "What's up with that?"

"Those are the little Di Palma girls. Remember them?" Tony asked.

"Damn. They grew up nicely," Steve commented, watching them walk away.

Tony punched Steve in the arm.

"What?" Steve asked. "What'd I do?"

Tony glared at Steve with disgust. "Quit looking at them. They're little girls. They're not even sixteen yet. Let's play ball."

However, before they could resume their game, Rose Lazaro leaned out the front door. In a loud and clear voice, she announced, "Boys, I just made brownies. Come and get them while they're hot."

Throwing the ball in the grass, John walked toward the house. "Awesome! I love your mom's brownies. I wish my mom still made brownies."

Retrieving the shirts from the grass, Joe tossed John his shirt. As they walked toward the house, Joe and John put their shirts back on. Like little boys, all four men bounded up the front steps for Rose's special double fudge brownies and tall glasses of milk.

Chapter 8

BACK at Misty Pines Institute, the floors had dried sufficiently, enabling the common room to be reopened for dinner. Most patients preferred to eat there, rather than in their cramped rooms. The head nurse surveyed the room, looking for Mark. Helga wanted to thank him for his help earlier in the day. Not seeing him, she approached one of the orderlies. "Have you seen Collins?"

"No, ma'am. I haven't seen him since we were hauling supplies this morning," the orderly replied.

"Please go check his room."

"Yes, ma'am," the orderly responded. He reached Collins' room. There was no sign of him. A search of the laundry room yielded the same result. Returning to the common area, the orderly addressed the head nurse. "Collins' room is empty, and he wasn't in the laundry room. You want me to check somewhere else?"

"No. I'm notifying security." She scurried to the nearest phone and pressed the red button.

"Security," the guard answered.

"This is Helga Braun. Mark Collins, a resident, did not report for dinner, and his room is empty."

"When was the last time he was seen?" the guard inquired.

"Around lunchtime."

"No one has seen him since? Is that correct?"

The nurse replied, "Yes."

"We'll get right on it," the guard assured her as he hung up and triggered the silent alarm in the building.

A silent alarm was necessary so that the patients wouldn't panic. Sets of lights in the hallways and at the nurses' stations alerted the staff. Unfortunately, they did sound an exterior alarm to alert the guards walking the grounds if an escape was suspected. Any time that alarm went off, which was rare, the staff informed the patients that there was an emergency at a nearby building and that the noise was a police siren. That seemed to placate the patients. No other excuse was ever required.

In minutes, the medical and security staffs were notified of the situation, and teams were formed. Lockdown commenced. No one could come in or go out without being escorted by a guard. The head of security, Larry Scruggs, assigned a team to search the interior of the facility. The other teams, equipped with German shepherds, searched the grounds.

The interior team searched each floor and concluded Mark Collins had vacated the building. Larry reassigned them to guarding the exits of the building in case Mark tried to gain reentry.

The dogs and the other guards scoured the grounds in teams of two. One team reached the woods and discovered Matt. The handler pulled hard to restrain his dog as he touched Matt's neck to check for a pulse.

"I don't detect a pulse. He doesn't seem to be breathing. I think he's dead. We should radio base," the male guard said.

The female guard agreed. She pressed the button on her radio and reported, "Team Two to base. Team Two to base. We found Collins. We need medical help immediately. Appears to be a suicide attempt. Copy?"

A static-laden male voice replied, "Base to Team Two. Collins down, medical needed. Copy."

Larry Scruggs accompanied the medical team. Shortly after their arrival, they pronounced Matt Collins dead. The coroner, Walt Jones, arrived thirty minutes later. He confirmed the death and offered, "I could schedule an autopsy for tomorrow."

Larry responded, "That won't be necessary, will it? This was this guy's fourth or fifth suicide attempt. Considering the evidence and the almost empty pill bottle, it's pretty clear he succeeded this time. Wouldn't you agree?"

Walt removed his gloves and replied, "Fine by me. No reason to waste the taxpayers' money if we don't have to."

Larry nodded. "Good. And another thing before you go—the media would have a field day with this if they knew a patient escaped and was roaming the grounds for the better part of a day before killing himself. They'd blow it all out of proportion and imply that we can't handle our patients. They'd claim that this facility and its residents pose a threat to the community. It will be bad for all of us. We could lose state funding. They could shut us down. And since no one got hurt, no harm, no foul, right?"

"No one got hurt?" the coroner asked incredulously. "A man is dead."

The guard brushed off the coroner's comment. "You know what I mean."

"I'm not sure I do. What are you asking me to do?" Walt inquired.

"Nothing much. I think we just need to get our story straight."

"And what story is that?"

"The story is that Collins slipped past security to obtain drugs with the commotion of today's water pipe mishap and committed suicide in the building."

"But there are several witnesses that can testify to the contrary."

"Only security and staff members. All residents were safe in their rooms. You leave the security guards and staff up to me. If you don't like the wording, we can change the word *building* to *facility*. Then, technically, you wouldn't really be lying."

The coroner face was stoic. "I will not do what you're asking."

Pausing, the guard proposed, "Fine. I've got a better idea. I'll say we found him in the common area right before dinner. We had to move his body outside to avoid upsetting the other residents. That way you won't have to lie about where you saw the body."

"I don't know."

"Hey, for all you know, that's exactly what we did."

The coroner repeated, "I don't know." He hesitated. "That might work. You better make sure I don't regret this."

"Don't worry. I'll take care of everything."

"See that you do."

"I owe you one."

"Uh huh. Someone will still have to notify next of kin."

"We'll contact the local authorities and let them handle the notification."

Mark heard the siren of the perimeter alarm as he drove home. *I guess they finally figured out I'm missing.* He whistled the rest of the way home. He parked the van behind the old red pickup truck, shut off the engine, and sat behind the wheel. His hands shook from the adrenaline rush. "I did it. I actually pulled it off. I can't believe it." Getting out, he closed the van door and walked silently to the kitchen door.

Once inside, he opened the refrigerator and pulled out the leftover chicken and mashed potatoes. He poured a tall glass of milk, emptying the carton. He transferred the food and milk to the kitchen table, where he ate everything cold. When he finished eating, his mind shifted into cleaning mode.

He dumped the contents of the lemonade pitcher down the drain. He washed and dried the dishes and glasses, including the ones from earlier, and put everything back in the cupboards. He also relocated the pills he had stolen into one of the cabinets.

After bleaching the sink and kitchen floor to remove any traces of urine or hair, he took out the garbage. Finally, he obtained his precious diary from the duffel bag before throwing the bag into the hall closet.

Settling onto the blue couch, he opened the diary.

Dear Diary,

Oh my God! I got out! I did it! No one saw me. I made the switch. Now Matt is going to have to suffer for a while. He should have let me do the outpatient program. Oh well. I'm one step closer to happiness. After I neutralize my competition, I'll win her back. I'm so excited!

After another fifteen minutes of writing, he closed the diary, brought it up to his bedroom, and placed it on his nightstand. When he returned to the couch to watch some television, headlights came into view.

Moving the drapes aside, he peered out the window. A police cruiser pulled in and parked in the driveway. His stomach lurched. Pacing back and forth, he swore. "Shit! Maybe Matt convinced them that he wasn't me. Stupid! Stupid! Stupid!" He kicked the couch.

The police knocked at the door. A voice called to him, "Mr. Collins? Are you home?"

Mark paced frantically. "I think I'm going to throw up." He leaned on his recliner for support. "What am I going to do?"

The police knocked louder. "Mr. Collins? Mr. Matt Collins? It's the police. We need to talk to you."

Mark took a deep breath. *Matt. He said Matt.*

"Hello?" the officer yelled, pounding on the door.

Mark shouted, "Coming!" Mark inhaled deeply, composed himself, and opened the door.

Two officers faced him on the porch, hats in hand. They were older men, solid in stature, approximately the same height, around six feet tall. The white officer was bald, while the Hispanic officer sported a crew cut.

Mark greeted them. "Can I help you, officers?"

"Mr. Collins, I am Officer Raul Gonzalez. This is my partner, Officer Rob Stone. We're from the sheriff's office. May we come in?"

Mark opened the door and stepped aside, allowing the two men to enter. "Sure. Is there a problem?"

"Sir, we have some news for you. We suggest that you sit down," Officer Gonzalez responded.

Mark sat in his favorite recliner, trying to conceal his shaking hands. The officers sat on either end of the blue couch.

Officer Stone broke the news. "We are sorry to inform you that your brother, Mark, committed suicide."

Mark was stunned. "What? What do you mean he committed suicide? Don't you mean he *attempted* suicide?"

"No, sir. This time he succeeded," Officer Gonzalez replied.

Mark could not process this information. In disbelief, he asked, "What?" Matt wasn't supposed to die. Mark just wanted to torment him a little. He didn't want him dead. Matt was his brother. "He was the only family I had left. Now he's dead, like my parents and grandparents." Mark stared at the floor.

The officers exchanged glances and sat quietly, allowing Mark time to absorb the news. After a few minutes, Officer Stone broke the silence, "Sir? Do you need us to call anyone for you?"

Confused, Mark asked, "Huh?"

"Anyone you want us to call?" the officer repeated.

"There's no one left to call. It's just me now. Oh my God! Oh my God! What have I done?" Tears ran down both cheeks.

"Sir?" Officer Stone questioned.

Despite his shock, Mark thought quickly. "I didn't agree to outpatient therapy. That must have been what drove him to do this. If only I had agreed, he would be here today."

At least that part of his statement was true. If Matt had agreed to the outpatient therapy, Mark would have already been a free man. The elaborate ruse wouldn't have been necessary.

"We're sorry for your loss. We don't have any detailed answers for you. His body will be released to you tomorrow for burial, unless you request an autopsy," Officer Stone stated.

Mark stammered, "No. There's no need for an autopsy. If they say it was suicide, it was suicide. I believe them. Can they have him cremated? Can they take care of that for me?"

"The funeral home usually takes care of the particulars. Don't you want to see the deceased before ... well ... you know?" asked Officer Gonzalez.

"No. I really don't want to see a reflection of myself dead. We're twins. Seeing him dead would be too creepy."

"Officer Stone and I will inform the coroner of your decision concerning the autopsy. Someone will contact you concerning the arrangements. Again, we're sorry for your loss."

Tears streamed down Mark's face as he ushered the policemen out of the house. "Thank you. Good night."

Mark gazed out the window until the gravel dust that had been kicked up by the police cruiser settled. All of his energy sapped, he collapsed on the floor, crying. He covered his face with his hands.

"I didn't mean to kill him. I just wanted him to see what it was like being locked up. Why did this happen? How did it all get so out of hand?" he said through his sobs.

If the urge to throw up hadn't struck, he probably would have stayed on the floor all night. Instead, he rushed to the bathroom, where he lost his dinner. After a complete purge, he staggered out of the bathroom and made his way to the kitchen. He opened the cupboard where the medications were stored. Scanning the pills, he decided to take two tranquilizers and chased them down with a gulp of whiskey. Mark had thought freedom would be the end of his nightmare. Instead, it was just the beginning of another one.

Chapter 9

THE next morning, Mark awoke to the sound of birds chirping. Slowly, he rolled out of bed, shuffled down the hall to the bathroom, and relieved himself. After washing his hands, he ran the tap cold and splashed water on his face. Returning to his bedroom, he sat on the bed and picked up his diary. A clean page beckoned to him. He unclipped the pen and wrote, unburdening his mind of the guilt it harbored.

> Dear Diary,
>
> There's blood on my hands. It's invisible, but I can see it. I don't think it will ever come off. I didn't mean to kill Matt. We were supposed to trade places for a while. That's all. I just wanted to punish him for messing with me all of our lives. He always got away with it. It was my turn to try. But it didn't work.
>
> I can't believe he's gone. It wasn't supposed to be this way. What am I going to do? If I turn myself in, I'll end up back in jail. They won't understand that I didn't mean to do it. I can't go back to that jail.
>
> I guess I just answered my own question.

Confessing to the diary proved cleansing. Content with the entry, he relegated the diary to the top drawer of the nightstand.

Mark yearned to resume a life of normalcy. A long, hot shower rejuvenated him. Savoring the feel of his own clothes against his skin, he dressed in gray shorts and his favorite Giants T-shirt and went downstairs. The morning's newspaper was visible from the front window. Mark crossed the lawn to retrieve the paper, shielding his eyes from the rising sun. With no activity on the street except for the birds and squirrels, he turned back to the house. Flinging the paper on the kitchen table, he hunted for breakfast.

A box of generic Raisin Bran cereal rested on the top of the refrigerator. Since he had consumed all of the milk on the previous day, he would have to eat the cereal dry. There wasn't any juice in the house either. Tap water would have to suffice until shopping day.

As he crunched on the dry cereal, he scanned the headline on the front page. There were more suicide bombings in the Middle East. Nothing new there. He decided to forgo the latest tales of bombing devastation and turned to the sports section. The Yankees were having a good season so far. Dale Jr. was moving up in the points race.

The comics section yielded a few strips worth reading. He turned the page over and was face-to-face with the obituary section. A lump formed in Mark's throat. At the top was the obituary bearing his name—a short and simple blurb.

> Mark Collins, 24, Clear Brook, NY. Died suddenly July 20. Preceded in death by his parents, Samuel and Marjorie Collins. Survived by a brother, Matthew. Arrangements pending.

The finality sunk in. Mark Collins was dead to the world. His identity was gone. In a cruel twist of fate, Mark was forced to assume his brother's life permanently. From that point on, Mark vowed to live a better life, to be a better man.

As Mark debated reading the rest of the paper or getting on with the day, an approaching silver Buick interrupted his solitude. The Buick turned into his driveway. Dust kicked up behind the vehicle as the tires rolled over the stones and dirt. The car came to a jerking halt. Three women Mark quickly recognized, armed with what Mark assumed were casseroles, climbed out of the car and paraded to the kitchen door. He dreaded the upcoming interaction.

Sister Nancy, instantly recognizable by any member of St. Peter's Church, had been his fourth grade math teacher. Approaching eighty years old, the years had bestowed white hair and many wrinkles upon her. The nun's daily uniform consisted of the cross pendant around her neck, a starched white blouse, a navy blue skirt that fell well below her knees, and ugly blue shoes. Her movements were slow but steady.

Kathy Delvecchio, the choir director, was in her fifties and wore a floral print dress and flat white shoes.

Lynda Menlo, the youth group coordinator, had graduated from college a mere three years ahead of Mark. She donned an orange T-shirt, jeans, and flip-flops. They were a motley crew.

Sister Nancy knocked softly on the door.

Mark greeted them. "Morning." He stretched to hold the screen door open, allowing them to enter.

"Good morning," they each replied in return, looking concerned.

Kathy Delvecchio said, "We are so sorry for your loss. As soon as we read the obituary on your brother in the paper, we just had to come over, to see if you needed anything."

"Losing your parents and now your brother, so early in life—such tragedy. If there's anything we can do, please feel free to ask," Sister Nancy offered.

He replied, "Thank you for your concern, but I'll be fine."

"Of course you will," Kathy concurred. She deposited her food container in the refrigerator and reached for the items the other women held.

Sister Nancy sat down on a kitchen chair. "At times like this, you must not lose faith. It is a difficult time, but God has plans for each of us."

"Yes, Sister," he replied, trying to appear respectful. He joined her at the table.

Lynda suggested, "We can help you get the house ready or help with the funeral arrangements. Whatever you need."

"Thank you, but there won't be a funeral mass or calling hours or anything," he stated.

Sister Nancy frowned. "We noticed the short obituary in the paper. We assumed more would follow in the coming days." The nun shifted uncomfortably in her chair. "We can help you plan the Catholic service."

Mark spoke tersely. "Sister, I appreciate what you're trying to do. We won't be going through the usual arrangements."

Patting his hand, Sister Nancy insisted, "It's no bother. We'll help you."

Kathy sat next to him and patted his back. "It must be very hard on you, now that you're alone here. I can understand if it's too much for you."

All of the patting and unwanted attention disturbed Mark. Although not claustrophobic, he felt as if the walls were closing in. He nodded and smiled weakly at her as a headache developed.

Not to be left out, Lynda pulled her chair closer to him and patted his opposite shoulder. She added, "We can take care of selecting the music and the readings. It wouldn't be any trouble at all."

Unable to tolerate the situation any longer, Mark jumped up. He moved away from the well-intentioned ladies. From the other end of the kitchen, he blurted out, "There's no need for any of this. He committed suicide. He's being cremated."

Stunned, Sister Nancy made a sign of the cross.

Mark lied. "He stated that he wanted to be cremated in his suicide note."

"Oh, he left a note," Kathy commented.

Mark quickly fabricated the note in his mind. "Yes. He felt ashamed. He said that he didn't deserve a Catholic funeral service, because he was killing himself. Suicide is a mortal sin."

Sister Nancy touched the pendant that hung from her neck. "You know that the Church has eased up on performing services in these cases. Of course, suicide is still a mortal sin. However, he wasn't in his right mind when he took his life. So he can still have a Catholic funeral. Mark attended church every week until he went away. It's the right thing to do."

The nun's last words echoed in Mark's mind—the right thing to do. Confessing his sins and exposing his perpetuating fraud was the right thing to do. But it was not an option in the plan to reunite with his one true love. He agonized over the situation. A funeral mass would provide closure. Closure would, in turn, help ease Mark's guilt. On the other hand, it would attract a great deal of attention in the parish community, not to mention all of the questions. There would be lots and lots of questions.

Kathy sneezed.

"God bless you," the nun said.

"Thank you," Kathy replied.

The exchange returned Mark's focus to the women in his kitchen.

Shakily, Mark explained, "This was my brother's last request. I have to honor it. Don't you understand that? Don't you understand how hard this is for me? Can you imagine what it would be like to stand alone, while people file in to pat me and hug me and offer me condolences?"

Lynda said, "You wouldn't be alone. We'd be there for you."

Mark argued, "*You* are not my family. I am all alone now. I'm the last one left. Everybody is dead. I can't pretend otherwise. I appreciate that you want to help, but you can't help me. No one can help me. All of the casseroles in the world aren't going to take away my pain. You can't magically bring my family back. This can't be fixed. I can't bear to do this. I can't deal with all of those people. They'll be staring at me and feeling sorry for me. Somebody will bring up how I'm the last one left to carry on the family name. I just can't do it."

Avoiding eye contact, Kathy fussed with the edge of the tablecloth.

On the verge of tears, Mark stated, "I just can't do what you're asking me."

"All right. Obviously, this is a delicate matter," Lynda declared definitively. Turning to Mark, she said, "Unfortunately, you do realize that people will want to pay their respects, regardless of what you or your brother wanted?"

That was true. He couldn't prevent people from seeking him out, despite his objections to the contrary. His angst concerning the entire situation grew.

Lynda offered, "We could modify the obituary announcement to include the name of a charity that people could make a donation to, in your brother's name. That way, you won't have to deal with the repeated intrusions on your privacy. You also won't feel forced to reveal the circumstances of his death. How does that sound?"

Actually, it sounded like an excellent suggestion to Mark. He felt badly that his brother wasn't going to get a proper Catholic service. However, it would be much easier this way. Keeping up the pretense was crucial. He accepted the recommendation. "It's fine."

Lynda inquired, "Is there a particular charity you have in mind?"

Proposing the first organization that came to mind, he asked, "How about the American Cancer Society?" *This might lead people to jump to the conclusion that he died from cancer. That would be better than everyone talking about suicide.*

"A wonderful choice," Sister Nancy admitted. "Matt, I am going to ask Father Francis to stop by and speak with you."

"That won't be necessary, Sister. You've all done enough already. I think I'd just like to be alone now."

Kathy stood up and pushed her chair under the table. "We've taken enough of your time this morning. I will take care of contacting the paper concerning this information. If you think of anything else, don't hesitate to call one of us."

Lynda followed Kathy's lead. "Oh, by the way, the food we brought can be frozen. The containers are disposable. You don't have to worry about returning them. We taped the heating directions on the lids. And there's a sheet with our phone numbers on it too, just in case."

Mark nodded, just wanting the women to leave the house.

Sister Nancy said, "I will continue to pray for you. May God comfort you in your time of sorrow." Looking into his eyes, the aging nun held Mark's hands in her own.

Mark pulled away uncomfortably. "Thank you, Sister. Thank you all for coming today."

"Remember, if there's anything you need ..." Lynda added, walking out the kitchen door.

"I know, I'll call. Thanks again."

The women piled back into the Buick in which they had arrived. After a discussion, they agreed not to reveal the information they had received. Out of respect for the boy's deceased parents, this tragic event did not have to become public knowledge. Marge and Sam Collins had been active members in the church community. The women felt this was the least they could do in their memory.

Lynda Menlo called the American Cancer Society to find out how to establish donations in Mark Collins' name. Kathy Delvecchio contacted the newspaper to modify the obituary notice. Sister Nancy retired to the convent chapel, lit a candle, and prayed.

Mark wandered over to one of the two bookshelves in the family room and removed one of the photo albums. Sitting on the hardwood floor, he leaned against the couch and opened the album to the first page. Three generations of the Collins family smiled from the pages. He missed his parents, despite the fact they had favored Matt. He missed the hugs and kisses his grandparents used to give him. He even missed his brother. Many times growing up, Mark had felt alone. Now he truly was alone.

Mark hadn't meant for his brother to die. It had been an accident. Not like the accident that killed his parents, but a worse kind of accident, because he inadvertently had caused it to happen.

After skimming through the snapshots, he slid the album back into its slot and traded it for another, more recent book. This album contained pictures of high school and college. Flipping to the halfway point in the book, he saw his sweetheart. She wore a light blue cotton dress that complemented his dark blue suit. Determined to win her back, the details of their wedding day were etched in his mind. They would be together forever. He would make sure of it this time.

Anna buttered her toast at the kitchen counter.

Laura poured a cup of strong coffee, added two teaspoons of sugar, and took a sip. "How are you feeling today? Any better?"

Anna nodded. "Much better, thank you. Almost as good as new. I already got the paper. It's there on the table."

"Glad to hear you're feeling better." Laura relaxed at the table with her coffee. After reading the lead stories, she passed the section to Anna, who had joined her at the table. Laura unfolded the next section and scanned the obituary section. She remarked, "Oh shit."

"Isn't it a little early in the morning to be shitting already?" Anna asked.

"No. Did you happen to read the obits yet?"

"No, they're too depressing," she stated, munching her toast.

"Well, things are about to get more depressing around here." Laura sipped her coffee.

"Why? Who died?"

"Psycho boy," Laura responded.

"No," Anna said, astonished.

"Unfortunately, yes."

"Does it say how?" Anna snatched the paper out of Laura's hands.

"No. It just says *suddenly*, but I'm sure it was suicide. He was still at Misty Pines. It's not like he was in a car accident. What else could it have been?"

Anna put the paper down. "Oh shit is right. How are we going to handle this?"

"There's only one way to handle it. We need to tell her."

"Do we have to? Couldn't we just hide that section?"

Laura drained her coffee cup. "No. The comics are on the other side. She'll miss it. We have to tell her."

"She's going to be a mess." Anna imagined the impact of the news on her friend.

"Better hearing it from us than from anybody else."

Sara emerged from her bedroom in a pink nightshirt, yawning the length of the hallway. She shuffled into the kitchen.

Laura and Anna stopped speaking.

Sara sensed something was wrong immediately. "What's going on?"

Laura rose and offered her a chair. "Why don't you sit?"

Suspicious, Sara asked, "How about if I don't want to sit?"

"You will," Anna muttered.

"Did I miss a phone call? Did something happen to my parents?" Worried about what she might hear, Sara sat down.

Laura sat next to her. "No, it's not your parents or your brother. But someone we know died yesterday."

Sara braced herself for the news.

Clasping Sara's hands in her own, Laura said, "It was Mark Collins. We're really sorry."

Sara yanked her hands out of Laura's grasp. "No!" she screamed. "It can't be. There has to be a mistake."

Offering her the paper, Anna pointed to the obituary. "It's not a mistake. The announcement is right here in the paper."

Sara ripped the paper out of her friend's hand. The first time Sara read the words, they didn't register. Concentrating, she reread the notice. "I ruined his life. Now I've killed him."

Laura put her arm around her friend, attempting to comfort her. Sara leaned onto her shoulder. Stroking Sara's hair, Laura reassured her. "It's not your fault."

"Yes, it *is* my fault. I did this to him. I set all of this in motion. I'm to blame for all of this." Sara sobbed into her hands.

Laura turned to Anna. "You better call in sick for the three of us today. The numbers are near the phone. I think we need to be here for Sara."

"Agreed. I'll take care of it," Anna replied, picking up the phone and the slip of paper containing the pertinent phone numbers. She disappeared into her bedroom and left a message for each supervisor. After completing the third call, she contacted Joe and explained the situation to him.

Joe responded, "I'll be over as soon as I can."

Anna answered the door when Joe arrived. They congregated in the family room. Sara was still crying. Laura made room for Joe on the couch.

As soon as Joe sat down, Sara turned to him. She buried her face in his chest. He held her until she stopped crying. He tenderly wiped away her tears. Anna and Laura sneaked out of the room, leaving Joe and Sara alone.

"Are you going to be all right?" Joe asked.

"I feel responsible." Sara struggled to maintain her composure.

"You know you aren't responsible. He had mental problems. He made his own decisions. I know you want to blame yourself, but it's not your fault. The girls and I are going to help you get through this. I promise. I'll stay here as long as you need me."

"Thanks. That's what I needed to hear. Will you just sit here with me?"

"Yeah, but is it okay if I take a piss first? I came right over as soon as Anna called. I didn't have time to do anything except call in to work."

Caught off-guard, Sara smirked through her tears. "Yes. Go. And thanks for putting me before your bodily functions."

Getting up from the couch, Joe kissed the top of her head. "And speaking of bodily functions, you are going to put some clothes on, right?"

"Huh?" she questioned.

"That nightshirt you're wearing is driving me crazy."

"Ugh! You're unbelievable," she responded, throwing a sofa pillow at him. The pillow hit the wall as he ducked out of its path.

Joe laughed and winked at her. "Got you to smile, didn't I?"

The four friends entertained each other all day. They watched Sara's favorite comedies, ordered pizza, and recalled happier times. By bedtime, Sara's spirits had improved. Although still upset about Mark's death, she acknowledged that she was not responsible for his actions. She announced, "I'm going to go to bed now. Thanks for staying with me all day. I appreciate it. You guys are the best."

"We know," Laura answered.

After a group hug and a round of good-byes, Anna and Laura retired to their rooms.

Sara walked Joe to the door. "Thanks for everything today, Joe."

"Don't mention it."

"I guess I'll see you around."

"Yeah, I guess so."

Sara reached out to Joe and gave him a bear hug. "Good night."

Joe held her in his arms and kissed the top of her head. "Good night."

Sara pulled back and opened the door.

Joe shook his head. "Damn."

"What?"

"I took my wallet out of my back pocket earlier and set it on the kitchen counter."

"I'll go get it." She closed the door and started to walk toward the kitchen.

"No. You're tired. You go to bed. I'll get it. Then I'll lock up behind me."

"You sure?"

"Yeah, I'm sure. Pleasant dreams, Sara."

"Thanks. Drive safely."

"You know me—I drive fast and take chances."

"That's what I'm afraid of. Good night again."

"Night."

Joe watched Sara disappear into the hall. After he retrieved his wallet, he returned to the foyer. He stopped at the front door. His heart wouldn't allow him to leave. Determined to set things right with Sara, he turned around and walked to her bedroom door and knocked.

"Come in," Sara called out.

As Joe opened the door, he said, "I just couldn't leave ..."

Sara was standing directly in front of him, naked, holding a T-shirt against her body.

Sara hadn't realized that Joe was still in the house. She had thought one of the girls was checking on her. Convinced this was a sign, she took advantage of the opportunity. Thinking quickly, she replied, "Then don't and close the door."

Joe complied.

Sara allowed her shirt to drop to the floor. Coyly, she said, "Oops."

Speechless, Joe decided the conversation could wait until later.

Sara advanced. She took his hand in hers, tilted her head, and gave him a sultry look. Licking her top lip, she led him to the bed.

After Sara assisted Joe in removing his clothes, they embraced tightly. The fire that had been smoldering between them erupted into a wildfire. Joe made love to Sara with renewed intensity.

Despite her efforts to the contrary, Sara couldn't suppress her pleasure. She moaned, "Oh! That feels *so* good."

"You like that?"

"Yes! Oh!" She exhaled deeply.

Joe shifted positions slightly.

Sara responded with a heavy, throaty sigh.

Joe slowed, in an effort to tease her.

"*Oh, Joe! Oh!*"

Both lovers were on the verge of ecstasy when the door opened.

Laura entered the room. "Sara, I heard you crying, and I didn't want you to be alone."

Sara yelled, "Get out! Get out!"

Laura covered her eyes. "Oh my God! I'm sorry. I didn't know. I knocked. You didn't answer. I heard noises. I thought you were crying. Sorry! Sorry!" She rushed out of the room and shut the door behind her.

Anna shouted from her room, "Laura, why are you yelling? What's going on?"

Laura answered, "Nothing. Go back to bed."

Anna yelled, "Are you sure?"

Laura reassured her. "Yes. Go to sleep."

Anna responded, "All right, good night."

Frustrated and out of breath, Joe commented, "That was awkward."

"To say the least," Sara replied. "God, I hate her right now."

"That makes two of us."

The moment ruined, Joe and Sara got dressed in silence. Joe had planned to explain why he had knocked on her door, after they had made love. However, he couldn't find the right words after Laura's interruption.

When Joe opened the door, Laura was standing in the hall.

Laura was still apologizing. "Sara, I am *so* mortified. Joe, I didn't know you were even in the house. I thought you left. I am *so* sorry."

"Please stop talking," Sara pleaded. "You're just making it worse. Go back to bed. I can't deal with you right now."

"Sorry." Remorseful, Laura returned to her room.

Joe thought, *Not half as sorry as I am. I really screwed this up.*

Sara escorted Joe to the foyer, where they said good night for the final time that evening.

Chapter 10

THE rest of the week passed without incident. Sara eventually forgave Laura for her ill-timed interruption. Anna found the story hysterical and said so. After that, the subject wasn't spoken of again. What really bothered Sara was that Joe didn't call all week, leading her to believe their relationship *was* only about sex.

The projects at work and the associated paperwork kept her focused and busy. In fact, she put in extra hours, because the upcoming two weeks were scheduled as vacation. She wanted everything to run smoothly in her absence.

Saturday night arrived. Sara prepared for her date with David Turner. She felt she owed it to herself to see if a real relationship with someone other than Joe was possible—especially since a relationship with Joe, other than a sexual one, seemed inconceivable at the present time.

After some deliberation, she slipped into a summer-weight black skirt with a light floral pattern. Falling just above the knee with a slit up the right side, it wasn't too conservative. The button-up blouse she wore matched the lavender color of one of the flowers on the skirt. Accessorizing with her diamond pendant necklace, black shoes, and purse, she was raring to go.

At six twenty-five, a rumbling noise shook the house's windows. Investigating the culprit, Sara observed a candy-red 1970 Chevelle SS, complete with black racing stripes, pull into her driveway.

"What's that noise?" Laura peeked over Sara's shoulder at the window.

"It's pretty loud, whatever it is," Anna chimed in.

Sara answered, "It's a Chevelle. Apparently, I'm getting involved with a muscle car guy. This should be interesting. Oh, he's getting out. Hide! I don't want him to see us looking at him."

Laura lingered for a moment. "Wow! Did you get a good look at him?"

Anna replied, "No. I'll wait until he comes in."

"Get away from the window," Sara ordered.

"Okay. Okay. Whatever you say. He's quite a hottie though. If you decide you don't want him, I'll take him," Laura remarked.

"Hey, I've got first dibs. Try not to drool when I introduce him," Sara replied.

"I'm not making any promises," Laura teased.

Anna returned to the family room. "You guys are crazy."

Laura giggled. "Wait until you see him."

Anna turned to Sara. "If I remember correctly, didn't you date a car guy before?"

Laura spoke first. "Sara dated a car guy once who paid way more attention to his car than to her. He didn't last long."

"Yes, but this one is older. Hopefully, he'll be more mature," Sara answered.

Laura laughed. "Good luck with that."

The doorbell rang. Sara took a deep breath and opened the door. To her surprise, David handed her flowers.

"These are for you."

"Thank you. They're lovely." She buried her nose in the colorful bouquet and inhaled deeply. She loved flowers, especially unexpected ones. "Please come in for a minute while I put these in a vase." She scurried to the kitchen to find a vase.

Laura fished a vase out of the cupboard.

Anna poured water into it and handed it to Sara.

Shaking her head, Sara said, "Thanks, girls."

"It was my pleasure," Anna replied.

Laura smiled. "No problem."

In the meantime, David had ventured into the family room and was examining the pictures on the walls and fireplace mantle.

Laura busied herself by checking out David in his beige khaki pants and light blue oxford shirt. She whispered, "He's got a really nice ass."

"Shh! He'll hear you!" Sara scolded.

"I'm sure it's something he already knows," Laura commented.

Hitting Laura's arm, Anna said, "You're terrible. You're right, but you're terrible." They giggled.

Oblivious to their conversation, David entered the kitchen. "You have a lot of nice pictures in there."

Laura and Anna composed themselves and simultaneously greeted David, "Hello."

"Hi. I'm David Turner."

"We know. I'm Laura. This is Anna. Nice to meet you."

"Nice to meet both of you."

Anna announced, "We were just about to watch a movie. Have a good time and have her home at a decent hour, will you?" Anna used her hands to shoo them away.

He replied, "I'll do my best."

Laura and Anna made their way to the couch as the couple walked to the foyer.

Reaching the front door, Sara asked, "What were we talking about before? Oh yeah, the pictures. I'm a nuisance with a camera. Sometimes people give me grief about it, but they're always happy when I get doubles so they can have a copy. I love taking pictures. At one point, I thought about working for *National Geographic*."

"That would have been an exciting career. Why didn't you pursue it?" David inquired.

"One word—bugs. Every interesting place they go has some nasty bugs. And those nasty bugs can give you terrible diseases. I wouldn't do well in that environment. Trust me. Trudging through swamps or hanging in trees for hours on end wouldn't work for me. It's just an idea I like to think about every now and then. So what about you?"

"When I was a kid, my uncle owned a mortuary. I thought that would be a cool job. I did actually help out one summer until my mother found out. She lectured my uncle and me for over an hour on how that wasn't a suitable job for an impressionable fourteen-year-old boy. And that was the end of that. But I decided to study biology as a result. So it wasn't a total loss."

"I guess. I don't like the idea of touching dead people. I didn't even like cutting up a frog in school. But I guess somebody has to do it, right? Your mom just didn't want the somebody to be you," she replied, picking up her purse.

"Right. But mom was a hypocrite. She always encouraged me to go hunting with my dad so we could bond, but working in a mortuary was taboo. Go figure. To freak her out, I took up taxidermy. That really got her going."

"Yeah, I can only imagine." She wrinkled her nose and changed the subject. "Don't you think we should get going? We wouldn't want to be late for our reservation." Sara yelled into the other room, "Bye. Don't wait up."

"We won't. Have a good time," Anna called back.

David and Sara approached the Chevelle. He went directly to his door, opened it, sat in the black bucket seat, and started the car. Disappointed he hadn't opened the door for her, Sara told herself it was trivial. She opened her door and slipped into the seat. However, she didn't pull the heavy door hard enough to close it. She managed to secure it on the second try.

David caressed the dashboard as he chided, "Hey, be careful. She's my baby."

The comment surprised Sara. She hoped he was joking. She didn't know him well enough to tell. She laughed nervously. "Sorry, I guess the doors are a little heavier than I'm used to."

"This is one fine American-made vehicle with doors of steel. They don't make them like this anymore. That's for sure. She's got a 454 under the hood and the LS-5 high performance package." David depressed the accelerator and revved the engine. "Hear that rumble? That's music to my ears."

David backed out of the driveway and turned on the radio. It blared loud enough that it felt as if the music was coming through the seat. Mick Jagger wanted to paint everything black. Not wanting to yell over the music, she motioned for him to lower the volume. Worried of his reaction, she didn't want to risk touching the knob. To her relief, he turned the volume down.

"Did you say something, Sara? Sorry if the music is a little loud. As a teenager, I damaged my eardrums listening to loud music. The irony is that now I still have to have the music on loud to hear it."

"I was wondering what kind of music you like."

"Rock and metal, like the Stones, Zeppelin, Boston, Queensrÿche, Metallica. You know, that kind of stuff. You can look through my CD collection if you want to hear something else. It's under your seat. The sound system is the only thing I modified in the car. Everything else is original. I just couldn't live with the old radio and speakers. I had to install a new system."

"Yeah, I know what you mean. The old speakers didn't have enough range and the bass was really flat."

David smiled. "Exactly."

Sara had learned enough about cars and sound systems to get by in a conversation, courtesy of her brothers.

"So where are we headed?" David asked.

"Mama Lena's. Do you know where it is?"

Arriving at the restaurant, David parked in the very last parking space in the lot. Apparently, he had never heard of dropping a woman off at the door, so she didn't have to navigate a gravel lot in heels. Sara ensured the car door closed the first time. David offered his arm for balance; she accepted.

Eventually, they reached the small paved section of the lot. Sara was impressed that she hadn't twisted an ankle or ruined her shoes. An older gentleman held the door as they mounted the steps. He motioned Sara to go through. She smiled and thanked him. Lively Italian music greeted them as they crossed the threshold.

The hostess couldn't be missed in her little black dress. Its plunging neckline left little to the imagination. It was cinched at the waist with a wide red belt. The well-endowed woman smiled. "Welcome to Mama Lena's."

Sara returned the smile. "Thank you. Reservations for Taylor."

The hostess motioned, menus in hand. "Please follow me to your table."

They were seated at one of the tables next to the windows. Sara thought they would have a great view of the sunset, which brought a smile to her face. "So have you ever been here before David?"

"Yes, a couple of times. The food was fantastic both times," he replied.

The waiter, clad in a white shirt, black pants, and red tie, introduced himself as Gianni and offered David the wine list.

David looked at it briefly and ordered. "We'll have a bottle of Chianti."

"Good choice, sir. Would you care for any appetizers?"

David looked at Sara. She shrugged her shoulders.

"The calamari looks good. How does calamari sound, Sara?"

"Fine with me."

"Calamari it is then."

"Another fine choice, sir. All meals come with a salad. What dressing would you like on your salads?"

"I'll take the balsamic vinaigrette," Sara responded.

"Make that two."

"Excellent. I'll return with your wine shortly."

David and Sara studied their menus. She craved the shrimp scampi but reconsidered. For a first date, that much garlic would not be a good choice. "I think I'm going to order the seafood linguine. What are you going to have?"

"I'm going back and forth between the lasagna and the eggplant parmigiana. So Joe told me that you are an industrial engineer."

Sara lowered her menu. "Yes, I work at DAGS Engineering. I try not to advertise it. I'm thinking about doing something different soon anyway."

"Why?" He closed his menu and set it aside.

"Because it's just not what I thought it would be. It's not like I thought it would be a glamorous job, but I always thought I would do something that would make a difference."

Sara unfolded her napkin and placed it across her lap. David followed suit.

"You could always volunteer at St. Peter's Mission. Spending time with the less fortunate makes a difference. As the volunteer coordinator, I volunteer as much as I can. You should join me. You'd be surprised at how much fun it can be."

"Working at the mission is fun? I never really thought about it that way." She continued, "We were forced to volunteer for things like that in grammar school. The nuns wanted to scare us so we wouldn't end up as prostitutes or homeless drug addicts."

David laughed. "God bless the nuns. Saving unsuspecting kids from becoming the dregs of the earth."

The waiter interrupted the conversation as he brought the wine. He removed the cork and poured some wine for David to sample.

Pleased with the wine, David asked the waiter to pour glasses for both of them.

"So what do you think about my idea of volunteering at the mission?" David persisted.

"Twist my arm, why don't you? Fine. I'll try it. Maybe I'll even bring some friends with me."

"Great—the more, the merrier. It's a good cause," he reminded her.

"I know. I just hope I don't have any Sister Bernice flashbacks."

"I'm not familiar with her. Who's Sister Bernice?"

"Let's not talk about her and ruin a perfectly nice evening."

"Agreed. However, if you do have any flashbacks, I'll take full responsibility. Deal?"

"Deal," Sara agreed.

Gianni returned with the calamari and bread. Sara ordered the seafood linguine. David decided on the lasagna.

"Your salads will be out shortly."

David offered Sara the calamari. She spooned some onto her dish and tried a small piece.

Dabbing her lips on her napkin, she remarked, "This calamari tastes great. It's not rubbery. Nothing is worse than rubbery calamari."

"I agree. The herb butter sauce is good too. I'm glad we ordered it."

Sara leaned in. "So what do you do when you're not volunteering or teaching?"

"I work on restoring cars. I've got a Camaro in my garage that I'm working on. The previous owner beat the shit out of it. I'm trying to save as much of the original equipment as possible, but the transmission and engine will have to be replaced."

"Sounds like a big job."

"It is, but it's satisfying. I wouldn't do it if I didn't want to. Most of the time, I resell the cars and make some money on them."

"I can't imagine putting in that much time and effort into something, only to turn around and sell it." She sliced a piece of bread for herself and offered to do so for David. He nodded affirmatively.

"I don't have the room to keep them all. But it's not like I just sell to anyone, though. I usually sell to friends or collectors that I know." David looked out the window; the sun was setting.

The horizon glowed shades of pink and red.

Sara's eyes followed David's and witnessed the spectacular sunset.

Gianni returned to the table. "Your salads. I see you have finished with the appetizer. Allow me to remove the plates."

"Thank you," they said in concert.

Gianni nodded.

"I love sunsets. Don't you, David?"

"Yes. I love the different colors in the sky during sunset. That goes for sunrise too, for that matter. I love how cloud cover impacts the colors."

"For some reason, I've always been partial to sunsets."

"That must be the romantic in you. Although the sunset represents the end of a day, it also gives hope that tomorrow is on its way."

Usually, Sara would have found a comment like that corny.

Tonight, she didn't. They stared out the window in silence for several minutes. The waiter interrupted the quiet moment.

"Ma'am, the seafood linguine. And for you, sir, the baked lasagna. Would either of you like some freshly grated cheese?"

"Yes, please," Sara replied.

The waiter nodded and retrieved the cheese. As he turned toward her, the grater hit David's wineglass. In a matter of seconds, the wine had spilled on the table and into David's lap. The napkin on his lap did not spare him.

"Oh, sir! I am terribly sorry. Let me get some soda water before the stain sets." The embarrassed waiter disappeared into the kitchen.

The tablecloth soaked up some of the wine. However, its saturation point was exceeded; the wine continued to drip onto David's legs. Backing away from the table, David looked down at his beige pants. "Looks like I had one hell of an accident."

"David, I'm sorry. I feel so bad."

"It's not your fault. It's only wine. Now if it had been flambé, *that* would have been a different story. I'd probably be hopping around grabbing strangers' water glasses and throwing water on myself."

Sara giggled. The wine had made quite a large stain on his crotch and thighs.

The waiter reluctantly informed Mama Lena of the mishap as he searched for soda water.

Mama Lena smacked her son on the back of the head, as she pushed open the swinging door and marched over to David and Sara's table.

"I apologize for my son. He takes after his father. God rest his soul," she said, making the sign of the cross. She continued, "The man was not good with his hands and always made a mess of everything. Your meals are on the house. And, of course, I'll pay for your dry cleaning."

"Thank you. That's not necessary. It's just a pair of pants."

"I insist." Mama clapped her hands twice.

Her son emerged sheepishly from the kitchen with soda water, a fresh tablecloth, and several cloth napkins. "Do you need help getting the stain out?" the waiter inquired.

"No. I think I'll handle that on my own in the bathroom. Thanks." David grabbed the soda water and napkins and departed for the men's room.

Gianni removed everything from the table, reset it, and replaced the wine-soaked chair. He informed Sara, "I am going to take this food back into the kitchen. Mama told the chef to make the meals fresh. I am so sorry for ruining your evening." He rushed back to the kitchen.

The sun finished setting. Just a hint of a red glow lingered on the horizon. Sara continued to stare out the window. She and Joe had loved watching the sun set on warm summer nights, complete with picnic dinners on the beach at a friend's parents' cottage. Joe had volunteered to housesit for the family while they travelled, once he learned of the secluded private beach. After sunset, they would make love under the stars.

The daydream progressed as she recalled the passionate evenings she had recently spent with him. There was no denying that their physical chemistry seemed stronger, hotter. The thought of his touch sent a shiver through her body. She closed her eyes and fantasized about her next encounter with Joe.

A patron at the next table coughed.

It startled her. She opened her eyes. *When did I close my eyes? I hope I wasn't doing anything weird. And I hope no one was watching me. Geez.*

Sara sighed and then chastised herself. *What am I doing? I'm here with David, not Joe. I need to focus on the here and now.*

She grabbed the bottle of wine. *I have to think of something that doesn't have to do with Joe. Only how am I going to do that? I love him so much it hurts.*

She topped off her wineglass and set the bottle back down. *Okay. Stop thinking about him. Concentrate on David and pull yourself together, Sara.*

After draining her glass, Sara switched gears mentally and pictured her own version of David's alternate accident scenario with the flambé—a man running around the restaurant with a flaming crotch and people throwing water at him. She laughed as David reappeared.

"Laughing at my misfortune, are you?"

She turned to say *no*, but when she saw him, she burst into laughter.

In addition to the wine stain in his crotch area, now there was a larger, pinkish colored stain that stretched almost to his knees. His shirt was wet as well. Apparently, David's attempt to remove the wine had gone poorly.

Sara lifted her napkin to cover her face, as heartier laughter overcame her.

"Sure. Go ahead. Laugh it up at my expense."

Sara brought the napkin down to her lap and struggled not to laugh. "I'm sorry. Really, it doesn't look that bad."

"Right, and the Grand Canyon is just a little hole in the ground." He pulled out his chair and joined her.

Sara attempted to regain her composure. "Should I ask why your shirt is wet?"

"Don't ask. If I told you, you wouldn't be able to stop laughing all night."

"I'm sure it's a great story."

"A story for another day. Where's the klutz?"

"He went back to the kitchen. He said the chef is making us fresh entrees."

"Great. After all that work, I'm starving. Looks like I missed the rest of the sunset too."

"It's too bad you missed it. It was beautiful." Sara leaned closer to David and whispered, "Hey, watch out. The waiter is coming back with the food."

"Thanks for the heads-up."

"Here are your entrees. I apologize again for creating a scene. The meals are on the house. We will pay your dry cleaning bill as well."

"That's not necessary."

"Yes, it is. Mama says it's necessary." Gianni reached for the cheese grater, but Sara stopped him.

She stated, "On second thought, I don't want any cheese. Thank you, anyway."

"Will there be anything else?"

"No. Thank you," David answered.

David and Sara ate their meals without any further drama.

"Did you save any room for dessert?" David asked.

"I couldn't eat another bite. The food was fantastic, and there was so much of it."

"I guess it's about time to flag down our waiter."

"Just try not to make any sudden movements. We wouldn't want another incident," Sara joked.

David caught the waiter's attention. The waiter reminded him that the meal was on the house. He left a decent tip for the clumsy waiter, despite the wine fiasco. As he stood, Sara couldn't help but look at the stained area. The stain had faded slightly, but the pants and shirt were still damp.

David commented, "Nice fashion statement, huh?"

"I've heard it's all the rage in Paris this season," Sara teased.

They walked through the dining room into the lobby. When they reached the bottom of the stairs, David said, "Stay here. I'll get the car."

Surprised and relieved, Sara waited. David pulled the Chevy right up to the stairs and held the door for her. After closing her door, he jogged to his side of the car, got in, and put the Chevelle in drive.

She looked at him puzzled.

"Is there a problem?" he asked, pulling out of the parking lot.

"No, no problem."

"I'm sure you're wondering why my manners were sporadic tonight. Am I right?"

Looking at him, Sara replied, "As a matter of fact, yes."

"Don't get mad. I was conducting a little test. You didn't complain a bit when I didn't hold your door or when you had to walk through the parking lot. A lot of women would have bitched about it. You didn't."

"So?"

"Please don't take it the wrong way. I am just sick of prima donnas who think they're God's gift to men. You're different. You're real. You actually ate your dinner."

"What?"

"You wouldn't believe how many women won't eat the dinner they order because they want to make a good impression. I've never understood that. Everybody needs to eat. All that tells me is that the woman isn't happy with who she is. Please don't be upset with me."

"Well, I am a little upset, but I'll get over it. I think God punished you enough with the wine incident."

"If you look at it that way, I guess God did. Sara, I had a really good time tonight. I'd like to see you again."

"I had a good time too. But I'm not going to take any more tests."

"Agreed. No more tests. I promise." David crossed his heart with his right hand.

"You better keep that promise, mister, if you know what's good for you."

"I was hoping that you would be good for me."

Sara blushed. "We'll just have to see what happens."

"I can live with that."

David pulled into Sara's driveway and turned off the car. He got out, opened her door, helped her out, and escorted her to the front door. "I meant it earlier when I said I had a nice time tonight."

"I did too. Would you like to come in?" she asked, unlocking the door.

"Actually, I'd love to come in, but these damp pants are driving me crazy. I think it would be better if I went home."

"Next time, then?"

"Yes, definitely next time. I'll even bring an extra set of clothes, just in case."

There was a moment of awkward silence. Then David moved toward Sara and kissed her. It was a sensual kiss. His lips were full and moist. She kissed him back. Her lips parted, as did his. They kissed for over a minute before he pulled back. Up until that moment, only one man had caused her to feel a rush of adrenaline like that. Now it seemed there were two.

"I think I'd better leave before this goes any further. Thank you again for a memorable evening."

"Thank you. I enjoyed it too."

"I'll call you soon. Good night."

"Good night."

Sara entered the house dazed. Her reaction to David's kiss had been totally unexpected. She watched him drive away. However, she did not see the white van parked across the street. She was still preoccupied with the kiss.

"Wow. If he kisses that well, I wonder how good he is at other things."

Sara smiled at the thought of things to come. The house was dark. Anna and Laura were already asleep. Any discussion would have to wait until tomorrow.

"Just my luck. No one awake to talk to. This is going to drive me crazy. I have all sorts of news to tell, and there's no one to share it with."

David drove home feeling pretty good about the evening, despite the wine incident. The kiss they shared had been intense. He assured himself she had felt it too. As he pondered the full impact of their kiss, it began to rain.

As he pulled onto his street, Crestview Lane, the wind and rain picked up sharply. Concerned by the inclement weather, he didn't notice the white van shadowing him.

Sara slipped into her bed, weighing the possibilities of a romance with David. That night, a vivid dream awaited her. She and David were in an amusement park on a merry-go-round. The multicolored strings of lights on the ride shined brilliantly. A calliope played in the background. Children scrambled to mount their favorite animals. The bell sounded. The ride started.

Standing next to an antique white jumper with gold hair, she mounted it. It had royal blue and candy apple red accents on the saddle and saddle blanket. David mounted a horse in front of her. He waved to her. His horse, a white jumper with golden hair, displayed saddle accents of purple and gold.

Sara glanced at the mirrors in the center of the merry-go-round. In their reflections, zebras, lions, and tigers loomed behind her. However, the children on them were missing. Each time she stared into the mirrors, the animals seemed to be approaching. But when she turned around, the animals would be in their appropriate positions, with the children atop them.

When the ride ended, David dismounted his horse and motioned for Sara to join him. His steed, no longer wooden, stepped gracefully off the platform. David adjusted the leather saddle. Floral garlands draped the creature's neck. The painted saddle blanket morphed into crushed purple velvet with gold fringe. The animal's breastplate, hip band, bit, and bridle shimmered with gold.

Sara dismounted her stallion. As she approached, David remounted his horse and galloped away into a meadow. She turned with the intention of jumping back on her steed to follow him. Alas, it was still a wooden carousel horse.

The children disembarked the ride. The lions and tigers, which previously had only moved in the mirrors, approached steadily, winding through other stationary animals on poles.

Sara looked back in David's direction. He had disappeared from view.

However, emerging in the distance, a figure on a black horse galloped toward her, riding bareback. Dressed completely in black, the mystery man donned a long, flowing cloak, which billowed in the breeze. He reached her with lightning quick speed. At a full gallop, the rider extended his arm.

Sara jumped off the platform and grabbed his arm. With great effort, she hoisted herself up on the back of the horse. They continued at full gallop until they reached the center of the park.

The faceless rider dismounted and motioned for her to jump down. It disturbed her that she could not see his face. Despite her misgivings, she jumped into his outstretched arms. They entered the house of mirrors, hand in hand. Through a labyrinth of corridors, he led her in silence.

Reaching a larger room, she tugged on his arm. Although he turned, the hood of the black cloak obscured his face. As she reached up to pull the hood off, the rider vanished. The cloak floated lifelessly to the ground. She spun around, only to see her own reflection in the mirrors. The rider was nowhere to be found.

She searched passage after passage for what seemed like hours, unable to find her way out. Exhausted, she sat on the cold, hard floor and wept into her hands. Suddenly, something moved underneath her. Startled, she opened her eyes and wiped away her tears.

No longer in the house of mirrors, she sat in a grassy meadow. A warm breeze blew her brown hair back, away from her face. A large tree grew alone in the distance. She stood up and walked toward it. As she approached, the wind blew increasingly stronger, making it difficult for her to gain ground. She fell numerous times. Her determination drove her onward. She would not give up.

Finally, within reach of the tree, she grasped a low-hanging branch to steady herself. As she touched the branch, the wind stopped completely. Birds, nesting in the tree, scattered in all directions. Sara noticed that the tree bore fruit. The apples were ripe and ready to be picked. One apple in particular appealed to her. She extended her hand to pick it. As she caressed the skin of the apple with her fingertips, it became hot to the touch. Suddenly, the tree was bathed in bright white light. And as quickly as the light appeared, it was extinguished, accompanied by a loud clap of thunder.

Sara awakened from her dream with a start. However, it only took seconds for her to determine the culprit was the rolling thunder of the evening's storm. Luckily, the sound of the steady rain lulled her back to sleep.

Chapter 11

BRIGHT sunlight peeked through the curtains Sunday morning. Sara rolled over. The clock displayed two minutes after seven. She groaned and pulled the covers over her head. It was too early to be awake on a Sunday. However, sleep eluded her. She was straining to remember the details of her dream when she heard a knock at the door.

"Sara? Sara? Are you awake?" whispered Anna, an early riser and cheerful morning person.

Emerging from under the covers, Sara groaned. "Yeah. Come in."

"There's someone at the door for you."

Sara popped up. "Who's looking for me on a Sunday at this hour?"

"For me to know and you to find out," Anna taunted. "Get out of bed and see for yourself, sleepyhead."

Sara griped as she got out of bed and pulled on her silk burgundy robe. She shuffled to the foyer. David was leaning against the front door.

He greeted her. "Morning. How'd you sleep?"

Sara stood up straight and pushed her hair behind her ears. She hoped it didn't look too wild. "Morning. Fine, I guess," she acknowledged.

"I know this is short notice. I was wondering if you'd like to work the breakfast crowd with me over at the mission today. It starts in about an hour. So we don't have much time. If you can't, I understand."

"Sure, why not? I'm awake. I might as well do something productive with my day. I'll be ready to go in twenty minutes."

Sara showered, tamed her wet hair in a ponytail, struggled

into a pair of blue jeans, and topped it off with a red V-neck T-shirt with a minute to spare.

Anna leaned into Sara's room as she dressed. "Apparently, your date went pretty well, huh?"

"You could say that. I'd love to tell you all about it, but I don't want to keep him waiting." Sara pushed past Anna in the doorway. "Excuse me."

"Fine. Just make sure Laura and I get all of the details later."

"You can count on it. See you later." Sara grabbed a blueberry bagel and a plastic bottle of orange juice on her way out the door.

David waited in the driveway and started the engine as soon as she got into the car. "I'm impressed," he admitted, backing out of the driveway.

"Did you doubt that I could get ready that fast?"

"I was skeptical, but now I believe anything is possible." David eyed the bagel. "You don't plan on eating that in my car, do you?"

Sara laughed and shook her head. "No, I'll wait until I get out. So what exactly am I going to have to do at the mission today?"

"We're serving breakfast. You'll plop hash browns, scrambled eggs, and other breakfast stuff on the plates held out in front of you. Then we'll help with cleanup."

"That doesn't sound too bad."

"Trust me, you'll have a good time, and you're helping the less fortunate."

"I know. I know. You don't have to remind me. I'm just not a morning person like Anna. Give me a few minutes. I'll perk up."

After driving several blocks, David pulled into the parking lot between the mission and St. Peter's Church.

St. Peter's Catholic Church was the predominant Catholic Church in the small town of Clear Brook, New York, which bordered Lake Ontario. The church had succeeded in establishing an educational powerhouse, as well as providing vital services to the community, starting with the church on the corner of Main Street and Third Avenue. Its elementary and high schools were positioned next to each other on Third Avenue, across from the church. The mission that served the community stood next door to the church on Third Avenue. The rectory and convent were located on the other side of the mission. However, because of space limitations, St. Peter's had erected its university four blocks away on Seventh Avenue. The college campus sprawled across five city blocks.

Sara exited the vehicle and took a large bite of her bagel. She chewed as they walked through the parking lot. Several people were perched on the steps of the mission.

After drinking some orange juice, she asked, "Aren't the doors open yet?"

"Yes, they're open. Why?"

"Then why are all of these people hanging out on the steps?"

David stated, "Smoking isn't allowed in the building."

"I don't understand how all of these people can be homeless and still afford to buy cigarettes."

David explained, "Not all of the people who come to the mission are homeless. Some come to hang out—to feel part of a group. Some are here to help serve food. Others offer a friendly ear to those who need it."

Sara followed him up the stairs.

David addressed the group. "Good morning."

He received a rousing good morning in return from the crowd.

"Everyone, I'd like to introduce our newest volunteer, Sara."

They all nodded.

Gesturing to the group, David said, "Sara, these are our fellow volunteers."

An elderly black man stood, removed his hat, and introduced himself. "My name is Lester Woods. I'm a retired furniture salesman from Bailey's. I volunteer here almost every day. It's a nice change of pace." Feeling the need to explain his smoking, he continued. "My wife won't let me smoke in the house. I come early to enjoy a cigarette before the day starts. I know I should quit, but I figure I've lasted this long. George Burns lasted until he was a hundred years old. He drank and smoked every day."

The burly man next to him loudly cleared his throat.

Lester apologized. "Pardon me, I ramble sometimes. The man who so tactfully cleared his throat next to me is Tom Grant."

"Thanks for the intro," Tom replied. "I worked at the appliance factory for seventeen years, until they transferred the equipment and the jobs to Mexico. Now I deliver newspapers and fix appliances out of my garage. If you need anything fixed, I'm your guy."

"Thanks. I'll keep that in mind," Sara responded.

A woman sitting at the top of the stairs on the other side spoke next. "Hi, my name is Sally Prado. I've got eight children at home—four of each. They range in age from eleven years to six months."

Sara thought that this woman took the Catholic Church's stand on birth control very seriously. Obviously, she relied on the Church-approved rhythm method. Not a risk taker, Sara had begun taking the pill as soon as she and Joe had started having sex.

Sally continued, "I'm a room mother at St. Peter's Grammar School. I come here on weekends to talk to some grown-ups."

The young woman sitting next to Sally stood up and shook Sara's hand. "Nicki Esperanza. I came from Mexico to this country with my parents a few years ago. I work with Lynda Menlo, the youth group coordinator. I talk to the at-risk teens. I used to be one myself. Since I'm nineteen, kids tell me things that they wouldn't want to say to an adult. Everyone here really helped me when I needed it, so I'm returning the favor."

The guilt associated with not staying involved with the church and the community crept into Sara's conscience. All of these people had made time in their lives to fit in some type of service. Sara's schedule wasn't that demanding. She couldn't legitimize a reason for avoiding her Christian duty. It was time to get involved and stay involved.

Lester disrupted her train of thought. "The young guy sitting on that old crate next to the stairway is James Dillon. He plays a mean guitar over at the jazz club on the corner of Second Street and Main. He's there every Friday and Saturday night with his band. On Sundays, he comes here to entertain the crowd. He's amazing. Once you've heard him play, I'm sure you'll agree. And I guess that's all of us."

Sara replied, "It's a pleasure to meet all of you."

Nicki asked Sara, "What's your story?"

Sara offered, "I'm an industrial engineer for DAGS Engineering here in town. I'm here today to help with breakfast."

Before anyone could ask a follow-up question, a loud booming voice filled the air. The voice proclaimed, "God loves his children. Repent and be saved! Repent, you sinners! Repent and feel the hand of God! Yes, my brothers and sisters, you too can be saved. Say Amen!"

"Crazy man," mumbled Tom Grant, extinguishing his cigarette.

Sara looked to David for an explanation. Before he could reply, the man with the booming voice rounded the corner into view. The overweight black man wore an ill-fitting light blue suit. He held a Bible in one hand. The other hand busied itself by pointing at sinners and waving at the heavens.

A teenage boy stood on the corner waiting for the light to change.

The loud man verbally accosted the boy. "My son, there is still time for you. You can achieve salvation if you reject the devil and fight worldly temptations. Repent! I say, repent! Can I get a hallelujah? You can be saved!"

The boy looked both ways and decided to cross the street, against the light, to escape.

Unfazed, the man proceeded down the sidewalk, shouting and yelling.

Lester happily offered an explanation. "Sara, it's your lucky day. That man right there is the Reverend Ezekiel Walker. He was the minister at the First Baptist Church until lightning struck him on the golf course. He hasn't been quite right since. He says getting struck was a sign from God. We all agree on the sign part, just not on the interpretation—if you know what I mean." He winked. "Now he just roams the streets, yelling at people all day."

Sara remembered meeting the Baptist minister years ago.

He had gained a tremendous amount of weight since their last encounter.

David spoke. "I hate to break up this party, but I need to go in and talk to Father Francis before breakfast starts. See you inside."

They nodded. The smokers finished their cigarettes and prepared to enter the mission.

Sara accompanied David up the marble steps into the mission. They crossed the large main room that functioned as a dining hall. She hadn't stepped foot in the mission in years. The walls were now painted a pretty sky blue, and an enormous rainbow stretched across the largest wall. It felt welcoming.

Long tables and folding chairs were set up for approximately one hundred people. Over half of the chairs were already occupied. Other people formed small groups along the walls.

Father Francis carried a tall stack of plates and positioned them on the end of the first food table.

David extended his hand to the priest. "Good morning, Father." They shook hands.

"Good morning, David. I see you brought a friend with you today. You look familiar. Are you a parishioner?"

"Yes and no. I'm Sara Taylor. Since my brother died several years ago and my parents took up missionary-type work, I haven't attended church regularly," she admitted.

"I remember your family well. I thought you had moved out of town with them since I haven't seen you in the confessional lately. And perhaps we can do something about your church attendance?"

"Yes, Father," Sara responded, looking down at the floor, feeling the full weight of the guilt. Guilt—the perfect weapon—wielded by Catholic priests, nuns, and mothers alike.

The priest continued. "Thank you for coming today, at any rate. Let's get started. We have hungry people to feed."

David gave her a sheepish look. "Sorry about that."

"It's my own fault for not coming to church more often." Sara finished her orange juice and threw the bottle in the recycling bin in the corner.

Tom Grant meandered through the main room with his toolbox. He made his way to the kitchen to examine the noisy dishwasher. Sally Prado accompanied Tom into the kitchen. She was one of the cooks for the day. Lester Woods chatted with the older people in the main room; whereas Nicki Esperanza sought out the teenagers. Jim Dillon settled in the back corner with his guitar and played familiar gospel tunes, unless someone made a special request.

Sister Josefina and Sister Renata, two nuns visiting from St. Peter's sister church in Brazil, served breakfast along with David and Sara. Father Francis and several altar boys hauled the food from the kitchen to the food line. The group served every person in line. Cleanup began immediately afterward. Everyone pitched in.

Father Francis announced, "Lunch starts in a little over an hour. I have to go prepare to celebrate the next service. There's plenty of room in the church. Everyone is welcome."

"Lunch? We have to do this all over again for lunch?" Sara asked.

"No. A new crew will come in for lunch."

"Thank goodness. I had forgotten how much work this was." She wiped the sweat from her forehead. "And, yes, I'm glad I did it," she admitted.

"See, I told you. Now how about catching the next Mass?"

"Maybe next time. I need to work up to it."

"I won't push. How about I treat you to lunch?"

"Sure. I've worked up an appetite."

They hopped in the Chevelle. David drove to the beach and parked in the general parking area.

"Um, I didn't bring a bathing suit. I thought we were going to lunch."

"Lunch by the beach. We can eat indoors or out, whichever you prefer."

Sara surveyed the burger places in the area. Some of the buildings looked pretty dilapidated. Although she came to the beach often, she didn't frequent the food vendors.

Noticing Sara's critical look, David said, "Don't get turned off by the appearances of these places. They make up in taste for what they lack in appearance. You won't get a better burger anywhere."

"If you say so."

"I do. If I'm wrong, sue me."

"I just might, you know. Go ahead, pick a place."

David selected Bob's Burger Barn and ordered a chilidog with cheese. Sara played it safe, opting for a hamburger with ketchup and relish. They split onion rings and fries. Neither noticed Mark Collins in the corner booth, watching them intensely. Mark had journeyed to the beach to clear his head. He was genuinely surprised to see Sara there with the mystery guy he had followed the previous evening. Mark was positive that their relationship had ended because Joe Lazaro had forced himself back into her life. This development had thrown him off. It didn't make any sense. He knew how he would handle Joe. Now Joe wasn't even in the picture. Mark realized he needed to learn more about this new adversary.

After eating, David and Sara headed toward the beach.

Mark followed at a safe distance.

Once they reached the sand, David and Sara removed their shoes. After twenty paces or so, she tripped and fell into him. They tumbled to the sand.

"Walk much?" David teased.

"Sorry. I lost my footing. Are you all right?"

"Uh huh, but you might want to roll off of me. This is a public beach with children around, you know. This probably isn't viewed as wholesome family entertainment."

Sara crawled off of him and stood up. "It was an accident."

"Oh, I believe you. But next time, try to wait until we're alone."

"Oh! Men! You're all alike."

"You say that like it's a bad thing."

Sara rolled her eyes, brushed herself off, and proceeded down the beach.

David brushed himself off, shook the sand out of his hair, and jogged to catch up with her. "You're cute when you're angry."

Sara glared at him. "I'm not angry."

"Fine then. You're just cute." He flashed a smile.

She smiled back. He took her hand. She squeezed his in return. They strolled along the water for a while, hand in hand.

David turned toward her. "You're being quiet all of a sudden."

"I've been thinking about how the beach differs during the day from at night. Children slathered in sunscreen run into the incoming waves, only to run back up the beach again because the water is cold. Other kids brave the water temperature and splash each other or play with water toys. Then there are those kids, over there." She pointed. "They build sandcastles and bury themselves in the sand. Days at the beach are noisy—laughter, screaming—an occasional crying fit. Nighttime on the beach is calm, peaceful, and serene. Screaming and commotion are almost nonexistent. There's quiet time to reflect and enjoy the sound of the water."

"You obviously like the beach better at night."

"Overall, yes. But being here now has its perks too. Like being here with you." She batted her eyelashes at him.

"The feeling is mutual."

Far from the screaming children, they found a place to sit. Sara absentmindedly drew shapes of nothing in particular in the sand. David picked up fistfuls of sand and let the grains slowly escape through his fingers.

Mark kept his distance. The couple appeared to be having a good time.

Two young boys played nearby with water guns.

Mark approached and offered them ten dollars each to play around the mystery man and Sara. The kids eagerly accepted the money and moved their fight. The kids did not disappoint. Running around David and Sara, they kicked up a fair amount of sand and drenched them with water. The children halfheartedly apologized for their behavior and happily ran down the beach.

Mark observed that the incident did not have the intended effect.

Instead, the couple laughed and resumed their stroll toward the pier.

Undaunted, Mark followed.

Eventually, David and Sara came upon a rocky area. They cleared the sand out from in between their toes before sliding their shoes back on.

The rocks led to the pier, where several older men fished. Seagulls glided overhead. A few birds forged in the rocks for discarded bait. The smell of dead fish was strong. However, it dissipated once they mounted the pier because of the steady breeze blowing across it.

Mark sat next to one of the fishermen and pulled the visor of his baseball hat down lower.

Sara glanced at her watch.

"Someplace you have to be?" David asked.

"No. Just a habit."

"If you've had enough, I could drive you home."

"I don't think I'm ready to go home quite yet. The weather is beautiful, and I'm having a nice time."

"Me too. What would you say about having a picnic in the park?"

"Sure. I know a deli that packs picnic lunches and dinners."

"Sounds like a plan."

They strolled off the pier to the parking lot and drove away in David's Chevy. Mark had parked in a different lot. He lost track of them—for now.

David and Sara ordered a picnic dinner for two at Carmine's Deli. The meal wouldn't be ready for twenty minutes, so David dropped Sara off at home to freshen up. He drove to the liquor store to buy some wine.

The white van slowly crept down Sara's street. Mark didn't see the Chevelle. There was movement in Sara's house. He was unsure whether it was Sara or one of her housemates.

Once again, Sara was disappointed. No one was home. Relaying last night's and today's stories would have to be shelved for later. After changing and freshening up, she selected a blanket from the hall closet to sit on.

As she waited, she attempted to cleanse her mind of Joe. *David is a really nice guy. You enjoyed going out with him last night. Today at the beach was fun. Tonight will probably be nice too. No more thinking about Joe. He's off-limits. Concentrate on David.*

On the street, two houses down, the van's driver-side door opened. Mark decided to approach Sara's house. As his left foot touched the pavement, the Chevelle rounded the corner and pulled into Sara's driveway. Mark slid back into the seat and closed the door. He watched Sara bound out of the house and into the car. Disappointed but undeterred, Mark restarted the van and pursued them from a distance.

David drove to Carmine's Deli. After they picked up dinner, they continued to the park. Once the contents of the backseat of the vehicle were unloaded, David popped the trunk to obtain an additional blanket, in case the temperature dropped. Predicting nighttime temperatures near the lake was tricky. Supplies and food in hand, they followed the gravel path into a wooded area of the park. They didn't want to be in view of the parking lot. Sara spread one blanket down under a tree. David placed the picnic basket, the bottle of wine, and the other blanket down on it. Getting comfortable, they opened the basket that held sandwiches, chips, fruit, and double chocolate brownies.

Mark tracked them into the woods, careful not to be seen or heard. Avoiding the path, he hid amid the trees in his dark shirt and jeans. An old tree with a thick trunk served as his observation station.

David popped the cork on the wine. Sara held the plastic cups as he poured.

She remarked, "I notice you bought white wine instead of red."

"Why tempt fate?" He wedged the cork back into the bottle.

"How about a toast?" she asked, holding up her plastic cup.

"How about this—to the future and the possibilities that it holds."

"I'll drink to that."

After they had consumed their dinners and most of the wine, they packed the empty wrappers into the picnic basket. Once the mess was cleaned up, they talked for a while before David began tickling Sara. They wrestled playfully on the blanket.

David was strongly attracted to Sara. His last relationship had ended badly, almost a year ago. He was finally ready for a new romantic interest. So he turned up the heat.

The chemistry between them surprised Sara. It wasn't the same type of heat as she had with Joe, but there was something tangible. Eager to learn where this might lead, she lowered her defenses.

Mark's stomach was in knots. The playful romp had turned into kissing. Mark became enraged the more he witnessed. The stranger's hands touched and caressed her. The rival kissed Sara's neck, and his right hand disappeared under Sara's shirt. Livid, Mark's body shook with contempt. Clammy and nauseated, he dug his fingernails into the tree and unwittingly picked at the bark.

When Sara pushed the man away, a glimmer of hope invigorated Mark. Alas, hope was dashed as he observed the man grab the other blanket and cover both of them with it. Mark could imagine the activity under that blanket.

At one point, the stranger's head disappeared under the blanket. The expression on Sara's face was too much for Mark to stomach. As his rival's head reappeared, kissing resumed. Mark struggled with his emotions. Despite the blanket, he could observe the couple's rhythmic movements.

Sara sighed audibly.

Mark covered his ears with his hands and looked down at the ground. A pile of bark chips appeared in front of him. He brought down his hands and saw blood on his fingers. His nails were split and jagged. Wiping his bloody hands on his jeans, he forced himself to turn around again.

The movement under the blanket continued. Depressed, confused, and enraged, he couldn't watch any longer. It was impossible to bear. He ran to the white van in the parking lot. Unable to control his stomach any longer, Mark dropped to his knees and vomited. "I don't understand. How could she betray me this way? I love her," he uttered, trembling as he stood up. Lightheaded, Mark leaned against the van. "I just have to remind her that she loves me too. That's all. I've been away too long. I love her." Tears streamed down his face.

Sara froze. "Did you hear something?"

David kept kissing her. "No. It's probably a squirrel or something."

"It sounded bigger than a squirrel," she insisted, pushing him away.

He paused. "I don't hear anything now. Do you?"

"No. But maybe we should pack up. It's awfully dark in the woods since the sun went down."

"If that will make you more comfortable, we can move this party elsewhere."

"Yes, please. Thank you."

"No, thank you. I'm really enjoying spending time with you."

"Me too," Sara responded.

After making themselves presentable, David picked up the remnants of their dinner. Sara folded the blankets. Upon reaching the car, they noticed only one additional car remained in the lot.

Mark had already left for home.

David drove toward Sara's house on Springhill Drive.

Sara asked, "Um, are you driving to my house?"

"Yes. I thought you'd be more comfortable there."

"Not really. I do have two roommates to contend with." *Not to mention all of the memories.*

"Good point."

"I never did ask you, do you live alone?"

"Yes, I do."

"Would it be too presumptuous of me to ask if we could go to your place?"

"Not at all." By turning right at the next intersection, he altered course and drove to his house on Crestview Lane.

David's house was a split-level structure, with a two-and-a-half-car garage. The large yard was big enough for kids to run around in. The garage door went up, revealing an older style Camaro. He pulled the Chevelle into the open spot to the right of the other vehicle.

"That's my latest project. I'd tell you all about it now, but I'd rather take you inside instead."

"I won't argue with that."

They navigated around the Camaro and entered the house. David gave Sara a quick tour, which ended in the family room. A gas fireplace occupied one wall. A flat-screen television was positioned above the mantle. Instead of a coffee table, a black bearskin rug lay between the fireplace and the black leather couch. A matching love seat, a recliner, and two oak end tables rounded out the rest of the furniture in the room.

David slid two of the hanging wineglasses out of the rack in the kitchen. "Have you ever made love on a bearskin rug before?" he asked, deftly balancing the glasses in his left hand, while filling them from the bottle of wine in his right hand.

Sara accepted the glass he offered to her. "No. But I'm sure you have, plenty of times." She sipped her wine.

David rested his glass on the mantle. Opening the fireplace's glass doors, he responded, "Actually, no."

With a flick of a switch, the fire ignited.

He continued, "I've thought about it a lot, and I'm thinking about it right now. I've decided that I'm done thinking."

"Oh really?" She kicked off her shoes.

"Yes, really. You don't have a problem with that, do you?" he asked, removing his shirt, revealing his muscular body.

Sara's pulse raced. "Not at all."

"Good. Because I can't wait any longer." David plucked the

wineglass out of her hand and deposited it next to his. Grabbing her by the waist, he pulled her to him. The heat radiating from his body rivaled the fire in intensity.

In a matter of minutes, the bearskin rug cradled Sara. The texture of the fur felt exhilarating on her naked flesh. David's fingers worked very quickly and effectively. His technique was unlike anything she had ever experienced. She gazed up at him. In the glow of the fire, his body glistened with sweat. The word *sexy* seemed inadequate to describe him. As she was about to compliment his physique, they became one. All thoughts escaped her mind. They had steamy sex on the bearskin rug for the first of what would be several times that night.

Chapter 12

DAVID Turner had taken the summer off from teaching to restore the Camaro in his garage. However, the past week had flown by with minimal progress. Sara had proven to be quite a distraction, spending a great deal of her first week of vacation with him. Although they had enjoyed walks on the beach and had gone to a couple of movies, sex prevailed as their primary activity. Her presence intoxicated him. He thought Sara might actually be the one for him.

After eating breakfast with David, Sara left to run errands. They would meet at St. Peter's Mission later for lunch duty.

When she arrived home, Sara yelled into the house, her arms full of grocery bags, "Can I get some help here please?"

Laura appeared and eased Sara's load. "Well, thanks for blessing us with your presence today. We weren't sure if you'd be able to tear yourself away." Laura heaved the bags onto the kitchen counter.

Sara carted her load to the counter as well. "I'm not going to apologize for anything. This has been an incredible week. I don't even know where to begin. David is unbelievable," she said with a sigh, emptying one of the bags.

Anna joined them. Transferring the newly purchased items to the pantry, she asked, "Did I miss anything?"

Laura replied, "Not really. All she's said so far is that he's unbelievable."

"Well, he is. I need to go change my shirt. It's got a stain on it. I must have rubbed up against something."

"Oh, I'm sure you did," Laura teased.

Sara played along. "For me to know and you to find out."

Physically pushing Sara out of the kitchen, Anna said, "Go get changed already. We're dying to hear your stories."

"All right. I'll try to hurry."

Sara changed into a purple T-shirt and an older, more comfortable pair of jeans. After freshening up in the bathroom, she entered the family room and sat on the mauve couch. She announced, "I'm back. Are you ready?"

Anna rushed over and sat next to her. "Since he's mechanically inclined, can we assume he's good with his hands?"

"He's good with more than just his hands. Oh my God! He is unbelievable."

"I think you said that already," Laura interjected as she joined them, sitting on the matching love seat.

"Well, he is," Sara bragged. "Let's see, I'll try to start at the beginning. We need to keep track of the time. We can't be late to St. Peter's Mission. Remember, you guys said you'd volunteer today."

"We remember," they responded.

Sara proceeded to relay the last week's events to her girlfriends. The girls listened intently. Time passed very quickly.

Anna asked, "So have you said the L word yet?"

"No, but neither has he."

"Well, do you love him?" Laura inquired.

Sara had asked herself that very same question every day for the past week. And each time, she couldn't answer it definitively. The physical chemistry between her and David was impressive. Physically, he satisfied all of her needs. However, he had been ineffectual at producing the highest level of desire—the one that touched her soul. Joe generated a fiery passion inside her that only he could quench.

However, if Joe remained unattainable, she would eventually have to settle for the next best option. It sounded crass, but that was the truth. So if she cast that one element aside, David was a contender for her lifelong affection.

Avoiding the question, Sara countered, "Did I mention that he's absolutely fantastic in bed?"

Annoyed, Laura replied, "Yes. And that's not what I asked."

"I haven't thought about it."

Laura challenged her. "I don't believe you."

"Neither do I," Anna added. "Do you have anything in common, aside from being sexually compatible?"

"There are plenty of things."

Laura rolled her eyes. "Uh huh. Name one."

"As I spend more time with him, the true love part will just happen."

Anna frowned. "I wouldn't count on it, if I were you."

"Well, good thing I'm not you then. I'm going to keep seeing him." Sara continued. "He's fun and interesting. I deserve to see if we have a future together. And he's just too good in bed to give up without giving him a chance."

Laura looked at her watch. "It's almost time to go. We're going to continue this conversation later today. You can't lead another guy on. It's not fair to him."

Sara folded her arms across her chest. "Who says I'm leading him on? I'm convinced that in time I'm going to love him."

"You shouldn't have to work at it. It should come naturally," Laura explained.

"Whatever." Sara looked away.

"Back at you. So is what we're wearing acceptable for today?" Laura asked.

Critiquing their clothes, Sara replied, "Your pink polo shirt and jean capris are fine. Anna, your white shorts and smiley face shirt will make a big hit."

"Good." Laura grabbed her designer purse. "We have to go now, or we're going to be late."

"Who's driving?" Anna inquired, searching for her purse.

Sara volunteered. "I'll drive."

"Do we need to bring anything?" Anna asked.

Sara slid her keys and big black purse off the counter. "Nope. Just yourselves."

As they settled into Sara's Impala, Laura asked, "Sara, isn't today going to be awkward for you?"

"Why should it be?" she asked, starting the car.

Laura replied, "Because Joe is going to be there."

Hesitating as she buckled her seat belt, Sara said slowly, "I forgot."

"Huh? You forgot?" Laura asked.

Sara thought, *I forgot he was going to be at the mission. It's not like I could ever forget, forget.*

"You're kidding, right?" Laura asked.

"No. I'm not kidding."

Astonished, Anna said, "Oh my God! David Turner actually succeeded in making you forget about Joe Lazaro."

"Anna, I guess we both have to agree that David *is* unbelievable," Laura joked.

Laura and Anna laughed.

"Damn. So what am I going to do?" Sara asked.

Laura shrugged. "Just play it cool and don't drool all over David. Joe knows you're seeing him. He just doesn't know how hot and heavy you guys are. So try to keep it that way, to maintain the peace."

"I'll try. I don't want any fighting or anything," Sara stated, backing out of the driveway and into the street.

Laura snickered. "The last thing the St. Peter's lunch crowd needs is a fist fight as a floorshow."

Anna added, "The nuns would kill us for sure."

While Sara was touting David's prowess to her girlfriends, David had ventured out into his garage to work on the Camaro. Some work needed to be accomplished before he left for the mission. He figured that he could replace the starter and arrive at St. Peter's in plenty of time.

The radio, tuned to classic rock, blared from the six-by-nines on the top shelf. The neighbors were mowing their lawns. They wouldn't hear his music over their mowers. The radio DJ ordered listeners to stay tuned. "We've got more music on the way in the next hour, including Foreigner, Aerosmith, .38 Special, CCR, and Boston."

"Cool. Sounds like a decent hour of music. It must be my lucky day," David said, opening the garage door for ventilation.

Before he began, he backed the Chevelle into the driveway to have better access to his tools and room to move around his project car. From his toolbox, he removed a few wrenches and a socket set. He positioned them on the garage floor next to the creeper.

The pegboard on the far wall held drills, air guns for compressors, and miscellaneous tools that didn't fit in the toolbox. Several shop lights hung at his disposal. While deciding on the proper light to use, David scrutinized the incomplete car.

Today's project involved replacing the starter, a relatively easy job. David strategically placed the hydraulic jack under the passenger side of the car and lifted the vehicle off the garage floor. Normally, jack stands provided extra support under the car. However, he had loaned them to his neighbor, who had forgotten to return them before going on vacation. David had worked on many cars without the proper jacks or stands over the years, so it didn't concern him.

David sat down on the creeper, reclined, and then rolled comfortably, headfirst, under the front of the car. Because it was rusted, the starter wouldn't budge without some elbow grease. The largest wrench worked double-duty as a hammer before the starter finally broke loose. After half an hour, the old starter disengaged from the vehicle. Triumphant, he rolled out from under the Chevy. To his surprise, a man, in a short-sleeved white shirt and blue jeans, was standing before him. The man clutched a clipboard. David sat up on the creeper. Unbeknownst to him, he was meeting Mark Collins.

Mark had soaked in the surroundings. The fully equipped garage would make things easier than he had originally thought. The plan unfolded before him. Deep in thought, he was actually startled when the man rolled out from under the vehicle.

"Hey, man. Can I help you?" David yelled over the music. He stood up and turned the music down.

Mark lied. "Oh, I'm just here to read your meter. But I saw

these cars, and I couldn't help myself. I can't believe you own a Chevelle and a classic Camaro."

"Yeah. These are my girls." David transferred the grease from his hands to a shop rag. "I'm restoring the Camaro. The last owner did quite a number on her."

"Some people just don't understand how to treat girls with the proper respect. They're precious, and we need to do what we can to protect them."

"Sure. Nothing is worse than guys who drive them really hard and then trade them in, or junk them, so they can move on to their next ride. It's just a shame."

"I must disagree with you on that. One thing is worse—when someone steals her away from you. *That* is the worst thing that could ever happen," Mark proclaimed through clenched teeth.

"I've never had one of my girls stolen. So I've never thought about it before. You're right. I'd be really pissed if someone stole one."

"Someone stole one from me. So I've learned a trick or two. Once you have a precious gem, you must protect her and hold on to her forever."

"Did you install a security system?"

"I'm working on it. I am putting myself in the perfect position to protect what's mine."

"Good for you. I can't afford a high-tech system. Luckily, I haven't needed one so far. I guess if I started keeping every car I restored, it might be another story. I probably would get some kind of system. My only concern now is to make sure the next owner appreciates her as much as I do. Then I get to do something I love and get paid for it."

"Well, I don't want to keep you any longer. I'll just go around back to read the meter."

"Have a good day, man."

"Oh, I will," Mark replied, touching the brim of his baseball hat. Walking around to the side of the house, he pretended to read the meter.

David removed the new starter from its box, turned the radio volume back up, and rolled back under the car.

The DJ spoke over the last few bars of the song. "And that was .38 Special. We have to break now to pay some bills. We'll be playing CCR when we come back, so don't touch that dial!" The station cut to commercial.

David proceeded to install the new starter. As he toiled, he sang along with John Fogerty about a bad moon rising. Connecting the new starter consumed considerably less time than had been required to remove the old one.

As David rolled out from under the car, a black 1977 Corvette Stingray pulled out of the road and into the middle of his driveway. The driver and passenger, both males, exited the vehicle.

Mark pretended to read meters at a few other houses. He wandered behind the Corvette on his way back to the van, nodding at the tall, blond newcomers. They reciprocated the nod before walking up the driveway. Mark slipped into the van and drove away.

David pulled a rag from his back pocket and wiped off his hands.

The Corvette driver extended his hand. "Hey, Dave! How's it going?"

David shook it. "Pretty good, Rick. Just working on the Camaro." He tossed the oily shop rag on the workbench behind him.

"It's looking pretty rough, dude," observed Rick's younger but taller, nineteen-year-old brother, Bill.

"She looks rough now, but wait until I'm finished with her. You'll be dying to drive her. So what are you guys doing over here so early on a Saturday morning?"

Rick said, "Actually, I wasn't sure if you'd be out here."

"Huh?"

"After what you've told me about your new girlfriend, Sara, I was expecting to see the garage door down."

"No. I needed to get some work done. She needed to run some errands."

"That's too bad. Sorry I missed her."

"You'll meet her next time. So what's up?"

"The Vette needs new plugs and wires, and I was wondering if you'd have some spare time to fix her up."

"Do you have the plugs and wires?"

"No. I wasn't sure what to get. I guess I'll need your help with that too."

"Why am I not surprised? I only have time to pick up the parts today. I'm volunteering at St. Peter's for the lunch shift. I could install them for you tomorrow," David offered.

Rick beamed. "Great. I've got to get back to the store anyway. Music stores don't run themselves."

"How's the business going?"

"Pretty well. I can't complain. I'm trying to convince Bill to come work for me. I even offered to change the name from Greenwood Music to Greenwood Brothers Music."

"Still not interested," Bill declared. "Me and my band are going to hit it big time. You'll see."

Changing the subject, David said, "Rick, you're blocking me in. You'll have to move your Vette, so we can all go in my Chevelle."

Bill hitched up his pants. "I can stay here. You guys will only be gone for what? A half-hour—tops? I think I can manage by myself while you go parts shopping."

"Are you sure?" his brother asked.

With an annoyed look, Bill replied, "Do I stutter?"

Rick warned him. "Fine. Just don't touch anything. We'll be back soon."

"Whatever."

David and Rick departed for the auto parts store.

Bill snooped around the garage and turned the radio volume up, searching for a hip-hop station. Finding it, he turned up the music even louder. Bored, Bill mounted the creeper and slid under the Camaro. He rationalized that although he had promised not to touch, he could still look.

The car's frame was rusted clean through in some areas, typical for a car suffering through decades of New York winters.

Salt and snow wreaked serious havoc on the undercarriage of the car. As Bill studied the rusty Camaro, Mark returned to the neighborhood. Observing the Corvette was gone, he parked across from the house. Mark smiled. Everything was falling neatly into place.

After a few minutes, the garage door closed. Bill didn't notice. The shop light provided plenty of light, the music boomed, and he was too preoccupied with the car to notice.

Mark positioned himself on the passenger side of the Camaro. He had never worked on a car before, but he had observed his father and brother work on various vehicles. So he knew how a jack worked. Once he released the pressure, the jack would collapse. From his back pocket, he pulled out a pair of gloves. He slipped them on, inhaled deeply, and released the pressure on the hydraulic jack.

The jack fell.

However, it stuck halfway down, partially pinning the unsuspecting teen. Bill screamed, *"Ow!* Fucking piece of fucking shit!" The frame fell on his left thigh, rendering him unable to move. The pain radiated up and down his leg. He yelled, "Somebody help me! Somebody! Anybody! Son of a bitch!"

Bill realized no one would hear him. The music was too loud. He couldn't believe his own stupidity. With all of his strength, he pushed up on the frame. It didn't budge. He inhaled deeply and tried again, this time using his good leg as well—another failed attempt. Pissed at himself, he screamed and pounded on the undercarriage of the car. He punctuated his temper tantrum with several swift kicks with his right leg. The energy expended was for naught; his predicament remained the same. The pain in his left leg steadily increased. He felt a warm trickle of blood run down it. To his relief, he saw blue jeans and work boots on the passenger side.

"Help! Guys! Help me!" Not receiving a response, he yelled louder, "Hey! Under here! I need help! Pump the jack back up! I'm pinned! I'm bleeding! Help!"

Mark bent down low, peering under the car. Expecting to see

his rival's face, he was disappointed and shocked to see a different face staring back at him. He had pinned the wrong guy.

Surprised to see someone other than David or Rick, Bill didn't care who helped him at this point. He pleaded, "Dude, I need help. Please get me out from under this thing."

Dumbfounded, Mark was faced with a conundrum. *The other guys are going to show up any minute. Being caught is not part of the plan. Think!*

Weighing the options, he decided to assist the boy. *The jack is faulty, so they'll blame it on that. No one will know I messed with it.*

He bent down and gave the teenager the thumbs up sign with his gloved hand.

Bill breathed a sigh of relief. "Thanks, dude. The guys won't let me ever hear the end of this. I can hear them now." His leg throbbed. He closed his eyes and thanked God that the worst part was over.

Then the passenger side of the car dropped completely.

Bill gasped, and his eyes flew open. The front axle fell on his chest and crushed his ribcage, rendering him unable to call out for help. The frame now rested firmly on both legs. Blood oozed out from the puncture wounds in his chest and his legs.

Mark had fully intended to lift the car back up. However, before he could touch the jack, it released the rest of the way by itself. Stunned, he watched the separate streams of blood merge together and trickle into the drain in the floor. He tried to make peace with it. Almost inaudibly, he muttered, "I'm sorry."

The scene reminded Mark of when the house fell on the wicked witch. All Dorothy could see were the witch's feet and the ruby slippers. A wave of nausea hit him. Mark hurried out the side door of the garage. He stumbled across the yard and into the street. Trembling, he retched as he reached the van. After the feeling passed, he climbed into the safety of the van and sipped some water. Taking several deep breaths, he attempted to calm down. *It was an accident. That kid was just in the wrong place at the wrong time. That's all.*

Mark was shaking from head to toe. *It was an accident. I'll write all about it in my journal when I get home. Then everything will be okay.*

As he drove, Mark decided to return the van to its owner. He didn't want it anymore. He altered course, to Ray's laundry business. After he parked, he caught a glimpse of his pallid reflection in the rearview mirror. He found it difficult to look at himself. Mark got out of the van and entered Chen's Laundry.

Ray was standing behind the counter, hanging up the phone. He said, "Matt, I'm really sorry to hear about your brother. If there's anything I can do, you just name it."

"Thanks. I'm good. I don't want to talk about it. I just wanted to return the van. Thanks for letting me borrow it."

"Any time, man. You sure there's nothing I can do?"

"Yeah, I'm sure."

"Well, I gotta head out. Troy Jenkins called in sick. I can't find anyone to do his route. I have to do it myself."

Mark needed to do something to clear his mind. The boy's face was etched in his memory. Helping Ray might ease his troubled mind. He considered it a self-imposed penance. "What's the route and how big is it?"

"Why?"

"Maybe I could help you out."

"You don't have to."

"I know. How big is it?"

Ray provided the names of the businesses and facilities on the route. It was a small and short route. Ray added, "You can use the van you're driving—the route doesn't require a bigger vehicle."

Mark pondered it for a minute. *It's the least I can do for my only current friend. Jenkins doesn't have the Misty Pines route. As long as I stay clear of that place, I'll be fine.*

Mark accepted the challenge. "I'll do it. It's the least I can do to repay you for lending me your van. Give me a map. And tell me what to do."

"Really?"

"Yeah. I was thinking about asking you for a job for the rest of the summer anyway."

"Weren't you taking this summer off to do stuff around the house?"

Mark snapped, "I changed my mind. Can't a guy change his mind?"

Ray held up his hands. "Relax, it was just a question. I'll give you the route map in a minute. Thanks for helping out."

Composing himself, Mark said, "Friends take care of each other. You were kind to me. I'm just repaying the favor." Mark had wanted to show kindness to the unknown boy. The jack prevented him from doing so. The guilt weighed on him.

Ray pulled a city map out from under the desk. After highlighting the route in yellow, he handed the map and a large envelope to Mark. He asked, "Are you feeling all right? You don't look good."

Mark replied, "I'm fine."

"You sure?"

"Yes, I'm fine. I'm just tired."

"Here's the map and some keys for a few of the businesses. The standard orders are written on the sheets in the envelope. If somebody requests something special, make a note of it. Got it?"

"I think I can handle it. I can always call if I have a problem."

Ray shook Mark's hand. "Thanks again. See you later."

The map guided Mark to area restaurants and a few motels. This job was a natural fit after his laundry job at Misty Pines. However, he struggled to remain focused. The boy's face haunted him.

At one of the motels, Mark saw a redheaded man exit one of the rooms. The man reminded him of Mercury. *I wonder how Mercury is doing. I wish I could have taken him with me. I really let him down by not helping him carry out his plan, whatever it was.*

He sighed. *I abandoned him. I let him down, like everybody else.*

A backfiring car snapped Mark back to the present. He drove to the next destination on the route.

The last stop was St. Peter's Mission. The note indicated he should use the key on the back door. There would be four to six bundles inside the door.

Mark turned down the narrow alley. He pulled the van up to the mission's back door. After opening the van's rear doors, he used the key to enter the building. A musty smell greeted him. The room was dimly lit. Five laundry bags waited by the door. After they were loaded, he replenished the supply of bags on the wall hooks located next to the one empty bag that wasn't used.

Music and laughter spilled into the room from beyond the interior door. It was happy laughter, not maniacal or forced laughter like at Misty Pines. Curiosity got the best of him. Gliding to the opposite end of the room, he made no notice of the contents of the shelves. He peeked out into the hall. It was deserted.

Poorly camouflaged by his baseball hat, he darted into the passageway, past the kitchen and bathrooms. At the end of the corridor, he gazed into the room. A guy was playing guitar in the far right-hand corner. People were gathered around him. Mark tapped his foot to the music until, out of the corner of his eye, he saw Sara. Time stood still. His heart leapt. His palms began to sweat. Although he desperately wanted to hold her, he knew he must wait. Retreating slightly, he watched her.

Rick and David returned from the auto parts store. As Rick pulled into the driveway, he muttered, "What's that kid up to now? The garage door is closed."

David shrugged. "I'm sure it's not a big deal. Maybe he was hot and went inside and just closed the door."

"Likely. He has a short attention span."

They could hear the booming music coming from inside the garage. David punched the garage door code on the keypad. The door opened.

Rick called out, "Bill? Are you out here, Bill?"

David walked toward the bench. He realized the car wasn't as high above the floor as it should have been. His eyes immediately focused on the jack—it was released. He rushed to the front of the car. Two lifeless legs protruded from under the car's frame. As David doubled back to raise the jack, he yelled to Rick, "Call 9-1-1! Call now!"

Rick dialed before his brain registered why he was doing it.

After raising the car, David reluctantly looked under it to see if Bill was attached to the undercarriage or if his body was free of it. He steeled himself for the horrific sight. The view wasn't good, but he ascertained that Bill's body could be moved.

Not knowing the full extent of the injuries, David didn't pull on Bill's legs. Instead, he grabbed a garden tool and snagged the edge of the creeper. Slowly, he pulled Bill out from under the car. Blood trickled from his motionless body. David felt a very weak pulse. Amazed, David yelled to Rick, "He's alive."

Rick provided the dispatcher with all of the pertinent information. An ambulance was on its way.

Rick and David stared at the unconscious boy. They reassured him that he would be fine—although neither man believed it to be true.

David fashioned tourniquets for Bill's legs from clean towels and rags. Rick held his brother's right hand. David applied light pressure to the puncture wounds in Bill's chest. He wanted to stop the bleeding but didn't want to risk pushing too hard. The teenager's breathing was labored. Bill had lost a great deal of blood. Just how much was difficult to calculate. Much of it had travelled down the floor drain. David silently said the rosary.

The ambulance and police arrived within minutes.

Rick stayed at his brother's side as the paramedics worked on him.

"Can you tell us your name and what happened here?" Officer Rob Stone asked David.

"My name is David Turner. It's my house. This is Rick Greenwood, my best friend. Bill is his younger brother. Rick and I went to the store for some parts for his car. When we left, the car was on the jack. The garage door was up. When we came back, the garage door was down. We found Bill under the car."

In a low voice, Rick added, "I told him not to touch anything."

"Unfortunately, it looks like he didn't heed your warning," Officer Raul Gonzalez commented.

David continued, "I don't understand how the jack could have failed with him under the car. It doesn't make any sense. I've never had that jack fail. *Ever*. It's a hydraulic jack. You have to release the pressure in order for it to fall. And he couldn't have accidentally done it from under the car."

"You're saying you don't think this was an accident," replied Officer Gonzalez.

David stood, arms crossed, shaking his head. "I'm just saying it's impossible for this to have happened without somebody messing with the jack."

"We'll dust for prints and see what we come up with," Officer Stone offered. He obtained the kit from the squad car and dusted the jack handle, the garage door wall unit, the keypad, and the doorknobs on the side garage door for prints.

The paramedics announced that they were leaving for the hospital. Not optimistic on Bill's chances of survival, they stated that a miracle could happen.

"Dave, I'm going to follow the ambulance to the hospital," Rick said.

David walked over to Rick and hugged him. "He's going to be all right. He's in good hands."

"I hope you're right. I better call my parents," Rick said, holding back tears.

"I can pick them up," David offered.

Officer Gonzalez held up his hand. "Sorry, we need you here for a few more minutes. We have more questions for you."

"Can't it wait?" David asked.

Officer Gonzalez responded, "No. We need to do this now. You can meet them at the hospital when we're done."

David urged, "You better get going, Rick. I'll see you there soon."

As the ambulance and Rick drove off, Officer Stone asked, "Mr. Turner, to your knowledge, were you the last person to touch the jack?"

"As far as I know. I set it this morning, so I could replace the starter. I worked under the car this morning. It didn't move an inch. It never does."

Officer Stone asked, "Could you demonstrate how you set the jack?"

"Sure." David walked over to the jack and set it.

Officer Stone inquired, "Do you ever wear gloves when setting the jack?"

"No. I don't wear gloves when I work. Why would I? You can't feel anything through gloves," David answered.

"Just asking. Did you touch the jack handle after you set it?" Office Stone asked.

"No. Once it's set, it's set. I don't touch it again until I plan to bring the car down," David responded.

"Thank you. Step away from the jack," Officer Stone instructed. He redusted the jack handle. "Interesting."

"What's interesting?" Officer Gonzalez inquired.

"The first time I dusted, I couldn't get a decent print from the handle. It wasn't wiped clean—it was smeared. But now I get full intact prints."

"Somebody did mess with it," David concluded.

"It's possible that someone wearing gloves could have made the prints smear," Officer Gonzalez concurred.

Officer Stone asked, "Do you have any enemies, Mr. Turner?"

"Not that I know of. I can't think of anyone," David responded, scratching his head.

"Any problems with anyone at work?" Officer Stone inquired.

"I took the summer off from teaching at St. Peter's University. I didn't fail anyone last semester. So I can't imagine any students holding a grudge. I've been doing a lot of volunteer work over at St. Peter's Church and Mission, but I haven't had any problems or confrontations there. I just can't imagine any reason why anyone would want to do this."

"Anyone have a problem with the victim or his brother?" Officer Gonzalez asked.

"Not that I know of. But I don't know all of their friends. Bill's a teenager. I have no idea who he hangs out with. Rick runs a music store in town. He hasn't mentioned having any problems there lately."

Officer Stone handed David his card. "Well, if you think of anything that might help in the investigation, please contact us."

David nodded. "I definitely will. Can I go to the hospital now?"

Chapter 13

BACK at St. Peter's Mission, the newly recruited volunteers served lunch to the hungry crowd. Because there were three extra people to help serve, Sister Josefina and Sister Renata mingled among the guests.

Looking at her watch, Sara complained, "I could see being a couple of minutes late, but this is ridiculous. I can't believe that David isn't here."

"Maybe he had car problems," Laura suggested, serving mixed vegetables to a person in line.

Sara scooped mashed potatoes onto another person's plate. "I called his house phone and his cell phone. I didn't get an answer on either."

Anna offered, "Maybe he forgot to turn on his cell phone. Or he could be in a service dead zone. That happens to me a lot." She served beef noodle casserole and dropped a little on the table. "Oops!"

"I guess," Sara admitted. "Anna, the food goes on the plates, not the table," she kidded.

"Sorry," Anna apologized. "I'll try to do better."

"We're running low on clean plates," Joe noted.

"I'll go to the kitchen and bring some back," Sara said. "Can you guys hold down the fort while I'm gone?"

"No sweat. I think we'll manage," Laura shot back.

Anna asked, "Can you bring me some paper towels or something to wipe up this mess?"

"Sure," Sara replied, walking toward the kitchen.

Mark saw her coming toward him. He turned and ran down the hallway, where he hid behind the back room door, out of sight. His heart quickened at the thought of being so close to Sara that he could touch her.

Sara entered the kitchen. Sally Prado hovered over the hot stove, cutting up a fresh casserole into serving-size portions. A tray of hot rolls rested on the counter. Across the room, Tom Grant was drinking a glass of water over the sink.

Sara asked, "Are there any clean plates ready? We're running low."

Tom nodded toward Sally. "There are some stacked up on the other side of Sally. I was going to bring them out in a minute."

Squeezing past Sally, Sara replied, "Since I'm here, I can do it."

Sally turned to Tom. "Tom, could you please take the rolls and this casserole out while they're still hot? I need to get the next casserole out of the oven."

Tom grabbed two potholders and picked up the rolls in one hand and the casserole dish in the other. "No problem. After I drop these off, I'll clear some tables."

Sara attempted to follow Tom out of the kitchen. However, Father Francis stopped her. The priest asked, "Before you carry those plates off, could you bring me a fresh set of sheets and towels for a new guest? They're in the storage room, past the pantry area. I want to get him settled after lunch. Right now, he's eating with the rest of the group."

Sara deposited the plates on the counter. She pushed her hair behind her ears. "Sure, Father. I'll take care of it."

The mission housed twenty-four homeless people in the upper levels of the building. The basics were provided for the temporarily disadvantaged. Sara strolled past the restrooms and stood in the doorway of the back room. She fumbled around for a light switch on the wall to her left and found one. Although the bare light bulbs didn't improve visibility much, she forged ahead. Several sturdy metal racks held boxes overflowing with old clothes and shoes. Other racks were crowded with rows of canned tomatoes, huge jars of mayonnaise, and boxes of dry cereal. The sheets and towels were stored in the back.

Mark faded into the shadows behind the door and stifled a sneeze. The dust in the room had triggered his allergies.

Sara heard the noise but couldn't identify it or from which direction it came. She stopped and called out loudly, "Is someone there? David Turner—is that you? Are you hiding from me?" She paused. "Did you lose track of time working on the Camaro? I'm not upset. Just come out; we're swamped."

Silence.

"Come on. It's not funny. We need an extra set of hands out there."

Mark remained immobile. Curiosity had led to more than he anticipated. Now he knew the name of his new foe—David Turner.

Sara waited a few seconds, and then dismissed the noise as her imagination or a mouse. Moving quickly, she reached the rack with towels and sheets. "Decisions, decisions. Should I pick dingy white or dingy white?" she asked aloud, lifting a set of sheets off the shelf. She held them against her body with her left arm. Then she plucked a hand towel, bath towel, and washcloth off the adjacent stacks and piled them on top of the sheets.

At that moment, Mark managed to suppress another sneeze. However, his right boot inadvertently bumped into the door. The door slammed shut.

Sara jumped.

A man stood between her and the door. The menacing figure was definitely too short to be David. The stranger's baseball cap was pulled down low. It shadowed his face. This didn't appear to be a practical joke.

Backing up, Sara spoke calmly to the intruder, in an attempt to defuse the situation. "Can I help you find something? If you want food, you can take it." She gestured openly with her right arm. "The same thing goes for the towels and sheets. They can get more. It's not a problem."

Unprepared for an actual encounter with Sara, Mark did not reply. The plan he had intended to implement wasn't formulated completely yet. Not wanting to scare her, he inched slowly toward her, his hands up, facing out, in a surrender position. He believed it would convey that he meant no harm.

As the stranger approached, Sara turned slightly and noticed the back door was ajar. If she could outrun him to the door, she would be safe. Deliberation took a few short seconds. Sara thrust the pile of sheets and towels in the stranger's face in an effort to slow him down while she ran for the door.

The diversion confused Mark. He batted the sheets and towels to the floor and trampled them in pursuit. He grasped Sara's left arm. At a full run, Mark couldn't stop fast enough. Consequently, as he swung her around, he ended up body-slamming her into the door, which banged shut on impact.

Pressed against her, Mark whispered, "I love you. I would never hurt you."

Face-to-face with her attacker, Sara stammered in disbelief, "You're dead. You're supposed to be dead."

"I'm not dead. It's a long story. I want to tell you everything—just not this way. I didn't want it to be this way. Sara, I love you. I just want to be with you."

Sara wanted nothing more than to get away from him. Squirming, she ordered, "Let me go!"

"Not until I explain everything," he pleaded.

"You're hurting me. Let me go," she demanded.

"I couldn't *hurt* you. I *love* you. Can't you see that?"

"If you love me, let me go!"

"No. I can't let you go again. I love you."

Sara saw nothing resembling love, only maniacal behavior. She thrust her knee into his groin. Wincing, Mark released her and fell to his knees. She pushed past him. In a desperate act, he grabbed the back of her shirt and yanked it. The motion jerked her backward. She fell on her tailbone.

"Ow!" she yelled, rubbing the area. "You son of a bitch!" As she rolled onto one knee in an effort to stand, he grabbed her foot. She kicked, making it hard to hold. She yelled, "Get the hell away from me!"

"You don't understand."

"I don't care!"

The kicking continued until he released her leg. Pulling herself up, she ran for the hallway door. However, she tripped on the sheets and towels that had fallen and landed sprawled across the sheets.

Mark pulled the edge of one of the sheets. Each pull delivered her closer to him, so she rolled off the sheet. Sara scooted backward, still facing him. Stepping on the discarded sheet, he lunged at her, tackling her like a football player. Her head snapped back and hit the floor. The world went dark as she lost consciousness.

Mark climbed off her. Staring at Sara's limp body, Mark deliberated. Someone might have heard the commotion and would come to investigate. At the very least, someone would miss her soon and look for her. Either way, there was no time to waste. This was his chance. Although he would have preferred a happier, more romantic reunion, this was better than nothing.

Mark kicked the dropped sheets aside. He grabbed an empty laundry bag from a hook on the back wall and enveloped Sara's body. The bag wasn't large enough to cover her completely. The top of her head stuck out.

He swiftly carried the bundle to the white van parked outside. After hoisting her into the back of the van, he closed the rear doors.

Returning to the mission, he secured the back door before returning to the vehicle. As he did so, he came face-to-face with Reverend Ezekiel Walker. Their eyes met. Ezekiel had seen enough to know that he didn't want to get close to this young man, so he backed away. He claimed, "I didn't see anything."

This was unacceptable to Mark. Obviously, the preacher had seen something. Mark needed to find out what he had seen and advanced.

The preacher panicked. "Lord, help me, Jesus!" The large man ran. However, the task proved difficult because of his size.

Mark shouted, "I just want to talk to you!"

Ezekiel ignored Mark's statement and pleaded to the heavens. "Lord, help me! I have done wrong in the past. Forgive me! I swear, I repent! I repent!" His chest heaved as he attempted to catch his breath. A pain in his side caused him to pause and lean against the grocery store's back wall. In his frenzied state, he failed to notice that his Bible had dropped to the ground.

Desperate to find out what the Baptist preacher had observed, Mark jumped into the van, started the engine, and pursued the preacher.

The Reverend Walker searched in vain for a way out of his predicament. The doors and windows on his side of the alley were locked. Wrought iron bars covered them—no sanctuary there. The parking lot on the opposite side of the alley, between the mission and the church, was bordered by a chain-link fence. The only door on that side of the alley, other than the mission's door, was the back entrance to St. Peter's Church.

Ignoring the nagging pain in his side, Ezekiel forged ahead toward a dumpster and some old metal garbage cans. He held his chest as he ran toward the dumpster. Stabbing pain radiated throughout his chest. Lightheaded and dizzy, he stumbled. Somehow, he managed to kick the cans into the middle of the alley to buy some time.

The van hit the cans and dented them. Garbage flew in every direction. Because the van was equipped with a cage protecting its grill, damage was negligible.

The preacher continued his awkward, waddle-run down the alley toward Main Street. Finally, he reached the back door of the church. He pulled on the handle with both hands. The door was locked. The effort had been futile. Panting hard, the preacher swore. "Damn Catholics. The First Baptist Church's doors are always open."

The preacher turned to locate his pursuer and lost his balance. He stretched out his arms to break his fall. As his left hand made contact with the pavement, his arm buckled under the weight and snapped. The Reverend Walker grunted as his arm gave way and his body hit the pavement. Excruciating pain shot through his arm. He struggled first to his knees, then to his feet. With his left arm dangling at an unnatural angle, he headed for the intersection.

Mark threw the van into reverse. Garbage flew off the hood. One of the metal cans got caught in the protective cage. Angrily, he rammed the vehicle against the dumpster in an attempt to dislodge the can. It worked. He resumed pursuit of the overweight man of God. As Mark gained speed, Ezekiel reached the intersection, clutching his chest.

For a moment, the preacher waved his right arm in an unsuccessful attempt to gain attention. The sound of brakes squealing caused him to turn in time to discover he had stepped into the path of an oncoming garbage truck. The truck could not stop in time. The preacher's body flew in the air like an overstuffed rag doll, landing several feet in front of the truck that hit him. The Reverend Walker sustained massive injuries to his vital organs at the moment of impact. His spleen and liver were heavily damaged, several ribs punctured his lungs, and the heart attack that had started moments earlier reached its climax. His skull cracked and fractured as it hit the asphalt. The head trauma he sustained was irreversible.

Mark halted the van in disbelief. An inner voice told him that, in all probability, the Baptist minister was dead. The consequences of his actions hit hard. He asked aloud, "What have I done? What have I become?"

The questions were met with silence.

Mark looked in the rear of the van. Sara's hair spilled out of the bundle. He had meant no harm to her, but there she was—unconscious. He had wanted to remove his rival from the picture. That had failed to materialize. Although events hadn't gone as planned, the end result was the same—Sara was his again. Torn, he wondered if the ends justified the means. Mark hadn't intended for the minister to die. He definitely didn't want that boy under the car to die. Nevertheless, reality could not be ignored. Two people had died today as a direct result of his actions. Adding his brother to the total, there were three deaths on his conscience.

The buildings in the alley created a tunnel effect. Its focus—the inert man's feet and the garbage truck. Mark watched as a garbage man in a blue jumpsuit climbed out. He was met in front of the truck by the vehicle's driver. They knelt next to the accident victim. If Mark stayed, he would be questioned. He couldn't risk that, especially considering Sara's current state. Mark felt a headache coming on. Things were spiraling out of control. None of this was supposed to happen. One thing he did know: he couldn't stay here. He would most surely get caught. Then all would be lost. Mark's unrelenting quest for love was taking its toll. He quickly composed himself, threw his right arm over the passenger headrest, and backed up past the mission. Turning left down a side alley, he disappeared into the maze of city streets.

Laura checked her watch. Sara should have returned with the plates by now. Laura said, "Joe, I'm going to see what's taking Sara so long."

Joe wiped the sweat off his forehead with his right arm. "Fine. I'll stay put since the women are all deserting."

Anna protested, "Hey, I'm still here."

"I stand corrected."

Laura skirted around the lunch line, composed of a variety of characters, down the hall to the kitchen. She hoped she wouldn't find Sara and David making out or having sex in a corner somewhere. Peering into the kitchen, she saw two stacks of clean plates on the counter. Farther into the room, a man was loading the dishwasher and a weary-looking woman was scrubbing the stove. Laura called out to them. "Excuse me. Do you know Sara Taylor?"

Sally blew the hair out of her eyes and nodded affirmatively.

"Yeah," Tom Grant answered, rearranging a group of dirty glasses on the top rack.

"Has she been in here lately?"

Tom answered, "She was here fifteen, twenty minutes ago. I left the kitchen for a few minutes. She was gone when I came back."

Sally chimed in. "Father Francis asked her to get some stuff out of the back room. I haven't seen her since."

"Do you know where Father Francis is?"

Sally replied, "Sorry. I don't."

"Thanks. If you see her, tell her Laura's looking for her."

"Will do," Sally confirmed.

Before leaving the kitchen, Laura opened the door to the pantry where they had left their purses. Sara's purse was still there, on top of Anna's purse. Laura announced, "Maybe she wasn't feeling well and went to the bathroom. I'll go see if she's in there."

Laura reached the ladies' restroom. She opened the door to the lavender-colored bathroom. "Sara, are you in here?"

She received no answer.

Laura proceeded into the bathroom. She bent over to see if any feet were visible in any of the stalls. All of the stalls were empty. She vacated the bathroom and continued down the hall to the back room. She tried the door, but it was locked. Praying David and Sara weren't in there doing something they shouldn't, she pounded on the door and yelled, "Anybody in there?"

Again, there was no answer.

She pounded again.

"Hey," said a voice behind her.

Laura jumped.

Tom laughed. "You scare easy, huh?"

"Apparently," Laura replied.

"You still looking for Father Francis?"

"Yes."

"Sister Renata saw him outside."

"Thank you." Laura grabbed a stack of plates from the kitchen and rushed to the dining area. She set the plates down on the first table. "Hey guys, I'm going to walk around the building and see if Sara's outside anywhere."

Stretching, Joe asked, "You haven't found her?"

"Not yet."

As Laura crossed the dining area, she scanned each person at every table. There was no sign of Sara. Laura exited the building. On the front steps, Nicki Esperanza was talking with a couple of teenagers. Laura addressed them. "Have any of you seen a girl with brown hair and a purple T-shirt leave the building in the last twenty minutes?"

Nicki spoke up. "If you're asking about Sara, no, we haven't."

"If you see her, can you tell her Laura's looking for her?"

"Sure. No problem."

The group resumed their conversation.

Laura bounded down the stairs. At the bottom, she stopped. "Duh, she has a cell phone. I'll call her on that." Laura pulled her cell phone out of her pocket and dialed Sara's number. There was no answer. It transferred to voice mail. "Sara, this is Laura. I'm just wondering where you went. Give me a call as soon as you get this message." She pressed the numbers one, two, and then one again, so it would be marked as urgent. She returned the phone to her pocket.

Laura walked around the building to find Father Francis and, hopefully, Sara. The parking lot to the left still held Sara's car. Laura continued down the sidewalk, approaching St. Peter's Church. People were running down Main Street to the side of the church she couldn't see. She sprinted to the intersection of Main Street and Third Avenue and rounded the corner. Traffic was stopped in all directions.

A crowd of people stood in a semicircle in the street, where an alley crossed Main Street. She ran the length of the church and pushed her way through the crowd. When Laura arrived, she saw the bleeding body of a large black man. Two men in dark blue jumpsuits, covered with blood, were performing CPR. Glancing down the alley, Laura saw dented garbage cans. Garbage was strewn everywhere.

Father Francis made the sign of the cross and stood up. Laura heard sirens. Moments later, an ambulance and a police cruiser arrived. The emergency medical technicians took over. They used their portable defibrillator numerous times. Alas, they were not able to revive the preacher.

"Poor Ezekiel. He is with God now," Father Francis proclaimed, kneeling beside the deceased man.

The garbage truck driver stammered, "I tried to stop. I really did. He just came out of that side street and stopped right in front of me. There was nothing I could do. I tried to stop." He looked at the priest. "I killed a preacher. I'm going to hell, aren't I?"

Father Francis consoled the man. "You're not going to hell, my son. It was an accident. God won't punish you for an accident."

The priest was clearly upset.

Laura addressed him as he stood. "Father, I hate to bother you in light of the current situation, but Sara Taylor is missing. I can't find her anywhere. A guy in the kitchen told me that you spoke to her."

"Yes. Yes, I did." The priest rubbed his temples. "I asked her to get some supplies from the back room."

Sirens wailed loudly as another police car approached.

Father Francis reassured Laura. "I'll be with you after I talk to the police."

Unsatisfied, Laura ran back to the front of the mission. The loiterers on the mission's steps had moved to the corner to get a better view of the accident scene. That provided her with a clear shot up the stairs.

Crossing the dining area, Laura yelled, "Anna! Joe! There's a dead man outside, and Sara's gone!"

The people standing in line didn't even turn to look at her. She wondered what was wrong with these people. If she heard someone yelling about a dead body, she'd want to know where it was so she could avoid it. Reaching the lunch line, she asked, "Are you listening to me? Sara's gone."

"Did you say dead body?" Joe inquired, astonished.

Laura tried to catch her breath. "Yes, and Sara's gone."

Joe ladled mashed potatoes and gravy. "What do you mean, gone? We're not done for another hour yet. Plus, where would she go? Is her car still here?"

"Yes. Her car is still in the parking lot, but she's nowhere to be found. I searched inside and outside. She's gone, you know, *missing*."

"She's probably powdering her nose," Joe offered.

"No. Don't you think that I would have already checked there? I'm not stupid."

Anna asked, "Did you try her cell phone?"

"Of course, and I left a message."

Joe added, "Check with the kitchen help or ..."

"Already did. And I checked the dining room and asked the people out front if they'd seen her. The only place I couldn't look was the back room. The door is locked. If I couldn't get in, she couldn't either. She probably went looking for the priest since he has a key. But he hasn't seen her since he asked her to get him supplies almost a half an hour ago. I'm telling you, I'm worried."

Anna stated, "There must be a rational explanation for this."

"If you two can come up with one, I'm all ears. All I can come up with is someone took her."

Joe joked, "Who'd want to take her? Think about it. If someone did take her, after a few minutes, they'd bring her back. Can you imagine the trouble she'd make? You've got to be kidding."

Laura insisted, "I'm not kidding. There's a dead body outside and a huge mess in the alley, and she's missing. Do you have a better idea to explain this? It's not like this is the greatest neighborhood."

He nodded. "Well, yeah. You've got a point."

Anna asked, "Do you think we should call the police?"

Laura glared at her. "They're already here because of the dead guy outside, genius."

As they argued, the priest and two police officers entered the dining room. Laura motioned them over to her.

"Officers, we need your help," Laura pleaded.

"I'm Officer Raul Gonzalez. This is my partner, Officer Rob Stone. Is this concerning the incident outside?"

"I believe it is related to it," Laura answered.

Officer Gonzalez flipped open his small notebook. "And you are?"

"I'm Laura. This is Anna, and that's Joe."

"Any of you have last names?" he asked.

Laura stated, "Delaney, Cristo, and Lazaro, in that order."

"Thank you. Now, what can you tell us?" Officer Gonzalez asked.

Laura stated, "I need to report a kidnapping of a twenty-three year-old female named Sara Taylor."

Officer Gonzalez wrote Sara's name on his pad. "Did you see the kidnapping?"

"No," Laura admitted.

He continued writing as he addressed them. "Any of you see the kidnapping?"

Anna and Joe responded in unison. "No."

Officer Gonzalez inquired, "Then how do you know this person was kidnapped? And why do you think it relates to the situation outside?"

Laura answered. "She was here a short while ago. She went to get plates. Then she got sidetracked to get sheets. No one has seen her since."

Joe lamented, "I should have gotten the plates myself. I shouldn't have let her go alone."

Laura continued, "Considering the mess in the alley and the dead guy outside, I believe something terrible happened to her."

"Uh huh," Officer Stone replied, surveying the dining area.

Joe said, "I'm never going to forgive myself for this."

Laura persisted. "Come to think of it, maybe that guy who was hit by the garbage truck saw what happened. Maybe he was trying to get help."

"Uh huh." Officer Gonzalez wrote without looking up.

"*I'm serious.* You've got to listen to me. I've looked everywhere. The only room I couldn't search was the back room. It's locked," Laura explained.

"That's odd," Father Francis commented.

"What's odd, Father?" Officer Gonzalez asked.

"The door to the back room is always open during this time of day. It's locked all night, as is this entire floor. We don't allow free roaming at night. Anyone sleeping upstairs must come through the front door and be checked in and out. It's for everyone's safety, you understand."

"Uh huh," Officer Stone commented. "How many people stay here?"

Father Francis said, "Right now, twenty-four. Some are children. Oh wait—with the new edition today, we now have twenty-five, total."

"Do you have the key?" Laura asked the priest.

"The key?"

Laura reminded, "For the back room."

"Oh, yes. It's right here on my key chain," the priest answered.

He quickly produced the key chain, which Laura ripped from his hand. With it, she ran down the corridor. The police officers pursued her. Anna, Joe, and Father Francis brought up the rear. Laura reached the door. She fumbled to identify the right key. By that time, everyone had caught up to her.

Officer Gonzalez directed her. "Miss, please turn over the keys, and step back from the door. This could be dangerous. We're trained to handle these situations. For your own safety, step away from the door. All of you, step away from the door."

Laura knitted her brow and begrudgingly turned over the keys. When everyone had moved down the hall to a safe distance, Officer Gonzalez and Officer Stone drew their weapons. Officer Stone inserted the key into the lock and opened the door. Signs of a struggle were evident—the sheets and towels lay trampled on the floor. The officers searched and secured the room.

Officer Stone announced, "All clear."

Joe stood in the doorway, shocked by the scene. He found it hard to breathe. Never before had he ever felt this helpless.

Officer Gonzalez resumed questioning. "Can any of you tell us what led up to this apparent kidnapping?"

Laura replied, "I'll tell you everything I know. Sara was working the lunch line with Anna, Joe, and me. She went to get more dishes."

The priest interrupted. "That's when I asked her to get some sheets and towels for me. I was busy, and David wasn't here yet. It is so unlike him. He is always here. He's usually early."

"Has anyone contacted this David person today?" Officer Gonzalez inquired.

"Sara called his home number and his cell. She wasn't able to reach him. It's odd, because this volunteering project was his idea," Laura replied.

"He's the volunteer coordinator," the priest stated.

"Was there a relationship between him and the alleged victim?" Officer Gonzalez questioned.

Joe leaned against the wall for support. "They've been dating for a week or so," he offered reluctantly.

Officer Stone asked, "Could he have whisked the alleged victim off for a romantic getaway of some sort?"

"And not tell anybody? And leave her purse and car here? No. I don't think so," Laura responded, annoyed.

"I have to ask the questions," Officer Stone explained. "Anyone know how I can contact this David character?"

Laura volunteered. "Yes, all of his contact information is in Sara's planner. It's in her purse. I can get it for you."

Officer Gonzalez turned to address Laura. "If you could obtain his information, we'll check on the residence when we're through here. In the meantime, Officer Stone and I need to gather evidence."

Officer Stone turned to the priest. "Father, we'll need a list of the people staying here and the names of anyone else who might have gained entry—like volunteers."

Laura went to the kitchen. She opened the pantry door that contained all of their purses. She obtained Sara's purse. As she opened the purse, Sara's cell phone fell out.

"I guess the voice mail I left won't do any good."

Extracting the planner, Laura ripped out a blank piece of paper, and then flipped to the address section. David's recently added information was written in red ink. Laura copied it down on the paper. She returned to the group with the purse and planner, in case the police needed any additional information. She handed the paper to Officer Stone.

Officer Stone glanced at it. He held it up so Laura could see her own handwriting. "Are you sure this information is correct?"

Laura replied, "Yes. Why?"

He flipped back a few pages in his notebook. "We were dispatched to that address right before we came here."

Surprised, Joe asked, "Why? What happened?"

As Laura transferred Sara's planner to her other hand, a picture of David fell out.

Officer Stone bent over and picked up the picture. Studying it, he said, "Sorry, we're not allowed to give out details. I can tell you that the man in this picture was not the injured party. It also means that he could not have been involved in the disappearance of your friend. He was with us at the time of her disappearance."

Chapter 14

MARK wrote in his diary for a long time to capture all of the day's events. Portions of the day had been extremely disturbing. Being responsible for two additional deaths burdened his heart and mind. However, the bright spot was that Sara was with him.

The last words he wrote in his diary were:

And Sara and I will live happily ever after.

That diary, the vessel into which he emptied his soul, served a vital purpose. Now that Mark had purged and confessed his sins, he imposed his own penance. He vowed to be a better man—for real this time. He would make amends for his sins and devote his life to a higher purpose. Only good things were yet to come. Starting out with a clean, fresh slate, he would make sure of it.

After much soul-searching, the diary was boxed up with some other mementos of his old life. Banishing the items from the house would provide a final cleansing. He carried the box to the loft in the barn, where all of his things were stored. After depositing the box, he returned to the house to check on Sara.

Sara awoke in a strange bed, disoriented and dizzy. Her head throbbed. She closed her eyes to stop the room from spinning and massaged her temples. The action provided no relief. The pain radiated from the base of her neck to the top of her head. As she reached around to massage her head, she felt a large knot on the back of her head. The lump was approximately the size of a half dollar. The skin didn't feel broken. Opening her eyes for the second time, she focused on her outstretched hand. That kept the dizziness at bay somewhat, but the incessant pounding continued. She attempted to sit up, but reconsidered after the room started spinning wildly.

What little she saw of the room seemed vaguely familiar—pale blue walls and white curtains with pink flowers on them. A small wooden chair flanked the bed on her right side. Closing her eyes, she breathed deeply, unsure of her location. Things were hazy. What she remembered played like a bizarre dream. She thought that perhaps she was still stuck in the dream.

As she struggled to make sense of her thoughts, she heard a squeaking noise, followed by running water. The noise emanated from an open door a few feet from the bed on the right. Knowing she couldn't resolve anything at the moment, she pretended to be unconscious. It would buy some time.

The water stopped.

Footsteps echoed loudly in her head like cannon blasts. The chair creaked as the person sat down next to her. A cold washcloth was applied to her forehead. The man started humming an unfamiliar tune. However, she recognized the scent of his cologne.

Mark gazed lovingly at Sara. He whispered, "Sleep now. Get your rest. I love you, Sara. I'm going to take care of you and protect you. I just wanted to talk to you, that's all. I didn't mean for you to get hurt. I'm going to nurse you back to health. Everything's going to be fine. You'll see." Believing that a darker room would be more comfortable for her, he rose to draw the drapes.

Sara recognized the voice immediately as Mark's. Perplexed, she wondered how that was possible. The paper had reported that he was dead. Clearly, he wasn't. Apparently, the authorities had made a mistake. The booming footsteps distracted her. Unraveling this mystery would have to wait.

As Mark drew the drapes, he saw the van in the driveway. Its presence triggered his memory. The unexpected encounter and excitement of being with Sara had interrupted the job he had promised to complete for Ray. If he didn't return, Ray would search for him. The only option was to finish the laundry run by dropping off the load.

Approaching Sara, he said, "I have to leave for a few minutes,

Sara. I'll be right back. I have an errand to run. You just sleep. You'll feel better in no time." Mark kissed her gently on the lips. He left the room, closing the door behind him.

Sara waited until she heard the sound of a vehicle driving away before moving. She noticed that his tone of voice had been hurried, as if there was something important requiring his attention. She tugged the washcloth off her forehead and sat up slowly. Feeling lousy, she deposited the washcloth on the back of her neck. She remained on the edge of the bed for a few minutes, until the room stopped spinning. She slowly stood up, leaning on the chair for balance. The dizziness kicked in again. Determined, she closed one eye and used the chair as a walker to cross the room.

The door on her right led to a bathroom. She lumbered by it to reach the window in front of her. She pulled back the curtains. There were no houses as far as she could see. Below the window were roses—red, pink, yellow, hybrids too—held up by sharpened garden stakes. If she jumped, she would be impaled for her efforts. The width of the flowerbed made it impossible to jump clear of it.

Sara hobbled over to the window directly in front of the bed. A vegetable garden bordered this side of the house. Tomato plants grew under this window with another full complement of sharpened garden stakes. At that moment, she realized where she was—the master bedroom in the Collins house. Nonetheless, she gave up on the idea that she was dreaming. All of this felt too real to be a dream.

Sara leaned on the chair and shuffled unsteadily to the bathroom door. Leaving the chair next to the bed, she held the doorjamb to enter the bathroom. On the toilet, she stretched, forgetting about the washcloth at the base of her neck. It fell into the toilet with an audible plop. She muttered, "Shit."

After she finished, she looked into the bowl. There was no way she was fishing out the washcloth. "Oh, the hell with it." She flushed. To her surprise, everything went down. It was a good old-fashioned toilet, not a new low-flow one.

After washing her hands, she studied her reflection in the mirror. It was definitely not her best hair day. "Looks like danger and disaster found me anyway." She pushed her hair behind her ears and splashed some cold water on her face. After blotting her face with a towel, she leaned on the sink. She asked her reflection, "What am I going to do? I was trying to be a better person. I was even volunteering at that stupid mission when this happened! God, why are you doing this to me?"

A car pulled into the gravel driveway, and a door slammed. Sara's head pounded. Unable to muster the energy to make it back to the window, she struggled back to the bed. Trapped in a house with a crazy person, she would do whatever was necessary to get out of this place alive.

Back at the mission, Joe paced up and down the corridor, while Father Francis, Laura, and Anna stared at the discarded linens on the floor. Tom and Sally rushed to the back room after they heard the disturbance.

Officer Stone held up a hand. "Stop! Don't come any further. Names?"

"Sally Prado."

"Tom Grant."

The officer continued. "Have either of you been in this room today?"

Sally said, "No. I haven't."

"Me either," Tom confirmed.

"Did you see anyone go in or out of this room?" Officer Stone inquired.

Sally replied, "No. I was at the stove, cooking. I couldn't see anything from there."

Tom added, "I walked back and forth in this hallway several times, carrying all sorts of stuff. I never saw anybody go anywhere except the bathrooms."

Officer Stone presented each of them with his card. "Fine. You two can go. We need to examine this room. If you remember anything, please contact me."

Officer Gonzalez noticed a large boot print on one of the sheets. "Did Ms. Taylor wear boots?"

Joe shot the officer a disgusted look. "Boots? In the middle of summer? No, she was wearing sneakers, and her feet aren't that big," Joe snapped.

Ignoring his tone, Officer Gonzalez continued, "Does anyone notice anything else out of place or missing?"

All sets of eyes canvassed the room.

Father Francis pointed at the corner. "One of the laundry bags is missing. We always have six large laundry bags for the sheets and towels. There are only five laundry bags now."

Officer Gonzalez flipped over to a new page in his notebook. He asked, "Couldn't they have shorted you one bag?"

Scratching his head, the priest replied, "I guess it's possible, but it's never happened before."

"So one missing girl and one missing laundry bag. Anything else?" Gonzalez inquired.

Enraged, Joe responded, "Sara's not inventory. You say that like she's a thing, a possession, and not a person."

Laura attempted to calm him. "Joe, I'm sure he didn't mean it like it sounded."

Joe walked away.

Officer Stone examined the back door. "It doesn't look like there was a forced entry. Who has keys to the back door?"

Father Francis rubbed his chin. "I have a key, David Turner has a key, and the laundry service has one."

"The laundry service has a key to the back door of this mission?" Officer Stone asked, looking away from the door.

"Why, yes. I did business with Mr. Chen for over thirty years. We had a wonderful relationship until he died. His family recently sold the business to Ray Peters. I never thought of asking for the key back. I've never had any problems, ever."

Officer Stone dusted for fingerprints. "Father, I would recommend that you change the lock on this door immediately, and only have a key made for yourself and one for Mr. Turner, if you feel that he still needs to have a key."

Father Francis was about to argue. But he realized he probably had been foolish to let outsiders have a key, considering the number of thefts at area businesses and churches lately. He reflected on the discomforting current state of affairs in the neighborhood. Years ago, they had kept St. Peter's Church and Mission unlocked. There had never been a worry about theft or vandalism.

Officer Stone continued with his assessment. "I agree with your initial reaction that Ms. Taylor was abducted. The discarded sheets with the boot prints on them provide ample evidence that she was not alone in this room. I've taken fingerprints off the door handles and doorjamb. We should be able to get preliminary results if the person is in the system. I'll need prints of anyone else who's been in this room."

Father Francis replied, "We had a disturbance here a few months ago. David's prints and my prints should already be on file."

Joe asked, "So what are we supposed to do in the meantime? We can't just sit here and do nothing. We've got to find her."

"Just let us handle it," Officer Gonzalez replied. "Do any of you have a picture of Ms. Taylor that we could use?"

Joe took out his wallet and opened it. He pulled out two pictures. The first was Sara's senior picture. The other was a snapshot of Joe and Sara together on the beach. "Take your pick."

Officer Gonzalez picked the photo of Sara alone.

Sara sat on the bed, holding her head. She thought about Eva Seville and the tarot card reading. She remembered laughing at the thought of danger lurking. She was not laughing now. There was no use crying about it either. The die had been cast. Danger and disaster were staring her in the face. Her current prospects looked bleak.

Mark quietly mounted the stairs. Lost in thought, Sara didn't hear him until he opened the door.

Surprised, she jumped. "You scared me."

"Sorry. I'm so glad you're awake. It's wonderful. How do you feel?" He rushed to her side.

"My head is killing me, and the room is spinning. Otherwise, I'm just peachy," she answered sarcastically.

He sat in the creaky wooden chair. "Sorry about that. I didn't mean to hurt you, but you kept running away and throwing things at me." He reached for her hand. He held it briefly before she yanked free of his grasp. A hurt look crossed his face.

"You're Mark?" Her words rang loudly in her head.

"Yes, I am."

Holding her head, she asked, "How are you alive? They said you were dead. Did they lock up the wrong brother?"

"No. I was in Misty Pines until the day of Matt's death. It's a long story. I don't want to talk about it now. You should eat something. Do you feel well enough to go downstairs?"

Raising her head to make eye contact with him, she inquired, "You're not keeping me locked in this room?"

With a carefree laugh, he replied, "No. Why would I? This is your house too."

"My house?"

"Yes. We'll be married soon. We'll live here together, forever. Just like we planned. We're going to be so happy."

Sara lacked the energy to contradict him. Until she knew more, she would play along.

At County General Hospital, Janet and Richard Greenwood arrived and joined their son, Rick, and his friend, David, in the hospital's main waiting area.

"How could something like this happen?" Janet asked, dabbing her green eyes with a tissue.

"The police are investigating," Rick replied.

"The police? Why are the police involved?" Richard asked.

Rick explained, "It might not have been an accident. We just don't know. All that's important right now is that Billy comes out of surgery."

David stood. "I'm going to get everybody something to drink. I'll be back in a sec."

They nodded as David departed in search of the vending area. During this quest, he checked his phone for messages. There were several. He attempted to return Sara's call. He got voice mail. On the message, he explained, "I'm sure you're upset with me. I'm really sorry. There was an accident at the house. I'm fine. But Bill, Rick Greenwood's brother, was hurt badly. I'm at the hospital now. Call me when you get this. Bye."

David called the rectory to talk to Father Francis. The housekeeper took a message. Disappointed that he was zero for two, David purchased some bottled water and soda pop and brought them back for the Greenwoods.

"Thanks, Dave," Rick said, accepting a soda.

David replied, "It's the least I can do." He positioned the other beverages on the table, in front of the family.

A doctor clad in a long, white coat appeared. "Family for Greenwood?"

Richard Sr. stood and held up his hand. "I'm his father."

The doctor nodded and joined the family. He introduced himself. "I'm Dr. Eli Horowitz. I'm treating your son. He's in guarded condition and has a ruptured spleen, punctured lungs, and other internal organ damage, not to mention the broken and crushed bones. We've managed to stop the bleeding and have repaired some of the bone fractures. We've given him several units of blood. He will require additional surgeries. That might lead to more transfusions. But for right now, it's more important to get him stable. We can worry about setting the rest of the bones later. The next twenty-four to forty-eight hours will be critical. We've put him in a medically-induced coma to improve his chances."

Sobbing, Janet asked, "What *are* his chances?"

Dr. Horowitz reiterated, "The next two days are critical. If he makes it through without any further complications, his chances will be much improved. I don't like to give out numbers. They don't serve much of a purpose at a time like this. A nurse will notify you when you can see him."

"Thank you, Doctor." Richard wiped away a tear.

David stood up and declared, "I'm going to donate blood."

"Good idea. I'm coming with you," Rick stated.

Janet rose and hugged them both. "You're such good boys."

Officer Gonzalez received word from the police lab that the fingerprint results from the St. Peter's crime scene were in. He and Officer Stone walked from their desks to the lab.

Officer Gonzalez picked up the report and thumbed through it.

Officer Stone asked the male technician, "Have you gotten the results from our earlier case yet?"

The technician replied, "Nope. I worked on the kidnapping case first. But I should have them in an hour or so."

Officer Gonzalez read the results. "There were four sets of prints on the back door of St. Peter's Mission. Three sets were in the system. Father Francis and David Turner account for two sets. The third set belonged to an unknown party."

Officer Stone interjected, "Hypothetically, let's say those are Sara Taylor's prints."

"Agreed."

"What about the fourth set?"

"Rob, you're going to love this."

"Why?"

"The fourth set belongs to a guy with a rap sheet by the name of Mark Collins," Officer Gonzalez finished.

"Raul, you're yanking my chain. Mark Collins? Wasn't he the suicide guy at Misty Pines?"

"Uh huh."

"We delivered the news to his next of kin."

"Yeah, we did. Look for yourself." He offered the report to his partner.

Reviewing the report, Rob asked, "But, remember, he didn't want to see his brother's body?"

Smiling, Raul replied, "Yeah. He said they were twins."

Pointing at his partner, Rob declared, "Bingo!"

"Can twins have identical fingerprints?"

"I don't think so."

"Would his brother have taken the rap and served time for him?"

"I don't know anyone who'd serve time in jail or a psych ward for something they didn't do."

"Yeah. Me either."

"So we're looking at him pulling off this kind of elaborate switch when he was locked up in a mental hospital?"

"I don't know. There's only one way to find out. First things first—we need to see if that dead body's been cremated yet."

Chapter 15

JOE, Laura, and Anna huddled together on the marble steps of St. Peter's Mission. They descended slowly, in shock from the day's events. Third Street, in front of St. Peter's Catholic Church and Mission, was deserted. The crowd that had migrated around the corner stayed there. The curious people gathered near the yellow crime tape, blocking the intersection of the alley and Main Street, where the Baptist preacher had died. His body had been taken away in a black body bag.

"This is crazy," Anna commented, looking around.

"I can't believe something like this could happen *here ... to us ... to Sara*," Joe stated in disbelief.

Holding her purse and Sara's purse, Laura said, "Well, it has. And we need to get off our asses and find her."

Shielding her eyes from the sun, Anna asked, "How?"

Laura paused for a moment before continuing. "I think we should go to the hospital to see what's going on. I'm guessing that's where David is. Maybe he can tell us what the police couldn't."

"And you think *that's* going to help us find Sara?" Joe asked.

"I don't have any other ideas at the moment. Do you?" Laura asked.

"No. I guess it's worth a try," Joe admitted.

"Fine. Let's go before something else happens. This place is giving me the creeps." Laura shuddered.

Anna asked, "What about Sara's car?"

Laura poked around in Sara's purse until she recovered the key chain. "I've got the keys. I'll drive it home. I don't want to leave it here."

Joe reached into his pocket for his keys. He twirled them

around. "I'll follow you home. Then we'll go to the hospital together from there."

David and Rick sat next to each other in County General Hospital's Outpatient Lab, drinking orange juice after donating blood. David hadn't experienced any ill effects. However, Rick felt lightheaded. The nurse wouldn't let him leave the area yet.

"I'm so sorry about what happened to Bill. I just don't know what to say," David apologized.

"It's not your fault," Rick answered.

"No matter what you say, I still feel responsible. It happened with my car, in my garage."

Rick drank the remainder of his juice and tilted his head back. "Just shut up about it. You can't fix it. And there's no use talking about blame at a time like this."

David and Rick waited in silence, watching the nurses work on the other half-dozen people in the white, cold room.

Joe, Laura, and Anna arrived at County General Hospital in less than thirty minutes. Joe parked in the outdoor visitor parking area. The outdoor parking was farther away from the building, but it was free. The ramp garage parking connected to the hospital wasn't. The three friends traversed the lot to the emergency room entrance. Not recognizing anyone in the ER waiting area, they decided to check the main waiting area. When they arrived, they didn't see David. However, Joe recognized Janet and Richard Greenwood. Joe approached them. "Hi, Mr. and Mrs. Greenwood."

Richard Greenwood greeted him. "Joe, we didn't expect to see you here."

Joe responded, "I didn't expect to see you either. We came here looking for David Turner. The police said there was an accident at his house."

Crying, Janet replied, "Yes, that was our Billy. He was crushed by a car."

"Oh, I'm so sorry. I didn't know. How bad is it?" Joe asked.

Janet blew her nose. "Very, very bad. He's guarded or critical or something like that. We haven't seen him yet. The doctor said something about the next day or two. We're waiting to see him."

As Janet finished speaking, her gaze shifted into the distance. Joe took a step back and turned. David and Rick were coming toward them. Rick looked pale. His mother noticed immediately. When the men reached the group, Janet exclaimed, "Richard, you look terrible!"

"I'm fine. I just got a little dizzy giving blood. They gave me some juice and told me to take it easy," Rick replied. He sat in the chair next to her.

Puzzled by the presence of the newcomers, David asked, "What's going on? Why are you guys here?"

Laura answered, "We need to talk to you about something."

"What?"

Putting her hand on his back, Laura guided him away from the grieving family. "Why don't we walk over to the vending area, so the Greenwoods can be alone?"

David agreeably accompanied Joe and the two girls to the vending area. There were four vending machines—one with hot beverages, one with cold beverages, and two other machines that held assorted snacks, candy, and gum. The well-worn, multicolored chairs were arranged in a boxy W-shaped pattern on the gray carpet. Faux wooden tables were strategically placed among them. David sat with the girls while Joe paced.

David settled into a chair, resting his arms on the armrests. "So what's up?"

Laura reported, "There was an incident at the mission today."

"Two incidents," Anna corrected.

"What kind of incidents?"

Anna stated flatly, "The old Baptist preacher, Ezekiel Walker, was killed outside the mission. He was hit by a garbage truck."

"Brutal," David commented, massaging the back of his neck with his right hand.

"And there was a kidnapping," Laura added.

David exclaimed, "A kidnapping? You're kidding. At the mission? In broad daylight?"

"Yes. Somebody took Sara," Joe answered.

David searched their facial expressions. He leaned forward, moving his hands to his thighs. "You're kidding."

"No. Dead serious. The police found signs of a struggle, and she's missing," Laura replied.

Gesturing toward him, Anna said, "The cops at first suggested that you might have come and taken her away for a getaway or something."

David shook his head vehemently and straightened up in the chair. "I didn't take her. I swear," David testified.

Joe stopped pacing. His gaze shifted from the window to David. "We know. After we gave them your information, the police vouched for you. They were the same cops who were at your house earlier."

"Do they have any leads? Or clues? Or anything?" David questioned.

Laura responded, "Not yet. They should be running the fingerprints they lifted from the scene. Hopefully, that will give them something to go on."

Suddenly, Janet Greenwood appeared and interrupted their conversation. "We can go see Billy now. Will you come with us, David? I don't like the way Rick looks. I need for my focus to be on Billy."

Joe encouraged David. "Go ahead. Go with them. We'll call you if we find out anything."

David was torn. Because of the nature of Bill's accident, he felt obligated to the Greenwood family. At the same time, he wanted to search for Sara. However, as he watched the tears stream down Janet's face, the decision was clear. David jumped up. "You'll keep me posted, right?"

Anna responded, "Sure. We're just waiting to hear something anyway. You might as well help the Greenwoods. At least you can do something for them."

"Do you have my number?"

Laura said, "Yes. I've got Sara's phone."

"Talk to you later," he replied, accompanying Janet back to the main area.

"Later," Joe acknowledged.

Laura and Anna exchanged glances. Joe sat in a chair. He bent over and covered his face with his hands.

Laura sighed. "This is so unreal. This whole freaking day has been unbelievable."

Anna asked, "Yeah, so now what?"

Joe looked up. "There's nothing that's going to help us here."

Laura nodded. "You're right. Let's go. Hospitals bother me anyway. And Anna needs to change out of that smiley face shirt."

Anna pulled on her shirt. "What's wrong with my shirt?"

Laura explained, "It was fine for earlier, but it just doesn't seem appropriate any more. It's really annoying."

"Fine. I'll change. We should probably get something to eat on the way home," Anna stated. "There's nothing in the fridge."

"You're hungry?" Laura asked.

"It's late. We haven't eaten in hours. We should try to eat," Anna reminded them.

"I'm not hungry," Laura said.

Joe stated, "Neither am I, but I am thirsty. I'll stop at a burger drive-through on the way back."

"Okay," Anna replied.

At County General Hospital, Officer Stone and Officer Gonzalez parked in the special section of the parking lot reserved for on-duty police officers. They marched into the hospital and proceeded directly to the elevators. They boarded the first available elevator to the basement, which housed the county morgue.

The elevator doors parted to reveal a dark, cold, gray hallway. The walls were cinderblock. The hallway led to a small, gray room. Filing cabinets filled most of it. In front of it all was a clerk's desk. The clerk stamped documents with a large red stamp as the officers approached.

"Where's Walt Jones?" Officer Gonzalez asked the scrawny male clerk.

Without speaking, the clerk turned and pointed to the coroner across the room.

Walt responded, "Over here. What can I do for you?"

"We need to know if a body has been cremated yet," Officer Stone stated.

Walt asked, "Do you have a name? Or is it a John Doe?"

"The name is Collins. Mark Collins," Officer Stone replied.

The coroner remembered that name. His decision to lie about this case was coming back to bite him. "Is there some sort of problem?" he inquired, fishing for details.

Officer Gonzalez answered, "We need to take his fingerprints."

"Fingerprints?"

"Yes. We need to verify the identity of the individual," Officer Gonzalez explained.

"Let me look through my records." The coroner flipped through his files. "You're in luck. He's still in cold storage."

"Good. Show us what drawer he's in," Officer Stone directed.

Walt nodded affirmatively. "Consider it done. Follow me through the double doors. He's in the next room."

One stainless steel autopsy table occupied the middle of the room. A variety of lights hung overhead. The stainless steel drawers, set into the walls to store the bodies, were stacked three high. No names identified any of the drawers' occupants, just numbers. The air felt heavy in the cold room.

The coroner quickly located Matt Collins' current resting place—a middle drawer on the right-hand wall. He winced as he pulled on the drawer. It screeched as it opened, sounding like fingernails on a chalkboard. Carefully, Walt Jones pulled back the sheet to expose the face.

The officers verified it was the correct subject.

Officer Stone hated touching dead bodies. Officer Gonzalez despised the task equally. However, he had drawn the short straw on the drive over to the morgue. He took a deep breath. The dead man's fingers were stiff and felt like cold marble. He moved as quickly as possible to complete all ten fingers. When the officer finished, he warned, "Don't cremate this body until you hear back from us."

After the coroner covered the body and closed the drawer, Officer Gonzalez handed him a piece of paper. "Here's an order stating there's an ongoing investigation. This body is evidence."

Walt replied, "I'll complete the paperwork and let the staff know. If you need anything else, let me know."

"Count on it," Officer Stone promised.

The two officers' footsteps echoed eerily in the cinderblock hallway to the elevator. When they reached the elevator, Officer Stone pressed the *Up* button and took a slip of paper from his pocket—a copy of Mark Collins' official fingerprint card.

Officer Gonzalez held up the newly created card from the dead body.

They studied the prints—they didn't match.

"Son of a bitch," Officer Gonzalez said.

"How the hell did he do it?" Officer Stone wondered.

"That's what we're going to have to figure out," Officer Gonzalez replied, as the elevator door opened.

Stepping inside the elevator and armed with this new information, they left the morgue. The elevator stopped on the main floor. The doors opened to reveal David Turner and Rick Greenwood. They were waiting to take the elevator to the third floor. The last elevator had been packed to capacity. They had sent the injured boy's parents up first.

Surprised to see the policemen, David asked, "Do you have any information on Sara Taylor yet?"

Rick looked at his friend, puzzled. David hadn't mentioned the kidnapping. His best friend was burdened with enough already.

Officer Gonzalez stated, "After a visit to the morgue, we now have a prime suspect."

"Who?" David pressed.

"Ever hear of Mark Collins?" Officer Stone asked.

"No," David answered.

"Make that two of us," Rick replied.

"Well, right now, he's our prime suspect. We need to get back to the station and put out an APB for him," Officer Gonzalez announced.

As the officers walked toward the exit, David and Rick entered the elevator. David pressed the button for the third floor.

"What's going on with Sara?" Rick asked as the doors closed.

"It's probably nothing. I didn't want to worry you," David replied.

"It has to be something. The cops came from the morgue. One of them said *prime suspect.* Something's wrong."

"Sara's friends think she's been kidnapped. The police are searching for her."

"Then what are you doing here?"

"I need to be here, with you."

"You need to be out there searching for her."

"Where am *I* going to look? If her closest friends and the cops can't find her, what chance do I have?"

"Good point."

The elevator stopped on the third floor. They walked to the small ICU waiting area. The nurse informed them that only two visitors were allowed at a time. Rick would have to wait for one of his parents to leave Bill's side before he could go in.

"Rick, I'm going to check my voice mail," David announced. "I'll be back in a few minutes."

Rick nodded.

As David walked down the hall, he dialed Sara's home phone number.

Laura answered on the third ring.

Before she finished saying hello, David asked, "Do you know who Mark Collins is?"

She hesitated. "David? Is that you?"

"Sorry. Yes, it's David. So do you? Do you know him?"

"Yeah. But psycho boy is dead," she replied.

"Psycho boy?"

"Yeah. That's what we called him. He recently committed suicide. It's a long story." She took a sip of her drink. Too nervous to eat, Laura had opted for a chocolate fix instead, in the form of a large milkshake.

David said impatiently, "Tell me the story. The police just told me he's their prime suspect."

"That doesn't make any sense. He died before this happened."

"They said *is* not *was,* and they're putting out an APB for him right now."

"Why? He's dead."

"I'm telling you that I just ran into the cops, who just came from the morgue. They said that *he* is their *prime suspect*. So maybe he's not dead."

"No," Laura blurted. "I don't believe it. How could he have done it? There's no way. It can't be."

"What?"

Laura explained, "He and his brother are twins."

Soaking in Laura's words, David demanded, "I need you to tell me everything."

"I'll give you the condensed version."

Laura divulged how Sara and Mark had met at a grief counseling meeting after Mark's parents died and Sara's brother died.

Joe threw up his hands and mouthed, "What's going on?" to Laura.

She waved him away, mouthed, "Not now," and walked into the family room. Laura continued her explanation to David. "They bonded through their common grief. They dated. It ended badly. He became obsessed with her. He stalked her for weeks. Sara ended up getting a restraining order against him. He violated the order, resisted arrest, and ended up in jail, where he tried to commit suicide. Then he was transferred to Misty Pines, where he was a patient until he killed himself a week or so ago. Or so we thought. Anyway, Sara was devastated when she found out he had died. She blamed herself for everything—including his death."

When Laura finished, David said, "Thanks for the info."

"So now what?"

"I don't know. I'm still at the hospital."

"I guess we just wait then."

"If you hear anything, let me know. I'll do the same. I'll be in touch." Then he hung up.

Laura stared at the phone before pressing the talk button to end the call.

Joe asked, "What did he want?"

"Well, you heard the conversation. He wanted to know about Mark."

Joe pressed, "Why?"

"He said he talked to the cops. They were coming from the morgue. They said that Mark is their prime suspect. They're issuing an APB for him."

"Their prime suspect is a dead guy? These guys wouldn't know their asses from a hole in the ground," Joe said through gritted teeth.

Anna, now wearing a plain white polo shirt, stated, "It doesn't make any sense."

"Unless Mark's not dead after all. Obviously, the cops found something that made them think he's still alive," Laura responded.

Anna asked, "Could it be his brother, Matt?"

Laura inquired, "The kidnapper or the dead guy?"

Joe deduced, "If the cops were coming from the morgue, I'm betting the dead guy is Matt. That's why they're looking for Mark."

"Wow!" Anna exclaimed. "How did psycho boy manage that?"

"Don't know. But I'm sure it will be one hell of a story," Laura said.

Mark and Sara ate a simple dinner in the bright yellow kitchen. Her head throbbed. She wasn't very hungry. The bright wall color wasn't helping matters.

Mark watched Sara eat toast covered with butter and strawberry jam. He ate a bowl of cereal. It wasn't the romantic dinner he had dreamt about. Nevertheless, he convinced himself that since they were together now, that was all that mattered.

After Sara finished her toast, she asked for some aspirin. Mark retrieved the aspirin and gave it to her. She swallowed two pills.

Holding her head, she looked around the kitchen. She needed access to a phone and would have sworn there used to be a wall phone in the kitchen. There wasn't one now. Sara announced, "I'm tired, and my head is still killing me. I'm going to bed—alone."

"I'll walk you up the stairs. I don't want you to fall," Mark replied.

Sara, too achy to argue, answered, "Fine."

Mark escorted Sara upstairs to the master bedroom.

At the doorway, she stopped. "Good night."

He responded, "Good night."

Sara shut the door.

He listened at the door and heard the springs squeak as she got into the bed. Satisfied, he went downstairs, poured himself a drink, and walked to the front door.

Mark looked through the front screen door. The smell of clean air delighted him, soothed him. His senses were no longer exposed to the institute's pungent combination of disinfectant, body odor, and urine. Although these odors were physically absent, they lingered in his memory. He shivered at the thought of ever having to smell those repulsive substances again. He inhaled again, slowly and deeply.

The sun hung low on the horizon, barely visible. The sun's rays cast hues of blue, purple, and a pinkish red behind the wispy clouds. The crickets engaged in their nightly serenade. Two robins flew from branch to branch.

The screen door slammed behind him as he moved to the front porch. One of the boards groaned under his weight. He made a mental note to fix it. For now, he would sit and enjoy the tranquil evening. He placed his whiskey on the porch railing and sat down on a rocking chair, rocking back and forth, back and forth.

A warm breeze blew. Fireflies appeared and danced in the air effortlessly. Mark was content for the first time in a long time. He and Sara were home together. A squirrel jumped from a nearby tree branch onto the porch railing. Its tail formed a question mark. Mark picked up his drink and swirled it. He spoke to the squirrel. "Everything worked out. Sara and I are together forever this time. We're going to have such a wonderful and happy life."

The disinterested squirrel ran the length of the railing and scampered down the porch steps. Mark drank the remaining liquid in his glass. He remained on the porch until after the sun set. He thought about his plans for the next day. When he could no longer tolerate being bitten by mosquitoes, he decided to turn in. Before retiring for the evening, he poured another drink, popped a tranquilizer, and washed it down in one gulp.

Chapter 16

JOE bargained with God silently. *God, please let Sara be okay. I'll start going to church every week. I'll even go to confession. Just please let her be all right.*

Laura stated, "So, for the sake of argument, we're assuming that Mark is still alive. Agreed?"

Frustrated, Joe replied, "I'd say yes, since they're putting an APB out for him. Are they going to check his house?"

"I don't know. David didn't say," Laura said.

As he got up from the table, Joe insisted, "I'm sure that's where that crazy loser is. If he's really alive, I'm sure that's where he took her."

Anna questioned, "Wouldn't he try to hide?"

Joe threw up his hands, pacing between the kitchen and family room. "Where else would he go? I don't picture him running around town with her. She'd make it too difficult. She'd kick and scream and make tons of noise. He couldn't risk it."

"Maybe he subdued her, so she's not able to scream," Laura interjected. "We didn't hear her, did we?"

Anna frowned. "No, we didn't. But that door was pretty thick, and there was crowd noise on top of it."

Laura said, "I think Joe's right. Mark's house is a farmhouse in the middle of nowhere."

Joe said, "It's a perfect place to keep a noisy captive. No one would hear her." Nervously, he twirled his keys.

Anna collected the empty food wrappers on the table, crumpled them into a ball, and deposited them in the trash. "I still think it's too obvious."

Joe ran his fingers through his hair as he walked back and

forth. "Yes and no. The guy's nuts. Who knows what he's thinking? But we need to start somewhere, don't we?"

"We should call the police," Anna stated.

"Whatever," Joe muttered, moving back into the kitchen. He opened the refrigerator and closed it without removing anything. "I should have protected her. I should have gone for the plates myself. Then none of this would have happened."

Laura argued, "He was willing to kill David. I'm sure he would have tried to kill you too. I think he would have gotten to Sara one way or another."

"Was that supposed to make me feel better? Because it didn't." Joe walked back into the family room.

Laura rummaged through her purse, located Officer Stone's number, and dialed it.

Joe shot her a look. "Calling them is just a waste of time."

"Sheriff's office, Stone speaking," Office Stone answered.

"Hi. This is Laura Delaney. We met earlier today at St. Peter's."

"Yes, I remember you." The officer cradled the phone on his shoulder as he typed on his computer keyboard.

"We heard that Mark Collins might not be dead after all."

"News travels fast."

"We were wondering if anyone has been out to his house yet."

"No. We're in the process of getting a search warrant. Why?" He ceased typing.

Nonchalantly, Laura replied, "No reason. Just thought I'd ask."

The officer removed the phone from his shoulder and held it in his right hand. His voice was low. "Don't you dare go over there. It's a bad idea. *Period*. We're aware of his past history with your friend. He could be armed. We know he's dangerous."

"Uh huh."

"Don't go over there," he warned. "I mean it. We could haul you and your friends in for obstruction of police business."

"Uh huh. Thanks. Bye." Laura disconnected the call.

"Damn kids." Officer Stone hung up his phone.

From his desk across the room, Officer Gonzalez inquired, "What?"

"Those kids from this afternoon are going to be trouble," Officer Stone responded.

Laura addressed Joe and Anna. "He told us we shouldn't go over there. They're getting a search warrant."

Joe stopped pacing. "That could take forever. I'm going now."

"We should let the police handle this," Anna pleaded, touching Joe's arm.

Joe pulled away from her.

Laura interpreted the look on his face. "Leave him alone."

Joe couldn't hold it in any longer. "This is stupid. I'm not just going to sit around here and do nothing. I've got a really bad feeling. I can't stay here. I'm going to lose my mind. I'm leaving."

Anna ignored Laura's advice. She attempted to stop Joe physically by planting herself between him and the door.

Joe grabbed Anna's upper arms and squeezed tightly. "Read my lips. I'm leaving—with or without you. And not you or any army is going to prevent me from leaving this house. I have to find her." Staring her down, he asked, "So are you going to move on your own, or am I going to move you?"

Anna received the message loud and clear. "I'll move."

Joe released her. She stepped aside and grimaced, rubbing her arms.

Pushing past Anna, Laura said, "I'm coming with you."

Anna rolled her eyes. "You're both crazy. I'm going on record that I think this is a bad idea."

"Duly noted. Are you coming?" Laura asked.

Joe didn't wait to hear Anna's response. He was halfway down the sidewalk.

Laura stood at the front door with her hand on the door handle. "Well?"

Defeated, Anna replied, "Yes."

As Joe drove toward the farmhouse, he spied David pumping gas at the corner gas station. He pulled in next to him. Joe rolled down his window. "Have you heard anything else from the cops?"

Topping off the tank, David replied, "No. I'm just coming back from the hospital."

"How's the Greenwood kid doing?"

"Not great." David returned the nozzle to the pump.

"Well, Laura talked to the cops. We're headed over to Mark Collins' house right now."

David looked hopeful. "They found her?" He secured the gas cap and wiped his hands on his jeans.

"No, they're still screwing around with paperwork. We're going without them."

"Count me in. I'll follow you."

Officer Stone leaned back in his chair. "Raul, I got a feeling that those kids are going over to Mark Collins' house."

"I heard you tell them not to, Rob," Officer Gonzalez replied.

A petite, dark-haired female officer entered the room and handed Officer Gonzalez two files.

Officer Stone commented, "I don't think that's going to stop them."

Addressing the female officer, Officer Gonzalez said, "Thanks for bringing them up, Joanie."

"No problem. Have a good night," Joanie replied, leaving the two men alone.

The top file contained the fingerprint results from the garage accident case. He reviewed the paperwork.

"Well? What's it say?" Officer Stone asked.

"I don't believe this."

"Believe what?"

"Two sets of prints were found in the garage. One set obviously belonged to the owner, Turner."

"No surprise there."

"The other set, found on the garage door opener wall unit, belonged to our man of the hour—Mark Collins."

"No way."

"Prints don't lie. See for yourself." Officer Gonzalez offered the file to his partner.

"For a dead guy, he's sure been busy." Stone perused the report. "Is the warrant in that other folder?"

"Yup. We're good to go."

On his feet, Officer Stone replied, "Hopefully, we'll beat those kids there."

Sara opened her eyes and looked at the clock on the nightstand. Three solid hours of sleep had improved her headache. She slipped out of bed and listened at the door for any noises. Not hearing any, she opened it. As she peered into the darkness, she observed Mark's closed bedroom door. The time for escape was upon her. It was now or never.

She steeled herself and crept downstairs, careful to walk on the far edges of the wood stairs to minimize any creaking noises. Slowly and quietly, she tiptoed through the foyer and hallway. She stopped in the family room. A quick search in the spaces around the couch and chair cushions didn't produce a cordless phone. Down the hall, in the downstairs bedroom, she found a cell phone charger plugged into the outlet. However, a search of the drawers and under the bed did not produce the cell phone. Resolute, she made her way to the kitchen. If she couldn't call for help, maybe she could escape on her own.

In the kitchen, Sara rummaged through the drawers in the dark. Her attempt failed to locate any car keys or cell phone. She turned to cross to the other side of the kitchen, tripped over the garbage pail, and fell against the old gas stove, inadvertently turning the oven on. Suddenly, she remembered there was an old rotary phone in the barn. That ringing phone had interrupted one of their hayloft romps.

She opened the kitchen door and held the screen door to make sure it didn't slam shut after she closed the interior door. Once clear of the house, she hurried across the gravel driveway to the barn. The door was unlocked. She passed through and secured the door behind her.

The moon shined brightly, and millions of stars lit the clear evening sky. A row of small, dirty windows on the ground floor let some light through—enough light to move around once her eyes adjusted. She remembered that the phone had been in a small office in the back of the barn. In daylight, she would have worked her way through the equipment. In darkness, there were too many shadows. She didn't want to risk getting injured. As she considered her options, the light in Mark's bedroom came on.

Sara scrambled to reach the office. She hugged the wall, bypassing the maze of farm equipment in the center of the barn until she reached the office door. The doorknob didn't turn. The office was locked. She kicked the door. It didn't budge. Sara looked around and then up at the loft. Backtracking to the wood ladder, she gave it a good shake, confirming it was solidly in place. She climbed it. At the top, she crawled over to the sole window in the loft that faced the house. Her head was beginning to bother her again.

Mark's bladder had awakened him. After taking care of business, he checked on Sara. The master bedroom door hung ajar. He approached the room and peered inside. She wasn't in bed. Entering the room cautiously, he called out, "Sara, are you all right?" There was no reply. The bathroom was empty as well. Retracing his steps, he shouted, "Sara! Where are you?"

Joe and David parked their cars behind the line of trees, just short of the driveway to Mark Collins' house. Joe popped his trunk and extricated two baseball bats. David got out of his Chevelle and walked over to the passenger side of Joe's Grand Prix. Joe offered him one of the bats. For a moment, they stood there in silence, protected by the tree line, leaning on the bats, staring at the house in the darkness.

"What are we waiting for?" Laura asked.

Joe leaned into his front passenger-side window, where Laura sat. "You girls need to stay in the car."

Laura objected with disgust in her voice. "Are you kidding? I'm going with you." She opened her door.

Joe closed it before she could get out.

"What the hell?" Laura protested, attempting to reopen the door.

Leaning on the door, Joe lectured, "You're not going with us. Dave and I can take care of ourselves. We can't worry about having to protect the two of you. Our focus has to be on Sara."

Laura glared at him. "We can take care of ourselves."

"I disagree," David stated, swinging the bat to get a better feel of it.

"Of course you do," Laura said, crossing her arms, refusing to abandon the idea of opening the door.

As they argued, a police car pulled in behind the Chevelle. Officers Raul Gonzalez and Rob Stone approached them.

Joe greeted them. "Nice night, Officers." Joe hid the bat behind him.

Officer Stone responded, "Evening, everybody. But I think we can cut the pleasantry bullshit. I see you didn't heed my warning."

"No. We didn't," Joe admitted.

"Good thing we got here when we did. We've got the search warrant." Officer Gonzalez waved the paper around. "We're going to do this properly. Understand?"

They all nodded.

"For some reason, I'm not getting a good feeling here." Officer Stone eyed them suspiciously.

"So Mark isn't dead after all?" Anna asked.

Officer Stone replied, "What we know for sure is that the dead body in the morgue is not Mark Collins. And, surprisingly, his fingerprints were found at both crime scenes."

"Both crime scenes?" David asked.

"Yes. The one in your garage, as well as the one at the mission," Officer Stone explained. "The way we figure it is that he went to your place to eliminate the competition. When that failed, he kidnapped her."

"Damn," Laura uttered.

"So what are we waiting for?" Joe asked.

Laura waved her hand to catch the men's attention. "Excuse

me." She pointed toward the house. "A light just went on in the house."

Everyone's attention shifted to the house.

Sara watched the house from the barn's loft. Mark's bedroom light was still on. She imagined him methodically searching for her, room by room. She scooted away from the window, into the shadows. To her surprise, she bumped into a cardboard box. Curious, she reached inside. She pulled out a book that rested on top. Interestingly, it wasn't dusty. The loft lacked sufficient light to identify the object she held. Sara inched closer to the window again. Sitting cross-legged, she opened the book. The discovery wasn't just any book. It was a diary—Mark's diary.

Laura reported, "A second light just came on upstairs."

"Stay here," Officer Stone ordered.

Joe and David exchanged glances.

Sensing dissension, Officer Stone asked, "You're not going to stay here, are you?"

"No. We're not," David and Joe replied truthfully.

Quickly, Joe added, "But the girls will stay here."

Officer Gonzalez said, "Good." He checked his service revolver. In doing so, he revealed a stun gun hanging from his belt.

"Hey, we didn't agree to that," Laura argued.

"It's four against two. You girls are staying here, in the car," David declared definitively.

The men headed up the driveway.

"You suck!" Laura called after them.

Joe waved in return.

Anna breathed a sigh of relief. "I'm glad that's settled."

"You're such a wuss," Laura replied.

Officer Gonzalez instructed Joe and David. "Just stay behind us, and stay out of the way."

Officer Stone checked his weapons as they approached the house. He said, "We've been using our stun guns with a high rate of success. We're hoping to subdue the target with them. We'd rather not have to use deadly force."

Office Gonzalez continued. "That means you guys have to stay way behind us, out of the line of fire. Fact is, you shouldn't even be here. This is against protocol. And by the way, ditch the bats."

"But ..." Joe protested.

"I don't want to hear it. Drop 'em," Officer Gonzalez demanded.

Joe and David dropped their bats in the grass.

"Good. Since you're staying behind us, you won't need them anyway," Officer Stone reminded them.

Joe said, "We'll stay behind you, but if he somehow gets by the two of you, Dave and I will tackle him."

"You've got that right," David replied.

"I don't think he'll get by both of us. If he does, have at it," Officer Stone said.

Having resolved that issue, the officers discussed the plan of attack as they surveyed the farmhouse. The men hugged the tree line that bordered the long driveway.

Mark received no response when he turned on the hallway light. He proceeded to the other bedroom. Then he switched on the downstairs light and climbed down the flight of stairs. The front door was still locked. He opened it and squinted into the dark night. Nothing could be seen past the front porch.

As soon as the front door opened, the four men halted abruptly. Motionless, they observed Mark's movements.

The outside temperature had cooled down considerably. Subsequently, Mark left the door open to let some air in. Not finding Sara in the family room, he searched the downstairs bathroom. He even pulled back the shower curtain. His brother's room and the kitchen were empty as well. That left only one place to search—the basement. Obtaining a flashlight from the utility drawer in the kitchen, Mark headed toward the basement door.

As Sara read, tears welled up in her eyes. Mark's diary entries revealed agonizing, internal torture. She read about the terror he had experienced in prison—how it had forced him to fake suicide attempts. Then came the drugs, the confusion, the intense bouts of rage, depression, and loneliness. It was all there in black and white. Hope, briefly mentioned, was only associated with her. She wiped away tears and continued reading. In great detail, Mark described how he had managed to switch places with his brother and that Matt had died unexpectedly. There was a lengthy passage concerning how he had set out to kill his new adversary with his own Camaro but had crushed someone else instead.

Sara realized David was in serious danger and wondered who had died in his place. Although appalled at what the journal revealed, she forced herself to continue reading. She discovered how Mark had abducted her earlier that day and the anguish he had felt about causing the Baptist preacher's death. Her heart ached for what his obsession had caused him to do in the name of love. His reality was twisted and sick. She pitied him. The pounding in her head increased the more she read.

As the four men resumed their approach to the house, they observed some long pauses between lights coming on.

Across from the front porch, Officer Stone instructed, "You two stay here, out of sight and harm's way. Gonzalez and I have it covered."

Officer Gonzalez crossed the gravel driveway and stationed himself near the open front door. He stood off to the side, so Mark couldn't see him through the screen door. Officer Stone bent low and reached the kitchen door without being detected.

Officer Stone peered through the kitchen door window. He radioed to Officer Gonzalez. "I've got a visual on the suspect. He's in the hallway, headed toward the kitchen."

"Copy."

Mark walked back to the kitchen, doubting himself. "There's no sign of her. Did I imagine that Sara was here? Was it all a dream? I thought she was here. I carried her upstairs when she arrived. Then we ate dinner together. When she got tired, we went to sleep in our separate rooms. We'll stay in separate rooms until we're married. That's the proper way to do it. But where is she now?"

He reconsidered. "Wait a minute. This is a nightmare. That's it! Duh. We went to sleep. This is just another nightmare of everyone leaving me. When I wake up, Sara will be here. Yes! That's exactly what's going on. I just have to wait until I wake up. Then everything will be perfect again. And Sara and I will be happy."

"We'll pound on the door on the count of three," Officer Stone said, stun gun in hand, safety lock off.

"Copy. On three," Officer Gonzalez confirmed, stun gun at the ready.

On the count of three, both officers pounded on the doors in front of them and shouted, "Police! Open up! We've got a warrant!"

Confused, Mark froze.

Laura squirmed in Joe's front seat. "I can't sit here any longer."

"We promised we'd stay here," Anna reminded.

"Actually, we didn't. This waiting is driving me crazy." Laura exited the vehicle.

"Where are you going?" Anna opened her door.

Laura lied, "Not far, just to the driveway."

Anna got out of the car. "Then I'm coming with you."

Silently, Joe and David joined the officers. Joe joined Officer Gonzalez at the front door. David coupled with Officer Stone at the kitchen door.

Sara heard men yelling and looked up from the diary. Wiping the glass with her hand to see more clearly, she saw two figures at the kitchen door.

Officer Gonzalez ordered from the front of the house, "Open up! Police! We've got a search warrant. We've got you surrounded. Open up, and nobody will get hurt."

From their posts, both officers watched Mark sit down on a kitchen chair. He clutched something shiny in his right hand.

Officer Gonzalez entered the house through the front door.

Officer Stone opened the screen door. David grabbed it. A glance was exchanged between the men, right before Officer Stone kicked in the kitchen door.

Joe followed Officer Gonzalez inside. "Do you smell something?"

"You were supposed to stay outside, on the other side of the driveway," Officer Gonzalez scolded.

The splintering of the kitchen door surprised Mark. He jumped up to avoid the flying debris, flashlight in hand.

Officer Stone barreled through the rough opening. He pressed the trigger on his stun gun.

Officer Gonzalez inhaled. He recognized the smell. "Gas."

The fiery explosion shook Sara in her perch. Instinct caused her to hold the diary up to shield her face. The barn shook and moaned.

Laura and Anna were halfway up the driveway when the flash lit up the sky. In an instant, fire engulfed the back of the house.

Sara lowered the diary and dropped it. She screamed and frantically scrambled across the loft floor to the top of the ladder. Trembling, she made her way down. She missed the last two rungs and fell to the ground, scraping her arms on the unfinished wood. She struggled to her feet.

Unlike earlier, she didn't need to feel for the wall. The light from the fire burned brightly enough that she could see clearly. She ran the length of the barn and tugged hard to open the door.

Laura and Anna were running toward the house when they heard Sara's screams. They couldn't pinpoint the direction of the screaming. They feared she was trapped inside.

"Sara!" Laura yelled.

Sara emerged from the barn. She collapsed, stunned, no longer crying.

Laura dashed to Sara. She tried to comfort her. "You're going to be fine. We're here now. You're safe."

"Oh my God!" Sara exclaimed, staring at the house in shock.

Laura held her. "You're going to be fine."

"But they're not," Sara stammered. "They're still in there."

Laura glanced at the inferno. Her heart sank. There was no sign of any of the men.

Anna said, "You stay here with her. I'm calling 9-1-1." She rushed to find the address number on the front of the house.

Sara pulled away from Laura. "What happened? Why did they blow the house up? They didn't have to blow it up."

Laura shook her head. "I don't think they meant to do that. I think that part was an accident."

"It was all a big mistake. He didn't want to hurt me. Mark loved me in his sick, twisted way. He's so screwed up. He's *really* mentally ill. I can't believe it. It seemed like he couldn't help himself. He did horrible things. He didn't mean to kill his brother or the preacher. They were accidents. He wanted to kill David, but somebody else died by mistake instead. We have to warn David."

Laura interrupted, "It was a teenager, Bill Greenwood. He's not dead, Sara. He's in the hospital. He's not dead. Mark thought he was, but he wasn't."

"It was supposed to be David. He tried to kill David."

Laura patted her best friend's back. "It's not your fault. Mark's crazy," Laura reminded her.

Ignoring her, Sara asked, "Who stormed the house?"

Laura didn't respond. She prayed that somehow all of the men would be fine.

"Who are they? Tell me," Sara pleaded. "Who went in there?"

"The police had a warrant. Mark kidnapped you."

"I only saw one man in uniform. The other was in regular clothes. Who was the other guy?"

From the front of the house, Anna yelled, "Help! Come quick! Help!"

Laura helped Sara to her feet. They hurried to join Anna. They arrived in time to see Anna dragging a man off the front porch. The fire was quickly advancing, enveloping the front portion of the house.

Anna called out, "Over there! I've got one of the cops." Using her head to gesture, she motioned toward a second man lying on the porch. "He dragged the cop out before collapsing. You need to grab him before the fire gets closer."

Laura sprinted up the steps. Sara followed at a much slower pace.

The unconscious man's ankles were closest to Sara. She grasped them. Laura lifted the man under his arms. When Laura heaved him up, Sara saw Joe's face.

Sara screamed, "It's Joe! Why didn't you tell me it was him?"

"There's no time to discuss this now. We've got to move him!" Laura yelled.

They carted Joe down the porch stairs. They placed him gently on the grass, next to Officer Gonzalez, well away from the house.

Anna performed CPR on the unconscious police officer. Laura assisted.

Sara brushed Joe's hair back with her fingers, off his forehead. She pressed her ear to his chest. She listened to his heartbeat, the rhythm of which she knew so well. The beat seemed strong and steady. His breathing was a bit labored. His clothes were singed. As far as she could tell though, his handsome face was dirty but unharmed. Sara gently caressed Joe's cheek and kissed his lips. She hovered over him until the emergency vehicles arrived.

Two fire trucks and an ambulance responded to the call. Firefighters dragged hoses toward the inferno.

Approaching one of the firefighters, Laura said, "There are still three people missing." Gazing at the burning house, Laura didn't believe they would be found alive. It would take a miracle to withstand the initial blast, the fire, the heat, and the smoke.

"Don't worry. We'll get them out," the firefighter responded. He rechecked his helmet and pulled the hose up the driveway.

Two emergency medical technicians rushed to the front lawn where the girls guarded the injured men. They split up to assess both victims. Anna stopped performing CPR. She moved away to let the medic take over. Sara didn't budge from Joe's side.

The EMTs quickly started IVs and intubated both victims. After several jolts from the defibrillator, Officer Gonzalez regained normal sinus heart rhythm.

Sara anxiously questioned the man working on Joe. "How is he? Is he going to be okay?"

"He's struggling for air. I've intubated him. He's getting 100 percent oxygen. We need to get him to the hospital for a full evaluation," the EMT responded.

"Thank God they got out in time," Sara said with a sigh.

As the girls sat in the grass, headlights blinded them momentarily. They squinted. The headlights darkened. A person approached the group.

John Lombardi tilted his head. "What are you guys doing here?"

"John?" Laura inquired.

"Yeah."

Sara said, "I'm so glad you're here."

John replied, "I'm sure the crew is fighting the fire fine without me. Today's my day off. I just heard about the call on my radio. I was close by. I figured I'd check it out. Then I saw Joe's car in the street. What's going on?"

Sara rushed over to John. "It was terrible." She became lightheaded, lost her balance, and fell toward him. He caught her in his arms and guided her to sit on the ground.

Kneeling beside her, John asked, "Sara? Are you okay?"

"I'll be fine. I'm just ... overwhelmed."

John looked up at Laura and Anna. "I'll ask again. What's going on?"

Sara pulled back. "Psycho boy went totally psycho this time. He kidnapped me. Joe tried to rescue me. Then the house blew up. Joe's unconscious."

"I'm confused. Didn't psycho boy die recently?" John questioned.

"We thought he did," Laura replied.

John looked over at Joe, lying motionless on a backboard. Sara crawled over to Joe and held his hand. Laura and Anna stood side by side. They didn't have the heart to tell Sara the rest of the story yet.

Joe's medic announced, "All right, people. We need to get out of here and get these two to a hospital."

"I want to come with you," Sara said.

"Sorry, there's not enough room. You can meet us there," the EMT replied.

John and the girls watched as Joe Lazaro and Officer Raul Gonzalez were loaded into the ambulance. The doors closed, and the ambulance departed with sirens blaring.

Sara begged, "We have to leave."

Laura stalled. "In a minute. I need to tell John something. Anna, you stay with Sara." She pulled John aside, so Sara wouldn't overhear their conversation.

John asked, "What?"

"There's a longer story. There are still three people inside that burning house. Sara doesn't know it yet. One of the guys is her current boyfriend."

"Turner?"

"Yes. I don't want her to see his car in the street."

"The car sandwiched between Joe's car and the squad car?"

"Exactly. That's why I need you to drive her to the hospital, but go the other way down the street. That way she won't see it."

"It's a longer way around. I'm sure she'll say something."

"Make up a story—like the cops blocked the road because of the fire or something. Be creative."

"She's going to find out sooner or later, you know."

"Later is better. I don't think she can take much more. You saw her. She can't even stand up. Can you please do this for me?"

"Yeah, it's no problem."

"Thank you. I'll drive Joe's car. He left the keys in it."

"Are you all right?"

"I will be. This has just been a horrible day for all of us. I just want this day to be over."

"Hang in there. If you need something, let me know."

"Thanks, John." Laura hugged him, to John's surprise. Before today, they had never shared a hug, but he gladly reciprocated.

Sara yelled to them, "What's taking so long? We need to get to the hospital!"

Laura answered, "John is going to take you to see Joe. I just wanted to let him know that Anna and I would follow you in Joe's car. He left the keys in the ignition."

"I need to go now. Can you take me? Please?" Sara implored.

"Sure," John replied.

As they walked toward the cars, they heard several firemen yelling. Turning, they witnessed something being carried out of the house.

John whispered, "Laura, I hope you have a Plan B."

"Damn. I was hoping we'd be gone before this," Laura answered.

Sara asked, "What are they yelling about?"

John wrapped his arm around Sara's waist and led her toward his blue Mustang. "It's just firefighting stuff. Probably nothing to worry about. Let's go."

In the background, a man loudly proclaimed, "We've got three bodies here!"

John cringed as Sara stopped dead in her tracks.

Sara looked at her friends. "There were three other people in the house?"

Anna answered, "Mark and another policeman."

"That's only two. Who's the third?" Sara pressed.

Her girlfriends looked at the ground, not wanting to answer.

Sara demanded, "Tell me!"

Laura put her arm around Sara. "We're so sorry, Sara."

"Why? Who else was in that house?"

"It was David," Anna finally admitted.

"No!" Sara screamed, tearing away from Laura's embrace. "No! It can't be. He didn't know about Mark. He didn't know!"

Laura explained, "He came with us to help rescue you. We're so sorry."

"No! I don't believe it! I need to see him!"

Adrenaline kicked in. Sara took off running.

John realized the girls weren't going to help. He ran after Sara, catching her just before she reached the bodies. He grabbed her and held her tightly. She squirmed and flailed wildly. John managed to physically restrain Sara, despite her attempts to the contrary.

"Sara! Stop!" John pleaded.

"No! I have to see him! You don't understand!" She pounded at him with clenched fists.

John squeezed her closer. "I *do* understand, believe me. *I do.* I can't let you look at him. He's burned too badly. You don't want to ruin the last memory you have of his face. *Trust me.* I've been doing this a long time. You won't be able to get the picture out of your head. I won't let you do that to yourself."

In her heart, Sara knew John was right. She sobbed and eventually went limp in his arms. "You win."

"It's not about winning. I care about you."

"I know. I'm so tired, and my head hurts."

Confident that Sara had given up on the notion of viewing David's body, John loosened his grip.

Sara leaned against him, unable to hold herself up. "Can we please go to the hospital now? I need to see Joe."

"Yeah, let's go. I'll help you to the car."

John held on to Sara as they made their way back to his Mustang. Anna and Laura waited for them. John opened the door. Sara slid into the passenger seat.

Laura said, "Thank you, John. I don't know what we would have done if you hadn't shown up when you did."

"No problem. Glad I was here to help. I'll take her over to County General. We'll see you there."

"Okay," Laura replied.

The girls walked to the cars in silence. Before getting into the Pontiac, Laura tested the Chevelle's door handle. The door didn't budge—it was locked. She knew that David would have taken his keys with him, but she felt the need to try.

Anna asked, "What's going to happen to the car?"

"They'll have to tow it."

"Sad."

"Yup. This whole day is tragically sad," Laura agreed.

Chapter 17

When Laura and Anna arrived at County General Hospital, they entered through the emergency room entrance. A swarm of people surrounded the main desk in front of them. The waiting areas to the left and right teemed with sick, broken, and bleeding people.

Anna turned to Laura. "It'll be quicker if we split up. I'll look over here on the left—you look on the other side."

After a brief search, Laura spotted John and Sara on her side of the waiting room, near the windows. "Hey, Anna!" Standing on her tiptoes, she waved and yelled, "They're over here."

Anna and Laura approached John and Sara. Sara sat hunched over, with her head in her hands.

Laura asked, "Any word yet?"

Sara was startled.

John answered, "No. But I just thought of something. Has anybody called Mrs. Lazaro?"

They exchanged glances.

Laura replied, "No. But I nominate you since you know Joe's family so well."

"Chicken," he challenged.

"You bet I am," she responded. "Think of it as taking one for the team."

"Uh huh. Nice spin." He held up his cell phone. No signal. The search for a signal ensued. Once he exited the ER doors, the phone registered a signal. He pressed speed dial number two. He tapped his right foot, waiting anxiously for someone to answer the phone. To his relief, Joe's brother, Tony, picked up the phone.

"Hello?"

"Hey, Tony, it's John."

"Hey. What's going on?" he asked, with a mouthful of salt and vinegar potato chips.

"Is your mother in the room with you?"

"No. Do you know what time it is?" Tony reached for his beer. He took several swigs to wash the chips down.

John said, "Yeah, I know. It can't be helped. Don't wake her yet though. I want to tell you the news without her seeing your face when you hear it."

"Huh?" Burping loudly, Tony emptied the beer can and placed it on the coaster his mother insisted he utilize.

"Joe was in an accident earlier tonight," John said, moving out of the way of a man walking toward him with a towel wrapped around a bleeding hand.

"How bad?" He transferred the bag of chips from his lap to the couch cushion next to him.

John moved farther away from the hospital doors. "We're not sure."

"What the hell does that mean?" Tony wiped the grease off his hands onto his jeans.

"He looked pretty good when I saw him. He didn't regain consciousness at the scene, but I'm sure he'll be fine in no time."

"Was the car totaled?"

"It wasn't a car accident." John walked along the sidewalk, toward the handicapped parking spots.

"Then what kind of accident was it?"

"He was in a house fire."

"A house fire? You're kidding." Tony switched the phone to his other ear.

"No. His burns weren't anything serious. He did breathe in a lot of smoke. He might have hit his head. We're not sure. He's at County General now."

"Anything else I need to know?"

"I don't know anything else. I just think you guys should get to the hospital. Then you'll be here when he wakes up."

"Thanks for calling."

"Thanks for answering. I was praying your mom didn't pick up."

"Yeah. Lucky for you."

"Good luck telling your mom. See you soon."

Tony Lazaro procrastinated. After rinsing the empty beer can, he threw it in the bag containing the cans and bottles to be returned to the store to get the deposits back. He returned the half-empty potato chip bag to the pantry.

Knowing he couldn't avoid the inevitable, Tony flipped on the upstairs hall light and trudged up the stairs and down the hallway to his parents' bedroom. He dreaded knocking on that door in the middle of the night, especially because it was bad news to relay to his parents. He rapped on the door as he turned the knob. He stuck his head in the opening and whispered, "Ma? You up?"

"I am now, Anthony. What is it?"

Opening the door fully, he stepped into the doorway.

Sal continued snoring.

"We just got a call. Joe was in an accident. He's in the hospital."

"Holy Mary, Mother of God!" she exclaimed. The covers flew upward on Rose's side of the bed. Swinging her feet over the side, she thrust her feet into her slippers and jumped out of bed. In her haste to turn the nightstand lamp on, she almost knocked it over. She grabbed the lampshade to steady the lamp, fumbled for the switch, and turned on the light.

"He's going to be fine, Ma."

Rose snapped, "So you're a doctor now? You know this, and you haven't even seen him." Rose opened a dresser drawer, removed undergarments and a pair of knee-high stockings, and threw them on the bed.

"John Lombardi is there. He said he thinks he'll be fine."

She rushed to the closet and selected a pair of dark blue polyester pants and a multicolored blouse. They landed next to the other items on the bed.

Standing with her hands on her hips, Rose looked at her son. "Well, what are you waiting for? I've got to get dressed. I can't go anywhere like this. And I can't get dressed with you in the room. *Out!* And close the door behind you!"

Tony gladly vacated the bedroom.

Rose glanced over at her inert husband. The exchange hadn't disturbed Sal at all. He remained sound asleep. Rose glared at her husband. She removed one of her slippers and threw it at him. The slipper hit him in the back of the head.

Sal awoke and rubbed his head. "Ow! What was that for?"

Satisfied with the result, Rose removed her nightgown and ignored his question.

Confused, Sal rolled over to look at his wife. "Why are the lights on? What time is it?"

"Get up and put some pants on," Rose demanded as she dressed.

"Why?"

"You can't go anywhere like that."

He looked at the clock on his nightstand. "Where the hell do you have to go at this hour?"

"I can't believe you slept through all of that!" she yelled, proceeding to the bathroom.

"Through all of what?" Sal sat up.

"Your son was in an accident. He's at the hospital." She fluffed her hair in front of the bathroom mirror.

"Which son?"

Rose leaned into the bedroom. Scowling at him from the doorway, she asked, "Does it matter?"

"Guess not."

"Well, for your information, it's Joseph. Get up and make yourself presentable. And don't wear a shirt with any holes in it. Comb your hair. We might see people we know."

Sal got out of his warm bed. He shuffled, naked and barefoot, into the bathroom. "What happened?"

"I don't have any details. We just need to get to the hospital."

Sal ran his fingers through his thinning hair. "It'll only take me a couple of minutes to get ready."

"Good." Rose pushed past him, obtained a pair of shoes from

the closet, and put them on. From her jewelry box, she selected a necklace and matching earrings. After completing a cursory once-over in the mirror, she scurried downstairs and into the kitchen. There, Tony stood by the garage door, ready to leave, holding her purse.

"I've got your purse. You don't have to look for it."

"Good," she said, scanning the kitchen. "We need to bring food."

"You want help?" Tony asked, moving forward.

"No. Just stay there, out of my way," she replied.

Tony returned to his original position and leaned against the door.

The stairs creaked, and moments later Sal appeared. He zipped up his pants as he entered the kitchen. "I'm ready to go," he announced, buckling his belt.

Rose said, "I have to wrap up these leftover brownies to bring with us."

"I don't think we're going to need them," Tony stated.

"*Oh really?* Now you're psychic? Obviously, you've been holding out on us all of these years." Rose exhaled loudly. "Anthony, make yourself useful. Get me something to put these in."

Not wanting to upset his mother, Tony didn't point out that she had just refused his offer to help. Instead, he put his mother's purse down on the kitchen table and hunted for a suitable container in the cupboard that held the ever-growing collection of plastic containers.

Rose saved every plastic container that crossed her path—whipped topping containers, take-out food containers, yogurt containers, and ice cream containers, to name a few. They stood in mini-towers—all stacked neatly by size and shape. Their corresponding lids were stacked in the same fashion and sequence next to them.

"We need drinks too." Rose selected a cooler from the floor of the pantry.

Tony chose a large food container. While he transferred the

brownies from the baking pan to the container, he shoved two squares into his mouth, justifying that they probably wouldn't have fit anyway.

Rose walked toward the refrigerator to obtain ice packs and drinks.

Determined to thwart her efforts, Sal positioned himself between his wife and the refrigerator.

Rose ordered, "Move. I need to get in there."

Sal crossed his arms and stood his ground. "No, you don't."

Bewildered, Rose unsuccessfully tried to push him aside. "Get out of my way."

Tony snatched the safely stored brownies. He retreated to his previous position, next to the garage door. This situation was about to turn ugly. He didn't want to be in the immediate vicinity when tempers exploded.

"Sal, I said move." Rose dropped the cooler and pushed her husband with both hands.

Sal didn't budge.

When she tired of pushing and shoving, she started beating his chest. "Why won't you move?"

Sal grasped both of her arms at her wrists. Slowly and forcefully, he said, "Rose, we are not going on a picnic. Our son is hurt. He's in the hospital. He needs us. He's not going to care if you bring brownies or soda pop. You can make him whatever you want when he comes home. So forget about all of this crap. Grab your purse, and let's go. *Now.*" Sal released her arms. They dropped to her sides.

Stunned, Rose stood as still as a statue. Then, as if nothing had happened, she stepped over the cooler, picked up her purse, and proceeded to the door.

Tony opened the door well before his mother reached it. Sal followed her out.

As Sal passed, Tony whispered, "Way to go, Dad."

"I've learned over the years to pick my battles."

Tony tucked the brownies under his arm and closed the door behind him.

Sal drove rapidly to County General Hospital in his champagne-colored Cadillac DTS. He had saved for years to buy this car. He had savored the moment when he rubbed it in his brother's face. Sal and his older brother, Mario, played a healthy game of one-upmanship. Sal truly loved his Cadillac. It had heated leather seats, a navigation system, and power-everything.

Sal had barely maneuvered the car into the parking spot at the hospital when Rose opened her door and jumped out. She rushed toward the emergency room entrance. Pushing her way through the crowd at the desk, she yelled, "Where is he? Where's my son? His name is Joseph Lazaro."

The heavyset, redheaded nurse at the desk replied, "Ma'am, you'll have to wait your turn. There are other people ahead of you."

Tony caught up to his mother at the desk. Sal was just making his way through the door when Rose lamented, "My son could be dying. She's telling me to wait. I might only have a few precious moments left."

The nurse leaned over the desk. "Ma'am, please calm down. You need to wait your turn." She motioned to the other people standing at the desk. "All of these people are in line ahead of you."

Rose ignored the nurse. She turned toward the crowd of people in line and pleaded to no one in particular. "For the love of God and all that is holy, somebody tell me where my Joey is!"

She received no reply.

The motley crowd nearest to her consisted of some coughing people, a few inconsolable babies, and a toddler who amused himself by spinning in circles until he fell. A little farther away, wheelchairs held people clutching injured body parts, while others bled on the floor.

Rose Lazaro, an expert in commanding attention, wasn't getting any of it now. She contemplated her options.

The nurse repeated, "Ma'am, calm down, and get in line."

Rose slowly turned just her head toward the nurse. "I don't have time to stand in that line."

"Ma'am ..."

Rose spun around and advanced to the desk. Perched on her toes, she lunged for the nurse.

The nurse jerked backward to avoid Rose's grasp. Her wheeled chair enabled her to scoot farther away. "I'm warning you, lady. If you don't calm down, I'm calling security."

"This *is* calm. You haven't seen *not calm* yet. I don't think you understand the seriousness of the situation."

"Everybody in line has a serious situation. Otherwise, they wouldn't be here."

"My son could be dying in some hospital bed. He's wondering why I'm not there with him. You need to find him. I need to see my son."

Luckily for everyone, John Lombardi heard Rose's voice. He rushed toward his best friend's mother. He waved and yelled, "Mrs. Lazaro, over here!"

At first, Rose couldn't determine where the voice was coming from. Tony, attempting to guide her, touched his mother's arm.

Pulling away, she screamed, "Unhand me! I'm being manhandled!"

"Ma!" Tony yelled back.

Irritated, Rose remarked, "Oh, it's you."

"Yeah, it's me. Let's go join the others over there," he said, pointing at Joe's friends. While Tony blazed a path through the crowd, he announced, "The show's over, folks. Excuse me. Pardon me. Thank you." Tony successfully guided his mother through the mob and ushered her toward John.

Sal followed.

The redheaded nurse breathed a sigh of relief.

Rose hugged John. "John, where is he? Have you seen him? What did the doctor say?"

"We don't know anything yet," he replied. "We're still waiting. He looked pretty good when I saw him."

Sal asked, "What happened? How did this happen?"

John turned toward the seats. "Why don't we all sit down?"

After they were all seated in the uncomfortable brown vinyl chairs, John attempted to allay their fears. He explained that Joe had been in a house fire and was probably suffering from smoke inhalation.

Rose asked, "His new condominium burned?" She repositioned her handbag, perched on her lap.

"No, it was somebody else's house."

Tony held out the container of brownies. Without speaking, he offered John and the girls some brownies. They all smiled and politely declined.

"Do we know this somebody whose house burned down?" Rose persisted.

At that moment, Sara said, "I don't feel well."

Everyone turned to look at her.

All of the color had drained out of Sara's face. Her eyes were no longer focused.

"You don't look good," Laura replied, moving closer to her.

Rose noted, "She looks lightheaded. Sara, honey, put your head between your knees."

"I'll get some water," Anna offered.

As Anna stood, Sara lost consciousness and slid off the vinyl chair onto the floor.

"Sara!" Laura exclaimed. Jumping up, she rushed to Sara's side.

Anna grabbed a magazine off the nearest table. She fanned Sara with it. Laura knelt on the floor and elevated Sara's head.

"Sara? Sara? Wake up," Laura pleaded, trying to revive her. "I can feel a huge bump on the back of her head." Laura gingerly felt the bump. "The skin isn't broken, but it's a pretty big lump. She didn't hit her head when she slid off that chair. I'm guessing she got it earlier today."

John felt for a pulse on Sara's scraped arms. "It's weak. This isn't good. She's not waking up. She's out cold."

At the top of her lungs, Rose yelled, "Help! We need help here! Help!"

Sal covered his face and shook his head.

Tony amused himself with another brownie.

Rose continued to wave and yell until a nurse and security guard appeared.

The nurse addressed Rose. "This is your last warning. If you don't tone it down, I'm having you escorted off the premises."

Rose stepped aside with her left hand on her hip and her right hand pointing to Sara on the floor. "I'd like to see you try. But right now, this poor girl needs help."

"What happened to her?" the heavyset nurse asked.

Laura answered, "She told us she wasn't feeling well. Then she collapsed."

"Is she on anything?"

"Not that we know of, but she was kidnapped today. I felt a big lump on the back of her head," Laura responded.

Anna added, "We don't know what the kidnapper did to her."

This latest development shocked Rose, Sal, and Tony.

Rose spoke, "*Kidnapped?* Was anyone going to tell us about this? Does this have anything to do with my Joey being in the hospital?"

John said, "Yes, but we need to take care of Sara right now. We'll tell you everything later."

"You bet you will, young man."

The nurse interrupted. "I'll go get a gurney."

John stood. "Forget it. I'll bring her to the gurney."

John scooped Sara off the floor. He accompanied the nurse to the double doors near the desk. Laura followed. The nurse pressed a button. The door opened. John commandeered an empty gurney in the hallway and placed Sara on it.

Laura quickly introduced herself to the nurse and briefed her on Sara's medical history and the day's events.

"Thank you for the information. Please return to the waiting room. We'll call for you shortly."

Helpless, John and Laura watched the nurse wheel Sara into an examination room.

"This day just keeps getting worse by the minute," Laura said.

John reached for Laura's hand and squeezed it. "I'm sure both Joe and Sara will be fine."

Laura unexpectedly blushed at the comforting touch of John's hand. She hoped he didn't notice. "I hope so. Now we have to go back out there and face the one-woman firing squad."

John laughed. "Don't let Mrs. Lazaro hear you call her that."

"I won't tell if you won't."

"Deal."

Exhausted, John and Laura returned to the waiting area.

Rose immediately resumed questioning. "So why did she faint? Was she in the fire too? And what's with this kidnapping nonsense?"

"It's a really long story, Mrs. Lazaro," John said.

Rose put down the tissue she was twisting. "Well, it looks like we have plenty of time to hear it. So start talking. All of you."

Laura explained in detail the beginning of the story with Sara's kidnapping at St. Peter's Mission. Anna picked up the story in the middle, when they realized that Mark Collins was involved. John finished the story, which brought them to where they were presently.

Rose Lazaro listened to the entire tale without interrupting. When they finished, she asked, "Let me get this straight, my Joey was trying to save Sara from the crazy boy?"

"Yes," John confirmed.

Rose raised her right arm and used her hand to punctuate her words. "That's my son—brave and noble—but terribly stupid. Obviously, God was looking out for him today."

"Did I hear someone mention God?" Father Francis asked from behind.

Rose greeted him. "Father! We didn't realize you were here."

"I was upstairs giving a boy his Last Rites," the priest replied.

Reluctantly Laura asked, "For the Greenwood boy?"

"Unfortunately, yes."

"Did he die?" Anna asked timidly.

"No. He's still with us. I must say, it's very grim. Is he the reason that brings you all here at this hour?"

Laura answered. "No. We were originally here for Joe Lazaro.

But while we were waiting, Sara Taylor collapsed here in the waiting room."

"My, my," the priest replied.

Laura continued, "Father, it turned out that Mark Collins was the one who kidnapped Sara. Joe Lazaro and David Turner tried to rescue her. There was a terrible fire. Mark and Officer Stone died in the fire."

"I don't understand. Mark died days ago."

"He actually didn't. It's complicated. And I hate to be the one to tell you ..." Laura couldn't maintain eye contact with the priest and looked down at the brown, stained carpet.

"Tell me what?"

Anna completed Laura's sentence. "David also died in the fire."

The priest made a sign of the cross and sat in a chair. "He was such a wonderful and giving man. It's a terrible, terrible loss. There's been so much pain and loss today."

Silently, everyone agreed. The last twenty-four hours had taken quite a toll. The Reverend Ezekiel Walker, Officer Rob Stone, and David Turner were dead. A teenage victim of a murder attempt, Bill Greenwood, received Last Rites. Joe, Sara, and Officer Gonzalez were hospitalized, their conditions yet unknown.

Father Francis broke the silence. "I'm going to go to the chapel. If anyone would like to join me, you're more than welcome."

Rose replied, "We need to wait here until we receive some word from the doctors on the kids."

"Oh, you're right. Let's pray together here then."

Sal said, "Thank you, Father. We could use a good prayer right now."

"Heavenly Father, hear our prayer in this time of distress. We ask that you bestow your healing power on those in need. Give us the strength and courage to face the trials ahead. We ask you for your guidance. May we feel your love, wherever we may be. We pray for the recovery of those close to us and for the safe delivery into heaven for those who are no longer with us. We ask this through Christ our Lord."

In unison, they responded, "Amen."

"Let us pray together now in the words our Father taught us."

Then Father Francis, Sal, Rose, Tony, Laura, Anna, and John joined hands and recited the Lord's Prayer. Several other people sitting nearby joined in reciting the prayer as well.

When they finished, the priest left for the chapel. As he did so, two uniformed police officers entered the ER. They didn't have to push their way to the desk—people parted for them.

"I'm Officer Vincent Varone. This is my partner, Officer Steve Caruso. We're looking for Officer Raul Gonzalez and Joe Lazaro. They should have been brought in a little while ago."

The desk nurse responded, "I'll see what I can find out. You can wait over there with the mouthy lady. I'll come get you when I know something."

The officers exchanged glances as they walked away.

John met them halfway. "Hey, Vinnie. Steve."

The officers returned his greeting with handshakes and one-armed hugs.

Vinnie said, "John. Long time, no see. Any word on Cousin Joe?"

"No. Nothing. And that's not making your aunt a happy camper."

"And if Aunt Rose ain't happy, nobody's happy."

John agreed, "You got that right."

Steve asked, "We're investigating the fire at the Collins' place. You know anything?"

John replied, "I got there after everything was over. The girls were there. I'm not sure how much they saw, though."

Vinnie said, "We'll need to get their statements."

John looked grim. "Can it wait until later? They're pretty stressed out right now."

Steve answered, "I guess tomorrow will be fine. Hopefully, Gonzalez will be awake soon. Then we can get the story from him."

"Hopefully," John said. "Sorry to hear about Rob. He was a good cop."

"Yeah, he was," Vinnie concurred.

Steve added, "We're going to miss him."

Vinnie stated, "Well, I better go say something to Aunt Rose."

"I'm sure she'd like that," John commented.

The three men walked over to where the group sat.

Vinnie removed his hat. "Hi, Aunt Rose." He bent down, hugged, and kissed her.

"Vinnie. How good of you to come. How's your mother?" Rose asked while giving him a bear hug.

"She's doing good. Hi, Uncle Sal. Tony."

Sal and Tony stood. Vinnie hugged them both.

Sal said, "Good to see you. Thanks for coming."

Rose said, "Join us. Your mother didn't call me yesterday. Should I be worried?"

"No. She's busy trying to get Dad to clean out the garage. I'm staying out of it."

Rose patted the chair next to her. "Here, sit down next to me. Anthony, get up and offer your cousin and his friend some brownies. You boys know the girls?" she asked, motioning to Laura and Anna.

Vinnie answered, "Sara's friends, Laura and Anna, right?"

Vinnie and Steve shook hands with the girls. They exchanged pleasantries.

Vinnie asked, "Where's Sara?"

Laura replied, "She collapsed. We're waiting to hear about her too."

"I didn't know that," Vinnie said.

John interrupted. "It's indirectly related to the fire. It's more we'll tell you about later."

Tony held out the half-empty container. Both officers plucked out brownies.

With a mouthful, Vinnie proclaimed, "Aunt Rose, you make the best brownies."

"Glad you like them." Rose smiled.

"Just don't tell my mother," Vinnie added.

"It will be our little secret." Rose winked at him and beamed.

A portly doctor with neatly combed blond hair emerged from the automatic double doors. "Family for Joe Lazaro?"

"Here." Rose waved. "Over here. I'm his mother."

The doctor glanced up from the chart in his hands. "I'm Dr. Dan Michaels. I'm treating your son. He's suffering from smoke inhalation and some minor burns. He also suffered some head trauma. The brain swelling is mild. We're going to monitor him closely to make sure it doesn't get any worse."

"Oh, dear God." Rose covered her face briefly with her hands. Then she laced her fingers and brought them together in her lap.

"We are using medications to draw the fluid out of his brain. We'll keep him sedated until the pressure subsides."

"My poor baby." She pulled a fresh tissue out of her purse.

"So far, everything is going smoothly. He's responding well to treatment."

Sal asked, "How long will he be like this?"

"Hard to say. He could be back to normal as early as morning. It all depends on how quickly his body recovers and the swelling decreases. But you need to be prepared—it could take days. Each person is different. And even when he goes home, he'll need to take anti-seizure medication for a while, as a precaution."

"Precaution against what?" Tony asked.

"Seizures that he might develop as a result of this injury. It doesn't happen in all cases. We just like to play it on the safe side."

"He'll take all of his medication. I'll see to that. When can we see him?" Rose inquired.

"They're transferring him to a room now. It shouldn't be too much longer. The nurse will let you know."

"Thank you, Doctor," Sal acknowledged.

As the doctor turned to leave, Rose stopped him. "Doctor, what about Sara Taylor? She was brought in too."

"I haven't seen a patient with that name. I'll check with the nurses," Dr. Michaels offered.

Vinnie asked, "How about a cop, Raul Gonzalez?"

"Sorry, I didn't treat him either. I'll check with the nurses."

The doctor disappeared behind the double doors.

The priest reappeared.

"Hello again, Father," Rose said.

"I was about to leave, but I didn't ask if anyone had notified David's parents."

Anna replied apologetically, "We don't know how to reach them."

"I can take care of it. I have their number at the rectory. I'll be back here tomorrow. Perhaps I'll see you then. Good night, everyone."

"Good night, Father," they replied.

Laura poked at Anna. "We didn't call Sara's parents."

"And what do you plan to tell them? We don't know what's wrong with her. I think we should wait until we know more."

"Yeah, I guess you're right."

Moments later, the double doors opened again. This time an older, thin nurse came out.

"Family for Sara Taylor?"

Laura stood up. "I'm her best friend. I have power of attorney."

Everyone looked at her. She explained, "Her parents are incommunicado. Her brother lives in Albany. She asked me if I would do this for her. I said *yes*."

"Follow me," the nurse instructed.

Laura followed the nurse, who ushered her to Sara's bedside. Sara, in a hospital gown, was still unconscious.

The nurse explained, "She was severely dehydrated. We're giving her fluids. She has a concussion, a lot of bruising, and some minor cuts."

"I told the other nurse that she was kidnapped this afternoon. We don't know what the kidnapper did to her. She didn't tell us. Did he ... you know?"

"She wasn't sexually assaulted, if that's what you're wondering."

"Thank God for that. She had to deal with so much today. Her current boyfriend died trying to save her, and her old boyfriend was almost killed in the same accident."

"That's awful. You can sit with her, if you want."

"Thanks. I will."

"My name is Vivian. I'll be around the corner if you need me." The nurse pulled the curtain forward, to separate them from the other patients.

"Thank you."

Laura stared at Sara, then at the monitors. Sara's blood pressure and heart rate were fine, as far as she could tell. She didn't know what all of the other things measured. Sara had suffered so much in one day. It was difficult to believe. Laura knew Sara would need a lot of love and support to recover from this ordeal.

Laura spoke to her unconscious friend. "Good news, Sara. Joe is doing well. They're moving him into a room. His family is here. As soon as they move you to a room, I'm going to call your parents. I figured you might want to talk to them, so they won't worry."

Sara moaned and whimpered softly.

"Sara? Wake up. It's me, Laura."

Laura lifted Sara's left hand and squeezed. Sara moaned louder.

"You're going to be fine. You're safe. I'm here." Laura pressed the call button on the bed.

Moments later, Vivian pulled the curtain back. "You rang?"

"Yes. She's waking up."

The nurse checked the monitors and rubbed her knuckles on Sara's upper torso. "Sara? Wake up, honey. Sara?"

Sara opened her eyes. "My head hurts."

Vivian nodded. "I'll give you something for the pain in a minute. How many fingers am I holding up?"

"Two."

"That's good. What's your name?"

"Sara Taylor."

"Do you know what day it is?"

"Yes." Sara started crying.

In a consoling tone of voice, Vivian said, "You're fine. You're safe now. You're in the hospital."

Sara's crying increased.

The nurse persisted, "Sara, you need to calm down."

"I can't. They're all dead because of me," she said, sobbing.

Laura and Vivian made several attempts to pacify her. However, Sara remained highly agitated.

Vivian turned to Laura. "I'm going to have to sedate her. She can't continue like this. It's not good for her. I'll be right back."

Waiting for the nurse to return, Laura held Sara's hand, not knowing what else to do. Sara continued to cry.

After a few minutes, Vivian returned with a syringe and injected the contents into Sara's IV. "She'll sleep now. Why don't you go stretch your legs? I'll have you paged if there's a change."

"Thanks."

Visibly shaken, Laura returned to the waiting room. She rejoined the Lazaro family and friends, minus the police officers. They were en route to find Officer Gonzalez.

John stood and offered her his chair next to Anna. "Laura, what happened?"

Laura accepted the chair. "She's unconscious again."

John sat on her other side.

"Again? So she was awake?" Rose asked.

"It was terrible. She was so upset. We couldn't calm her down. The nurse had to sedate her. She thought it was best, considering what Sara went through today."

"I'd say so. You look like you need a hug." Rose navigated around the table and hugged Laura.

"Thank you, Mrs. Lazaro."

"It's what any mother would do, dear," she said, reassuring her.

A different nurse with long, straight, blonde hair emerged from the double doors. "Family for Lazaro?"

Sal held up his hand. "Over here."

The nurse stated, "He's settled in his room. You can see him now. Follow me."

The entourage's search for Joe's room number ended on the fifth floor. The nurse entered the room. The visitors remained in the hallway. From the doorway, they could see inside the private room. In addition to the bed, there were two chairs and a wide window ledge for flowers and cards. A small television was positioned near the ceiling in a corner of the room. Joe had numerous monitor wires and tubes sticking out of him.

The nurse stood at the door. "You can come in. He's unconscious, but he can hear you. Don't be afraid to talk to him."

John said, "I think Mr. and Mrs. Lazaro should go in first. We'll stay out here for now."

"We can take shifts," Laura suggested.

"That's a good idea," Anna concurred.

Tony told his parents, "They got a point. You two go in. I'll relieve you when you need a break."

Sal and Rose entered their son's room.

Laura went to the nurse's station. She asked if Sara was in a room yet. The nurse picked up the phone and dialed.

Salvatore and Rose Lazaro hovered over their son.

"Sal, he's so still. He's never been this still in his whole life. He's always in motion, this one."

Sal put his arm around his wife. "He's going to be all right. He's a fighter. He's in good hands. You'll see." He kissed her forehead.

Rose hugged her husband. "I don't know what I'd do if anything happened to him."

"Forget about it. He's going to be up and around and driving you crazy in no time."

Vinnie Varone drove home after checking on Raul Gonzalez. Raul was awake but still intubated. He was able to relay the events that led up to the fire at the Collins' house, by writing them on paper. The doctors believed he would make a full recovery.

Vinnie arrived home in time for breakfast. He apprised his mother, Carm, and his grandmother, Marie, of the evening's events. By midmorning, the entire extended family had been notified.

Vinnie's mother and grandmother busied themselves in the kitchen. As soon as visiting hours at County General started, Rose's and Sal's relatives filled the two waiting rooms on the fifth floor. Carm carried in a large cooler with a variety of sandwiches. Marie brought several containers of homemade cookies. Cousin

Gina had picked up various salads at Carmine's Deli. Mario, his wife, Jeanine, and their boys, Bobby and Jimmy, carried in pastries. The relatives who couldn't come sent flowers or fruit baskets.

Joe's room was overflowing with food, flowers, and well-wishers. Nurses could barely squeeze through the mob to take Joe's vital signs. The staff was forced to order people out of the room.

Chapter 18

JOHN Lombardi spent the day shuttling between Joe's room and Sara's room. When he entered Sara's room again, he suggested that Laura and Anna take a break. "Why don't you come over and eat with Joe's family? They've got enough food to feed an army and then some."

Laura replied, "Sara's nurse is about to fill us in on Sara's lack of progress. I need to hear what she has to say."

John looked at the nurse. "Well, Vivian, you can come too. I'm sure you wouldn't mind having a sandwich or a cookie while you explain things."

"Actually, I'm due for a break. So I'd love to," Vivian said.

They were greeted warmly by the family. Offers of food came at them from every direction. As they ate, the nurse described how Sara became hysterical each time they brought her out of sedation.

Rose overheard. "Let me talk to her the next time."

Anna said, "You've already got your hands full with Joe."

Rose spread out her arms. "Look around. There's a sea of people here to see my son. I think I can spare some time for my future daughter-in-law."

"Um, they're not dating," Laura responded.

"I know all about their stupid *arrangement*. I'm going to take care of *that* too. So let me know when I need to go see her."

Vivian suggested, "We can try again at the top of the hour."

"Good. I'll be there."

A plethora of relatives were in Joe's room laughing and carrying on. The noise greatly exceeded an acceptable level. A nurse marched in and ordered them to keep it down. She also instituted a limit of three visitors at a time. She waited while they determined who would leave.

Vivian alerted Rose that she was going to bring Sara out of sedation again.

Before Rose marched off to Sara's room, she announced, "I've got something to take care of. I'll be right back."

The noisy crowd didn't seem to notice.

Rose sat in the uncomfortable chair next to Sara's bed.

Vivian cut off the sedative to Sara's IV.

After a few minutes, Sara awoke, groggy. Rose's presence surprised her. "Mrs. Lazaro?"

"Yes, dear."

Sara panicked. "Did something happen to Joe?"

"He's the same. He's going to be fine." Rose patted Sara's hand.

Sara relaxed.

Rose continued, "Right now, I'm concerned about you."

"Me? Why?"

"From what your friends tell me, you had quite the trying day."

Sara started to weep again.

"Stop! You stop that crying, *right now,*" Rose ordered. She handed Sara a tissue.

"But …"

"But nothing. Do you realize how lucky you are?"

"But I'm responsible. It's all my fault." Sara sobbed.

"That crazy boy was responsible for everything that happened. So you get that idea right out of your mind."

"If it wasn't for me, they'd still be alive."

"Maybe. Maybe not. God has plans for all of us. And since you're still alive, God still has plans for you."

Sara continued to cry.

Rose handed her the box of tissues on the table. "Blow your nose and stop that sniveling. You think you've been through a lot? We've all been through a lot. Do you think you're the only person suffering right now?"

"No," Sara replied.

"That's right. There's a whole hospital full of people suffering—in these beds and in the waiting rooms. You've got to pull yourself together."

"It's hard."

"Of course it is. But you're alive, and you need to make the most of your life. And as far as your lost loved ones are concerned, don't you think you owe them at least that much?"

"Yes."

"Let me tell you something personal. I don't go around broadcasting this to non-family members. It's very upsetting. So this is between you and me. *Capisce?*"

"Yes, I understand."

Rose took a deep breath. "Before Anthony and Joseph were born, I lost my first child during childbirth, after eighteen hours of labor, because of a doctor's error. We were going to name her Theresa. I should have a daughter. But it wasn't to be. Instead, I have two beautiful sons. And *that* ... *that* is what I concentrate on. Trust me, we all have our crosses to bear."

"I'm so sorry. I didn't know." Sara blew her nose.

"My point is that some of us have to deal with terrible, almost unspeakable things at times. God doesn't give us more than we can bear. Didn't you pull yourself together after your brother died?"

"Yes."

"And you're going to get through this too. Do you know why?"

Sara played with the edge of her sheet.

"Sara, look at me."

Sara lifted her tear-stained face.

Rose took Sara's hands in her own and held them tightly. "You are going to get through this because you are a young, beautiful, and strong girl. And because, by God, I'm going to help you."

"Why would you do that?" Sara asked incredulously.

"Because my son loves you and wants to spend the rest of his life with you. You're destined to be together. That's why."

"Did he tell you that?"

"Silly girl, he didn't need to *tell* me that. I *know it* in my heart."

"But ..."

"Don't you argue with me, young lady. He loves you. He came back from Italy for you. I'm telling you this is the way it is. So that's the way it is. *Capisce?*"

Sara nodded.

"Good. Now let's get you on the mend. No more crying for you. You need to be strong."

Rose stood up and warmly embraced Sara. When they separated, Rose pointed her right index finger at Sara. "Now you remember what I said."

"I will."

"If you don't, you'll have to deal with me. Now you rest and recuperate. I want you to think about the beautiful life you have ahead of you with my son and my grandchildren."

"I'll try."

"*No.* There's no trying. Just do it! I know you have it in you. You will find your inner strength. Remember that God will see you through this."

"Thank you, Mrs. Lazaro."

"You're welcome, dear. Now get some rest. I can check on you again later if you'd like."

"I'd really like that. Thank you."

Rose departed, leaving Sara alone with her thoughts.

Sara sat in quiet contemplation, reflecting on her life. This ordeal had provided a sorely needed wake up call. For years, she spoke of wanting to make a difference in the world. She never knew how. Today, she realized what she must do. Fate had stepped in to help her decide. A sense of calm washed over her, giving her the confidence to make a change.

After her epiphany, she dwelled on Rose's words—she and Joe were destined to be together. She believed it to be true. Following Rose's instructions, Sara imagined her wedding day—her dress and the flowers. She pictured Joe, dressed to impress, in a black tuxedo. She didn't care where they went on their honeymoon. As long as they were together, it would be perfect. They would have two children, a boy and a girl. Both would have Joe's dimples and wavy black hair. The future would hold wonderful opportunities if she would just embrace her destiny.

Rose checked in on her son after her counseling session with Sara.

Sal happily informed her, "While you were gone, they removed his ventilator. They've replaced it with an oxygen tube. The doctor said they'll continue to reduce his medications too."

Rose said, "Thank God. It's a miracle! I'm going to the chapel to light a candle."

Sal asked, "Do you want company?"

"No. I'm good."

Laura stopped her. "How did it go with Sara?"

"As far as I'm concerned, it's problem solved."

"How did you manage that?" Laura asked.

"For me to know, dear. I can't give away all of my secrets."

Anna said, "I don't care how you did it, as long as she's going to be all right."

"She'll be fine. She just needs a little time. I just reminded her of what a wonderful future she has ahead of her. She needs to concentrate on that."

"I'm glad you were able to reach her, Mrs. Lazaro," Laura said.

"All in a day's work as a mother. You girls will know what that's like some day. I'm going to the chapel. I'll be back."

Exiting the chapel, Rose ran into her nephew, Vinnie, in the hallway. He was carrying a cake container. "This is my second trip from the car. I had to go back out for the cake. After Grandma Marie made three more batches of cookies, she made this chocolate cake. She said it couldn't hurt."

"That's Mama for you."

They arrived to find a smattering of relatives, as well as Laura, Anna, and John, eating dinner in the waiting room.

"Who brought dinner?" Rose asked.

Sal answered with his mouth full. "I don't know. I can't keep track. People are coming and going like it's Grand Central Station. Somebody brought salads, pasta, and garlic bread. You know I don't turn down free food."

Wiping his mouth, John said, "I think it was Cousin Gina."

"At least somebody was paying attention. Thank you. You're a good boy." Rose patted John's shoulder.

Sal asked Vinnie, "What have you got there?"

Rose answered, "My mother made dessert for later."

"To Marie." Sal raised his plastic cup and toasted his mother-in-law.

Marie replied, "Baking is what I do. It's love."

Sara buzzed for a nurse. Doug, a male nurse, answered the call.

Sara asked, "Can I go visit another patient?"

Doug answered, "I don't see why not. Let me get a wheelchair. We'll transfer the IV bag."

Doug wheeled her down to Joe's room.

Carrie, the nurse in Joe's room, said to Doug, "I just got paged. A patient fell. I need to help lift him. I backed off of this one's sedation meds right before the pager went off. Can you watch him?"

"Sure," Doug replied. "I can lift the patient, if you'd rather have me do that."

"No. I'll do it. I'll be back in a couple minutes." Carrie rushed off.

Sara was surprised and relieved that Joe wasn't surrounded by family members. She wondered where they were hiding. Wherever they were now, they were sure to return at any time. She scooted closer to the bed. She stared at Joe for a few minutes in silence.

Cookies in hand, Laura and Anna visited Sara's room and found it empty. They deposited the cookies on Sara's tray.

Anna suggested, "Maybe she's in the bathroom."

"No, the door's open. We would have seen her as we walked in," Laura refuted. "Maybe they took her for more tests. Let's check with a nurse."

Reaching the nurses' station, Laura asked the nurse closest to her, "Has Sara Taylor been taken for testing or something?"

"No. I think she went to another patient's room," the nurse responded.

Laura replied, "Thanks. I know where to find her. By the way, could you tell me the status of a patient named Bill Greenwood?"

The nurse checked the computer. "Looks like he's been upgraded from guarded to critical."

"That's great news. Thanks."

Doug checked Joe's monitor. "He looks stable, and his numbers are good. If anything changes, use the call button. I need to get back."

Sara replied, "No problem. I will."

Then the nurse left Sara alone with Joe.

Sara pressed the latch on the bed and lowered the side bar. "Joe, I'm *so* sorry." She took his hand and kissed it. "I can't believe everything that happened. It was awful. I'm so sorry. Your mom came to talk to me. She got me thinking. I need to focus on what's really important, and that's you. She says we're destined to be together. She says you came back from Italy because of me. You are the most important person in my life. You always have been, and you always will be." She raised his hand and pressed it against her cheek.

She continued, "Remember how I always said I wanted to do something meaningful and make a difference? Well, I've made a decision. I'm going to take over all of David's volunteer duties at St. Peter's Church and Mission. I owe him that much. At least it's a step in the right direction. Maybe I can finally make a difference in somebody's life."

She paused for a minute and squeezed Joe's hand. "I should have told you the night of the beach party that I loved you. I was just scared. I didn't think you loved me. I was afraid you were going to hurt me again. But I'm not afraid anymore. Then there was the night that Laura barged in—I'm sure I would have told you I loved you that night if we hadn't been interrupted. I felt so close to you, so connected. I love you, Joe. I want to be with you. So, *please* wake up. I won't be able to go on without you. I love you so much." Sara kissed his hand.

Weakly and without opening his eyes, Joe said, "The things I have to do so that you'll say you love me."

Sara sat up straight. "Joe?"

"What?" he responded. He opened his eyes and coughed.

Overcome with emotion, Sara sprang out of the wheelchair. Her face was now inches from his.

In a raspy voice, Joe managed to say, "Hey, baby."

"Oh, Joe! *You're awake!* I have to ring for the nurse." She fumbled for the call button.

"No." Joe coughed. "Not yet. Just let me look at you."

Sara smiled.

Joe attempted to clear his throat and coughed again.

"I look like hell." Sara picked at her hospital gown.

He struggled to speak. "I love you, no matter what."

"You should save your strength."

"Why? Are you going to join me in this bed?" He coughed again.

"Now, I *know* you're fine."

Joe smirked. "These gowns do allow for easy access." The twinkle returned to his blue eyes.

Laura and Anna reached the waiting room. The Lazaros were still eating dinner with family and friends.

Laura commented, "We found out that Bill Greenwood is doing better. He got upgraded to critical."

Rose thanked God.

John added, "That's good to hear."

Laura said, "It's nice that you're letting Sara and Joe have time alone together."

John asked, "What are you talking about?"

"The nurse said Sara was visiting another patient. We assumed it was Joe."

Sal said, "We haven't seen her."

Rose questioned the girls. "Did the two of you see her in there?"

Anna answered, "No, we came from the other direction. We didn't pass by Joe's room."

"I'll go check to make sure," John offered. He wiped his mouth with a napkin and squeezed by Tony and Vinnie.

"Like we're letting you go by yourself. Silly boy," Rose said, standing up.

"I'll stay here to guard the food." Tony extended the not-so-magnanimous gesture.

The procession, consisting of John, Rose, Laura, and Anna, journeyed to Joe's room. Rose assumed the lead.

Sara held the straw close to Joe's mouth so he could drink water from his cup. After he took a few sips, she returned the cup to the tray. Joe confessed to Sara, "I've always loved you. I never stopped. *Never.* I'm sorry for hurting you. I was stupid to ever let you go."

"Yes, you were."

"Can you forgive me? I promise I'll *never* do anything to hurt you ever again."

"I'm going to hold you to that." Sara thought for a moment. "And if you screw up, I'll tell your mother. *Then* you'll have to deal with *her* too."

"Bringing out the big guns, aren't you?"

Sara smiled. "Joe, I can't imagine my life without you in it." As she kissed his lips, the search party materialized in the doorway.

Joe replied, "You'll never have to. I promise. I swear I'll spend the rest of my life making it up to you. I know this isn't the right time or place. But I have to make up for lost time." He paused. "Give me your hand."

Sara enveloped his hand in both of hers.

Joe cleared his throat. "I love you, Sara. Will you marry me?"

Rose held her arms out to block anyone from interrupting the moment. They waited anxiously for Sara's reply.

Sara showered Joe's face with kisses. "Yes! Yes! Yes! I can't wait to marry you!"

The voyeurs in the doorway erupted with cheers and clapping. John whistled.

Startled, Joe and Sara turned toward the noise.

"Finally," Laura declared.

"Congratulations, you guys! You deserve each other. And I mean that in a good way," John declared.

"This is wonderful," Anna commented. Then whispering to Laura, she added, "Now she can call her parents herself."

Rose beamed as she crossed her arms in front of her. "I told you it was problem solved. Look at how well things turn out when I get involved. When I'm right, I'm right."

Sara kissed Joe again. "I'm so happy."

Joe replied, "Me too."

"Of course, out of all of the times I dreamt about this moment, I never once imagined you'd propose to me from a hospital bed."

"Well, once we get out of here, I'm sure we'll find a more romantic, secluded setting. Someplace where we can express our love in a more physical and intimate way."

Anna interrupted, "Hello! There's a mother in the room."

Sara blushed and buried her face in Joe's chest.

Joe said, "I could say I'm sorry. But I'm really not. If you don't like it, I'm sure there's a waiting room you could all go to."

Laura agreed. "Good idea. Let's leave them alone."

Rose said, "I knew if I talked to her, I could undo that stupid friend arrangement they had. I should've intervened sooner. I could have had grandchildren by now. Oh well, better late than never. Now I've got a wedding to plan."

Everyone laughed.

Rose wondered aloud. "And speaking of weddings, what are we going to do about the rest of you?"

John, Laura, and Anna looked away from Rose, hoping she'd drop the subject.

Rose studied the body language between Laura and John. "Hmm." She pointed at Laura, then at John. "The two of you make a handsome couple."

Laura blushed.

Rose nodded. "Tell you what I'm going to do. You're all invited to Sunday dinner. Then we'll see what we can do with the two of you." Turning to Anna, she questioned, "You've met my good-looking nephew, Vinnie, right?"

Anna replied, "Yes, ma'am."

Rose continued, "He's a policeman and makes a very good living, you know. He's quite a catch."

Joe interrupted. "Ma ..."

Rose held up her hands. "*What?* All right. I'll stop with the matchmaking for now. Let's leave these two lovebirds alone and go tell the others the good news."

After another round of congratulatory wishes, the group departed for the waiting area.

As they reached their family and friends, Rose proclaimed, "I've got an announcement to make. Everybody, listen up."

The crowd quieted down.

"Joey is awake ..."

"Thank God," Sal interrupted.

"That wasn't the *big* news," Rose stated.

Sal asked, "What's bigger than our son coming out of a coma?"

"If you let me finish, I'll tell you." She cleared her throat for dramatic effect. "Our Joey and Sara Taylor are getting married! He proposed from his hospital bed."

Tony stated, "Wow. I didn't see that one coming."

Vinnie concurred, "Me either."

Marie stood and hugged her daughter, Rose. "My prayers have been answered. I'm going to be a great-grandmother after all."

Carm jumped in. "We've got a bridal shower to plan. Has she picked colors yet? How about a date? Have they picked a date?"

Laura asked, "Aren't we getting a little ahead of ourselves?"

Rose replied, "Honey, it's never too early to plan these things. You'll find that out soon enough."

Tony stood. "Let's go congratulate them."

Rose stopped him. "Wait. Let's give them some time alone together."

"Okay." Tony reclaimed his chair.

Rose looked around, pleased with what she saw. "I just want to say how wonderful it is the way our family and friends come together to celebrate the good times and support us during the not-so-good times. When it comes down to it, the love we have for each other, in our hearts, binds us together. It's the only thing that matters."

Laura agreed. "You're right. Love is the most important thing you can share."

Rose smiled. "So what do you say? Let's share the love. Who wants cake?"

About the Author

Suzanne grew up in Webster, NY. She is a graduate of Our Lady of Mercy High School, Rochester, NY. Although music and writing were her passions, she attended GMI Engineering & Management Institute, Flint, MI, to pursue a career with General Motors.

Never far from the surface, creativity beckoned, and she became a contributor and the editor of the school's underground paper. Shortly thereafter, she was asked to edit the school's official paper.

After graduation, she continued to further her career by earning a Master of Science degree from Kettering University, formerly known as GMI Engineering & Management Institute. Suzanne worked for General Motors and Delphi for a combined twenty-two years.

Over the years, she entertained coworkers with descriptive stories. They encouraged her to write a book. She didn't seriously consider it, until she was diagnosed with cancer. During her battle against the disease, she started writing again.

Embracing Destiny is the first of Suzanne's novels to be published. In her free time, she enjoys hiking, singing, and playing the guitar and piano. She now resides in Noblesville, IN, with her husband, Kulbinder.